DEAD SISTERS

DEAD SISTERS

The Thunder: Perfect Mind

Debra L. Manion

Copyright © 2015 Mute Apache Press

All rights reserved.

ISBN: 1499549741
ISBN 13: 9781499549744

*Dedicated to
Deirdre,
whose unconditional love
brought her sister back to life.*

I think of the story
of the goose girl
who passed through the high gate
where the head of her favorite mare
was nailed to the arch
and in a human voice
      If she could see thee now,
      thy mother's heart would break
Said the head
      of Falada.

                        Adrienne Rich

The italicized verse preceding each chapter is taken from the enigmatic Gnostic tractate labeled *The Thunder: Perfect Mind,* Codex VI in the Nag Hammadi Library, found in a clay jar in Egypt in 1945, where it lay buried for almost two thousand years. In this text, a feminine deity reveals herself through a mixture of paradox and injunction as a coherent strategy towards a single end. The author remains unknown, though the original text was most likely written in Greek. The ellipses indicate places where the Coptic version (the only extant manuscript) is unreadable, due to decay or scholarly dispute, but ultimately due to hallowed intention: I will contend that we must, indeed, maintain our spaces of ambiguity.

Connecticut 1988 A.D.

ONE

The Thunder: Perfect Mind
VI 13, 1-21, 32

I was sent forth from [the] power,
and I have come to those who reflect upon me,
You who are waiting for me, take me to yourselves.
Be on your guard!
Do not be ignorant of me.

from the Nag Hammadi Library

I married a man with a perfect mind. I knew it was perfect when I bandaged his hand in college and saw the gratitude in his face. I knew it was perfect when I stood shaking by his side before the dark altar of Saint Leo's Abbey, God smiling down from black tailcoats, my anorexic fairy body draped in diaphanous white gauze. I knew it was perfect when I sashayed my fuller hips to the car six years later, threw my sandals in the back and left him.

Not only was his mind perfect—his way with me was flawless, too. The soft way he'd wrap his long arms and soul around me when I was sad. The quiet way he'd bring me a glass of Cabernet before dinner. The whispery way he'd read Yeats to me in bed at night until I drifted asleep *brown penny, brown penny, I am looped in the loops of your hair.*

His body contained a "holy spot," he called it, near his left shoulder, a perfect fit for the curve of my cheek, and when I'd lie there, his beautiful long brown hair would drape over me like my grandmother's comforter. Often I would gaze up at his finely chiseled face and I couldn't look away, so reminiscent he was of the Sacred Heart Jesus that hung above my mother's bed.

And if all this wasn't proof enough, his name was Mikhail, which means "one like God."

I loved Mikhail so much I worked several jobs to finance him through Yale. My business exec father wouldn't let me major in literature—too impractical he said—so I fell in love and married the degree. And I lived the life I wanted through my husband. For six years I helped develop his perfect mind to even greater perfection. He read, thought and wrote; I card-catalogued his books. He earned fellowships, scholarships and the highest honors; I sewed his linen shirts and earned minimum wage.

Halfway through his program, however, Mikhail switched his specialty from W.B. Yeats to Ezra Pound. The treason almost killed me. Editing his papers changed from lyric delight to tedious chore. Footnoting his research changed from pleasing intrigue to grueling errand. And any woman can fall asleep to the verse of Ezra, but not with a languid smile upon her lips. Mine looked more like a grit.

After Mikhail finished his doctorate, he was immediately hired by the coveted Ivy league university. And within months, he became their brilliant baby, lauded and powerful, just like grad school. Me, I got to watch.

"Maybe you should keep working," he'd say. "We could use the money, Bernadette." I loved the way he always said my full name. But still this made me mad. Our original plan entailed his Ph.D., then mine. But since this wasn't coming to pass, I ditched him in order to get my turn.

So although I left ostensibly to attend graduate school, (in Religion, though. I'd read enough essays on Semiotics and Phenomenology to slay any love of literature), why I didn't enroll in grad school while remaining married remains a mystery.

Even my Jungian psychoanalyst, a Ph.D. herself (and her name was Psyche, really), said she couldn't comprehend leaving a lovely husband, a 56-window Victorian home, an idyllic life. Yes, she used the word 'idyllic.' It is my memory of this dagger adjective that encourages my guilt, lifting the balm of atonement just out of reach.

"Can't you read Yeats to yourself to go to sleep?" she'd ask.

"Listen," I'd say gravely, sitting up straighter in her archetypally red brocade chaise, completely ignorant of the magnitude of the crime I was about to commit. "I already told you I wasn't allowed to major in English."

"Okay," she said with a melodramatic sigh. She really hated it when I got obtuse and sarcastic. "This is our last session and you don't want to talk about the end of your marriage."

"I don't mind talking about it. There's just nothing to say. We had fun, it's over. Now I get to read the books."

She ignored me. "Any more dreams about the operation?"

I slipped down into the cushions of the chaise and gazed out the window to her rolling backyard of forest and hyacinth. I wanted to go to a foreign country, a desert maybe, a place of complete anonymity where my decisions carried no weight.

I mindlessly toyed with the Saint Christopher medal around my neck. "They've stopped," I whispered, glancing back to see how she was taking this.

She lifted one eyebrow. Damn, she wasn't buying it. She'd scrutinized me for too long, knew all my lies and escape routes. "Then tell me," she continued, "tell me if you're going to have it."

I hesitated. But something about the serenity of that forest, the way I could just glide out her open window and fade into green, made me feel secure. I could blur myself right into that bucolic watercolor and vanish. Emotional indifference takes away the ambiguity of any intellectual decision. Aloofness allows resolve. Moreover, this decision involved only the body, so who cared. "I've decided to do it," I said dreamily. "Madeline needs me. I have to."

She wrote something on her notepad. I closed my eyes to drown it all out, but I could hear her pen scratching. "Tell me how Madeline needs you," she murmured, thereby giving the question weight.

"Maddie can't have children," I said, shrugging my shoulders, relishing the easy answers, how rarely they manifest themselves. "This is something I can give her. Like a gift."

She just sat there, waiting for my mouth to trip up and reveal some deeply unconscious motive, some sort of primordial ooze that would leak out and allow us to see the real reason I was leaving Mikhail. "The operation has nothing to do with my divorce," I said firmly. How's that for nuance.

She nodded and continued to say nothing. This discomforting silence routine always struck me as so silly, even though it's clearly part of the game. But still, was I not the one forking out the cash for her to figure me out? Wasn't she supposed to know, after all these sessions, why I was really leaving my marriage? Don't we pay these people to be omniscient? Isn't subtext their job?

"I'm having the operation for Madeline," I repeated. "It has nothing to do with me. It has nothing to do with my sister. It has nothing to do with loving Mikhail." Her pen stopped mid-scratch.

"I mean, leaving Mikhail."

Her pen renewed its mission with a fury. Damn. I reached for my checkbook.

TWO

I am the barren one
and many are her sons.
I am she whose wedding is great,
and I have not taken a husband.
I am the midwife and she who does not bear.
I am the solace of my labor pains.

"Isn't your asshole husband disturbed about this operation?" my bedlamite sister asked me in typically sardonic fashion. "They're going to cram needles into you for Christ's sake."

"He couldn't care less about the operation," I said. "He just steps over the packing boxes and shoots me dagger looks."

"Well, who in the hell is Madeline anyway?" she snarled. Mary hates anyone she doesn't know personally, a character trait that makes entering public places with her somewhat unnerving. "I mean, do you really even know this woman?"

I changed the subject to Mary's new baby, and as she droned on I thought yes, I do know Madeline. Not intimately, not even in the sense of a good friend, but I know her laughter. I know the sincerity of her smile. I know this is a woman who should have many children.

I'd met her at one of my dreaded secretarial jobs. She was reaching for the coffee pot the same time as our boss.

"Nor but in merriment begin a chase,' Madeline said to him, laughing.

"Nor but in merriment a quarrel," I leaned in.

Well, she turned around and shot me a smile so big, I wondered how I could have missed such an exuberant person in this office building. "Prayer for My Daughter," she beamed.

"Yeats is my favorite," I said, returning the sugar. "You have a daughter?"

"Not yet, but I hope to someday," she grinned. "You?"

"No, no children. I take ballet instead. But still, that poem undoes me."

We ate together in the lunch room everyday after that, trading poetry under the table so the other workers wouldn't see and start asking questions, pretending to be interested, but really only making fun of us. We all got along, but Madeline and I definitely stuck out as different. We'd lower our vocabulary, never saying words like genre or indeed or paradigm, but it didn't help much. Everyone knew we was educated girls.

In November, Maddie began coming to work in a sweat, even though winter quasimoded the rest of us. Ten minutes later she'd be asking to borrow my sweater. By lunch, she'd give it back, beads of perspiration on her forehead.

"Keep it over your chair," I finally told her. "Save yourself the walk."

"Dette," she said one morning. "My therapist says these mood swings are related to job stress. I've got to quit." So she handed me my black mohair cardigan and I didn't see her much anymore, but I heard from the lunch crowd that her symptoms continued. That's when she quit the shrink and went to a neurologist.

After reams of tests, the doctor discovered her job did not cause her symptoms. She had, in fact, been experiencing menopause. At twenty-nine years old, she was barren. Menopause at such a young age was rare, he said, but it happened. Madeline could never have children.

"Maddie," I said on the phone. "I'm so sorry."

She was trying not to cry. "If I'd gone to the neurologist even six months earlier, when I still had some eggs left," she said, "I could have conceived. I could have had a baby." I bit my tongue to keep from lashing out the obvious irony—that six months earlier some idiot shrink with a PhD. was homeworking her to explore the inner child.

"Why?" I asked sweetly instead, repressing the urge for unsolicited commentary. "Do you know why this happened?"

"Why anything happens, I don't know," she whispered. "But I dug into my medical history—it's from a prescription my mother took for morning sickness when she was pregnant with me."

"Before you were even born. Have you told her?"

"She's the one who remembered. Pills prescribed by her physician come back now to haunt her daughter and she's completely unable to help. The knowledge that her actions are the cause of my pain, well, I mean," she hesitated. "There's nothing she can do."

"Madeline, she listened to her doctor in good faith. She was well-intentioned."

"Her original intention doesn't matter to her. She says she should have been more conscious, more careful. Now, years later, she watches her child pay a heavy price."

I never knew Maddie's mother, but I had this image of an aristocratic old woman, a retired docent from the Chase Museum, gray hair back in a bun, sitting at an antique and worn kitchen table with her arms hanging straight down from her shoulders, eyes staring at *The New York Times Book Review*, reading nothing.

And I wonder if there is a greater grief. The death of a child is said to be the most painful experience, but I don't think so. In death, there's safety. But to have unintentionally harmed your child in a permanent way, to have created suffering because of your actions; moreover, to know there is nothing you can do alleviate the pain, this would be unmitigated anguish.

One day at the office, months after she'd quit, Madeline visited the lunchroom. Her auburn curls were cut off and her hair didn't sway anymore when she walked, but there was a lightness to her step and a relief to her hello. She sat between Wilma and me. I gave her half my bagel and Wilma slid over some pork rinds.

"My mom has offered to pay whatever it takes to make me a mother," she announced.

At first no one said anything, but then we all began tossing around ideas about adoption and surrogate monkeys. The conversation sort of stopped, however, when Wilma asked if she'd ever considered in-vitro fertilization.

"What in hell's tarnation is that?" asked Edna, our manager. Edna wore polyester stretch shells and only read wicked loving lips bodice busters.

"You get some other woman's eggs," said Wilma, smoothing her beehive, "and they're mixed with Maddie's husband's, uh, you know what, in a dish or something, of course. Then it's all put in Maddie's body, and she has a baby."

Edna just sat there, stunned. "A dish?"

"C'mon Edna, one of those test tube things."

"Don't you Edna me, since when are you the science person?"

"I read about it in McCalls, a very interesting article."

Edna stood up from the table with a jolt. "Well," she said, like her dignity was at stake, "I don't think Barney would have appreciated it if I'd had little Eddie like that."

Wilma put down her corn dog, widened her eyes and leaned across the table. "We're talkin' about Madeline here, not you, Edna," she whispered with a growl. "Her ovaries dead and gone and you're hurtin' her feelings, so shut the hell up."

But Edna would not repent. "Well, I still say it sounds like a damn near retarded way to have a baby," she shouted, slamming down her Mountain Dew.

I looked at Madeline and she looked at me and we both had to cover our mouths. Meanwhile, the whole lunch table gets into the fray, arguing back and forth the paradigms of perversity and the laws of medical ethics. It's a moment I may never forget, but not because of the vehemence with which my colleagues debated, but because of the unexpected release I felt when I imagined myself the donor. Me, donating my eggs. It was like an answer to a nagging quandary, a weight being lifted from the smallness of my back. I straightened up. And although at the time I couldn't articulate why it felt so right, intuition took over: I would offer Madeline my body.

"I'll do it," I said, laying down my saltine.

Bags of cheese puffs froze in mid-air, the arguing stopped, and the forensic team just sat there, eyes wider than the loudly clicking lunchroom clock, mouths hanging open like stuffed fish.

Madeline didn't even flinch. Her arms folded across her chest, her brows knitted, she gazed at me with equanimity akin to God. And then she smiled that same big grin I hadn't seen for a long, long time. "I'll talk to Bob," she beamed.

Bob jumped at the chance. He said Maddie and I looked alike anyway, so the baby could easily resemble their own child, a thought that had already occurred to me. My concern, however, centered on a somewhat unmentionable item, namely, Bob's role. Too chicken to ask for specifics, I kept quiet and hoped Wilma was right about the petri dish.

So while my imagination wildly carried on, my hands busily packed moving boxes to keep it in check. This packing/imagination partnership worked out well. Thinking about donating my eggs kept me from lamenting over the sentimental significance of every single book or earring Mikhail had given me, gifts that were now being wrapped and moved apart from him. And packing boxes kept me from getting too deeply into my potentially perverse mental wanderings about just what donating my body to fertility science with Maddie and Bob actually meant.

Mikhail hardly spoke to me, and my therapy sessions had ended, so I turned to my sister for companionship. She was not, however, supportive. But her typical running commentary did keep me somewhat distracted. Cradling the phone every night while I packed, I listened to her warped slant on my life.

"What kind of a twisted sister do you have to be to let some asshole doctor do this to your body for no good reason? Are you insane? Divorcing Mikhail, yes, this I can see, but needles and operating rooms as contrition?"

"It's not contrition, Mary." Had she been talking with my analyst? Does everything good have to be based upon ulterior motive or psychological flaw? Is no act simple? Charitable? Maybe even altruistic?

"You just want to punish yourself for leaving Mikhail, for leaving God the hell Almighty." She never liked Mikhail, thought he was a snob. "Teach some Appalachian kids ballet for free or something. Teach piano in the ghetto. Or just volunteer at the Junior League for a few weeks. Seems like damn atonement enough to me. I love working there, get the good consignments first, some real bitch-notch designers."

I ran my fingers over a cloisonné piece Mikhail had given me one Valentine's Day years ago. He loved to buy the delicate and artful for my hair, waist-length and wavy then, held up by combs or barrettes or those jeweled sticks. The sticks were always my favorite, especially once I learned to weave them through knotted strands so well that even a string of pirouettes found them still in place. "I'm not punishing myself, Mary," I argue. "It's just something I can give."

"Do you know I got an Armani suit for thirty bucks? Armani, for Christ's sake."

I wrap the comb in tissue paper and put it in the box. "So where's Mikhail now?" she continues. "At the Faculty Club, no doubt. Have you folded all his damn underwear? Cooked chicken the fuck cordon bleu? If you just would have hired some damn help in that huge house you roam around in, maybe you wouldn't be…"

Normally I tuned my sister out when she ran on like this, which wasn't too often. It usually only occurred when she was nervous, and I think my impending divorce scared her somewhat, her own marriage to Brad being a bit shaky. In general, though, I appreciated her nightly phone calls. They kept me tethered to the task at hand.

And as I threw out my marriage with every old joint-checking account statement, my prospective parental friends gathered their marriage together by diligently researching fertility clinics. Madeline and Bob wanted the best, regardless of cost. At first, they met only with disappointment. The fertility success rate at most clinics hovered around twenty percent, paltry when you considered there were no refunds. If you were in the eighty percent that didn't get pregnant, you just shook hands and left. You paid money for a baby whether you got one or not.

Madeline slowly became so frustrated and uninspired with her search that I thought my chance to donate a child was not meant to be. But soon they found a clinic in southern California that claimed a pregnancy success rate of seventy five percent, the best in the country, the best on the planet. They flew out to UCLA immediately, and the physicians who examined Madeline determined that she was eligible for their fertility program, GIFT. I found myself relieved, but still didn't have the gumption to ask if they examined Bob.

GIFT, Gamete Intrafallopian Transfer, was similar to in-vitro fertilization, but one step better because the egg/sperm mixture, yes, prepared in a petri dish, would be injected directly into her fallopian tubes, where fertilization naturally occurs. Then the pregnancy would be supported with hormonal injections and careful medical monitoring for the entire nine months. The new procedure was developed by Doctor Asch, an Argentinean, now head research physician at the clinic. He was the one who coined the acronym GIFT, suggesting that his revolutionary procedure "gave the gift of life." Rumor had it he was being nominated for a Nobel Prize.

Dr. Asch told Madeline if she had an egg donor who passed their stringent physical standards, they could plant the donor's eggs in her tubes. So the plan involved my eggs, Bob's sperm, Maddie's body. No one spoke about the normal way of making a baby, a relief to me, considering. Not to say that Bob wasn't cute, he just wasn't mine to be cute with.

But again Madeline asked me if I was certain I wanted to go through with it. "It's not only extremely expensive for my mother," she said, "it's going to be physically demanding for you. And then there's the most strenuous issue: the result."

"You mean the child."

"Bernadette, you have to be so positive about this."

"I've thought it through carefully. There are no reservations."

After weeks of tests and physical examinations at the local university hospital required by the fertility specialists to determine my reproductive worth, they expressed my records to the California clinic, approving me as viable egg donor. I was guaranteed fertile, easily full of eggs, a regular Easter basket. As usual, the universal irony refused to stop haunting me: my friend wanted the children her body would not let her have while my body overflowed with children I didn't want.

"You're an angel to do this," Madeline kept saying. "I'll thank you forever." She even sent me a card with a brooding Yeats on the front and indebted words within.

> *Dear Bernadette,*
> *I don't know how to thank you. Everything I think of saying sounds so feeble compared to how I feel. What you have offered, few would ever take time to consider. For a long time I've known that it would take an incredibly caring, generous woman to donate an egg to a woman without her own. It has moved me when I contemplate the truly special nature of such a gift, one that no one can ever match in return. We all hope to give of ourselves, to someone, to the community, to society, but rarely can we give a gift that will mean so much to the recipient as this will mean to me. And while I offer my deepest and most heartfelt thanks, I know, and I want you to know, that you have not made a decision you're locked into. You have to listen to your instincts.*

If you change your mind you owe no explanation. It is not that I wouldn't be deeply disappointed, or feel set back, but I would recover, and would never think less of you for changing your mind (and that shouldn't matter in your decision anyway). It is important that you feel as confident as we feel that you want to participate. We are overjoyed with the prospect of having you as a donor.

Wishing you excellent health,
Madeline

Once the L.A. plane tickets were in hand, however, fear took me by the throat. So I dug the phone book out of the bottom drawer and held the receiver in my hand, just staring at it. Five long minutes passed before I broke down and dialed the number. It was time to ask my gynecologist what I could not bring myself to ask before now: Is this safe?

At first he wouldn't answer. He coughed, pretended to ask his nurse something, then cleared his throat. "Bernadette," he said slowly, "I've wanted to say this to you from the beginning, but I knew you didn't want to hear it. Any kind of operation is dangerous. But this kind of reproductive research is new to the medical profession. These doctors will be injecting you with fertility drugs, putting you on an operating table, and with an ultra-sound guided hollow needle, removing as many of your eggs as they can get. Not only is this operation a serious risk; the long-term effects for you are simply unknown."

"I, uh…I'm not sure," I stuttered, sort of tingling from the glamour of self-crucifixion. Maybe my sister's theories were right after all. "I've never heard it explained quite that way."

"Here's all I can add, Bernadette: if you were my daughter, I'd never let you do it."

I flew to UCLA the following Friday.

Southern California
1989 A.D.

THREE

*I am the bride and the bridegroom,
and it is my husband who begot me.*

Dr. Asch and Dr. Balmaceda, the award-winning fertility specialists at UCLA, extracted my blood, examined my estrogen levels, tested my urine, and shot me up with Pergonal and Clomid, fertility drugs, every day, sometimes twice a day, for the longest fortnight of my life. I felt constantly bloated. I lost all desire for food. But the drugs were working hard to stimulate my ovaries and develop those follicles numerous and large. They called it "superovulation," a term that prompted Madeline to rename the doctors Fred Neitzsche and Clark Kent.

Everyday after my fertility shots, the research team examined my ovaries to look for eggs. My gowned body lay flat on the table, my feet rose up in those ubiquitous stirrups and the team of dour-faced nurses brought out what Madeline and I called "the wand." It was a long thin cylindrical device with a camera at the end. I hated it.

One of the physicians would grasp the handle of the wand and put the would-be star up into my body to count my eggs. The overhead monitor displayed the blurred sonogram pictures of my insides. Unfortunately for me, things were hard to see. Everything on the TV appeared grainy and indistinct, like a movie when you put a cheap VCR on pause, and this hazy reception made it difficult to count just how many eggs were developing inside me. The physicians in their white coats and clipboards would shout, "Over there, move the wand more to the left, I see an egg." Or "Look, we've got another one; there's four, not three today!" Sometimes it felt like that special Spring Sunday, people excitedly hunting colored eggs in a park dense with fog. But sometimes it was Vietnam, overzealous soldiers rooting out the Viet Cong. I decided that this qualitative difference directly related to the amount of space Mikhail had taken up in my dreams the night before.

I preferred the female doctors to hold the wand because they were more gentle, they seemed to understand the humiliation factor. But usually, before the end of the egg-counting session, Dr. Asch would get frustrated with the amount of time it was taking. He'd mumble gruffly as he pushed back his gold cuff-linked sleeves and stalk over to the female physician. He'd grab the wand from her hand and begin to move it around inside me with a bit more vibrato. Actually, he was rough, which surprised me because he was otherwise so tall and tan and noble. I guess he had things to do. But I didn't mind too much. I would pretend I was numb from the neck down, and I'd just lie there like a dead carp and let him jab and thrust. I had much to think about anyway, things such as what life would be like without my perfect man to cheer on. Things like what I could do with a paycheck that went entirely to myself. Things like what I would do with my own doctorate. But mostly I focused my attention on biting my lower lip to keep from crying.

However, comic relief did come. It happened whenever Madeline and I sat in the hallway, waiting for our shots, and we'd see these blushing men come out of the bathroom carrying small plastic cups. We tried not to giggle, but we couldn't help it. Their role was just so small.

Near the end of the week, Bob flew in for the day. I was so out of it that I thought he was visiting Madeline to give her some moral support. Then Madeline and I were sitting in the same hallway waiting for our fertility shots when the men's bathroom door opened. I peeked to see what chagrined soul carried the cup today. The swift conclusion that divorce creates dementia occurred when I saw that the blushing bathroom groom of that afternoon, the bearer of his one true gift, our beloved Lancelot with the Holy Grail, was none other than ol' Bob himself.

I don't know why that wigged me out. It's not like we did anything. But it was still weird. We were making a child together, but not really. Were we? I didn't even know Bob, and I don't mean in the biblical sense, I mean *at all*. We'd said hello a few times, but that was it. And now we were creating a child together, half him, half me.

When our ten days of probing were over, they dressed me in a blue gown and puffy hat and laid me out on a stretcher. A nurse walks up with a form. "A week and a half after this transvaginal aspiration," she said," the doctors need an endometrial biopsy—that's from the lining of your uterus. This gives them information about the eggs they've taken. You need to sign this now, before the operation." She placed a pen in my hand and turned to the back page with the signature line. Above it was a list entitled *Risks and Complications*. I took the form and skimmed it while she waited, sort of tapping her foot.

1. *Ovulation induction*: ovarian cysts, internal hemorrhage, vaginal bleeding, failure to ovulate, abdominal swelling, pelvic pain, follicular rupture and possible hospitalization.
2. *Egg Retrieval*: death, paralysis, sore throat, nausea, vomiting, perforation of vessels, bowel or bladder, pain, infection, blood in urine, bleeding ovaries, colos-tomy (bringing the bowel out through the skin on a temporary basis)

Transvaginal aspiration? Follicular rupture? I may have earned a seriously low C in college Biology, but concepts such as hemorrhage, paralysis and death were fairly clear.

It didn't matter. I signed the form, I asked no questions. And Madeline and I were wheeled into the operating room and injected with the dreamy-thick anesthesia. "*May she be granted beauty*," Madeline said as she drifted off to sleep.

"In courtesy I'd have her chiefly learned," I murmured.

Dr. Asch and Balmaceda, gowned in Virgin Mary blue and oblivious to our Irish prayer, got a different kind of wand with a long thin hollow needle attached, and vacuumed out all the colored eggs in my Viet Nam they could find. I wondered if I'd know if they missed with the needle along the way up, if I'd feel it if I had tiny holes, like a colander, on the insides of my body. "Oops," I can hear Dr. Asch exclaim from behind his blue mask, "just a pinhole, she'll never know. Oops, another one, oh well. We'll just keep going 'til we get to the ovaries."

The physicians called this vacuuming procedure the "harvesting" of the eggs. Like I was a field of alfalfa.

"No," Madeline smiled before the operation, "neither alfalfa nor tobacco nor millet. Your body has become my daisy-covered field of dreams."

I don't know what happened to most of my eggs. Apparently some were put in Madeline and some were frozen. But I didn't pay much attention to anything after the operation. I was too sick from anesthetic—throwing up and dizzy and dreading the plane ride to Virginia where my small apartment and being single and starting school, all in a new city, awaited me. And to make matters worse, I took Advil before the operation, for a headache no less, so my abdomen was a lovely shade of indigo. No one ever told me taking ibuprofen even a month before surgery causes internal bleeding.

To get a better perspective, I kept saying to myself, over and over, the Tibetan mantra: "No more shots in my ass, no more shots in my ass…" It was just my body, frame and flesh, that's all. And this thought did raise my spirits—did make getting on the plane easier. But it didn't help with the new dreams I was having—those of me in my black ballet leotard lying back on Psyche's red brocade chaise with my arms full of new-born babies who all looked just like Mikhail.

Madeline did get pregnant, but despite the hormone injections and tens of thousands of dollars in clinic bills, her body wouldn't carry the pregnancy through. I heard she tried again with some of my frozen eggs, but, again, she miscarried. I lost track of her, but I've always felt badly about her not being a mother. And now, I must selfishly admit, now I'll never know what a baby of mine might have looked like. I decided that she was my one chance to see because I'm certainly not ever going to have any children. I don't know why. I just don't want to.

My sister says it's because I want to castigate myself. She's so opinionated. "You *want* to be barren," she says, "Nobody else on the entire planet does, but you do. Yet another proof of your eternal self-flagellation for leaving the Holy One."

But I don't think her mea culpa theory holds water. I suspect that not wanting children has more to do with taking care of a grown man for years. Now that I'm back in school, actually doing my own graduate work, living just fine with student loans and fellowships and loneliness, I can't imagine packing someone else's lunch again.

But my sister, well, my sister has this thing with men. Since her divorce, she has an endless run of boyfriends, but she complains about every one. Her favorite cliche is *"can't live with 'em, can't shoot 'em,"* which is a bit sick since she did try to kill her own husband. But not with a gun. My sister, she used a knife.

Virginia
1990 A.D.

FOUR

*And do not make your voice hate me, nor your hearing.
Do not be ignorant of me anywhere or any time.
Be on your guard.*

I sat deep in the stacks of the university library, way back in an obscure section of the fifth floor, hunched securely over an old Buddhism treatise, when my sister tried to kill Brad. I tell myself this is meaningful, that there's synchronicity here, because her attitude was so unattached, so like the Buddhist concept of upekkha.

Mary fixed his favorite meatloaf with sun-dried tomato sauce, but he came in so late that the watercress wilted and the loaf itself sagged. He didn't apologize. He stood, instead, at the edge of their Baluchi rug, his head hang-dog down and his Birkenstocks pointing toes at each other and he told her he didn't love her anymore.

My sister stayed still on the sofa and just looked at him. When he added that he wished their new baby had never been born, she stood up, walked calmly into the kitchen, slid open the utensil drawer, and took out the ginsu.

Brad backed out of the house clutching the baby's car seat in front of his face, threw it in the azalea bushes and ran for his champagne Mercedes. My sister changed all the locks and phoned me. She would raise the baby herself.

I heaved a sigh and fell back into my chair. "Ah, Mary, we always told you Brad was a slug. So now it's proven. Any blood?" My sister, she was no victim.

"No," she growled. "And that's what really makes me mad. The bastard got away."

"Did the baby wake up?" I tried to press the space bar quietly so she wouldn't hear it. My sister was always in some bourgeois crisis and I had to get my paper written.

"Not until—hey! You're working on the computer, aren't you? That is so rude."

My free hand flew off the keyboard and landed behind my ponytail. "No, I'm not, really."

"I don't believe this," she said. "I listened to you about your divorce and now you're caving on me about mine."

"Oh c'mon. What about Suzanna?" I put my hand down on the mouse and stared at the photo taped to my monitor, my great aunt Grace, my muse. Please let me research and write, Grace. Find out the facts. Go far away from men and separation and the confusion inherent in human connection. Don't drag me into this soap opera. I don't want to hear it. Keep me focused on my work, Grace. Please, just my work.

"After I'd finally fallen asleep," Mary continues, "the baby started crying. So I brought her into our bed. I mean *my* bed." Her voice dropped to a whisper. "She seemed so tiny, so sad, like she knew what Brad said. I tucked her in the quilt, then I laid awake all night and held onto her tight as I could."

I remember when my sister was four, she wore all the dresses in her closet at the same time, one on top of the other. We lived in a God-forsaken part of southern Texas, so you know how she must have felt out there in the backyard, with her bent spoon, digging to China in that summer heat.

Mary Catherine was skinny, but with all those dresses on and her brown hair cut short, she looked like an overweight dwarf with an embryonic head. Pinhead, we called her. She hated that. She'd stop digging and stalk off to play dolls with Bitsy, our whining cocker spaniel Mom kept chained up by the swingset.

Bitsy was brain-damaged and my little brother and I reveled in this fact. To deter boredom when swinging, we made it a game not to whack her in the head. Bitsy would bark at us frantically, trying to nip at our moving swing, but the chain didn't quite reach, so with every one of her leaps into the air, the chain would straighten, the collar would choke, and she'd fall back to the ground gagging. Failure, however, did not stop that dog from trying again. And again. And though our game involved a number of unique moves to avoid her, either by twisting the swing mid-flight, or maneuvering our feet, invariably, one of us would always nail her with an outstretched cowboy boot.

The worst part was Mom in her horn-rimmed glasses coming out after us. Between our screaming at Bitsy to get out of the way and Mary Catherine Pinhead squealing at us to leave the dog alone, and Bitsy going off like an alarm bell, Mom heard us. That meant we interrupted ironing Dad's handkerchiefs during *As The World Turns.*

When we heard the screen door slam, we knew we'd gone into overtime. Mom would grab the garden hose (Dad made it extra long so that it reached the swingset, our "base," useless as it was), turn on the faucet and blast all of us, especially the dog. I think she resented the dog the most. It's not respectful to resent your own flesh and blood, but a mutt you can blame.

What I noticed, though, was not how Bitsy got the worst of it, but how Mary Catherine never got any. She never got wet. And I don't remember her running away or anything. I just remember that after Mom went back in to her ironing board, Mary Catherine had on twelve dry dresses while the dog and my punk brother, Todd, and I were soaked. I'd just stand there, dripping, looking at her.

Invariably, Mary Catherine Pinhead The Dry would stomp over to Bitsy, unwrap her chain from around the base of the slide (before Todd and I could slide down and land on barking Bitsy's head) and put that muddy, smelly, flea-bitten mutt right in her lap, right in the middle of her twelve layers of dresses. And she'd kiss and snuggle that dog like it was born from her.

And here she stood all over again, in the middle of a muddy mess, holding tight to her child, alone. Brad scrambled out the marriage door fast, shedding fatherhood with the toss of a car seat. How easily he left her. How easily she recovered.

Wasting no time, she found a job. One that paid money. She walked straight into the Alternative High School for Boys, a euphemism for the prison that hides the city's choice juvenile delinquents and they told her she could start Monday.

"Way to do it," I exclaimed with elderly sister patronization. "How did you convince them to hire you on the spot, without an appointment, a transcript, anything?"

"Do you know what teacher turn-over is at schools like this?" she reminded me, bubbling. "They're desperate."

"Good point," I said. I knew she learned this sort of resourcefulness from me, but now was not the time to point that out. I let her luxuriate in my compliment.

"Actually," she said, "what made them sit up in their seats was when I grabbed a straight jacket hanging on the Principal's wall, and strapped the secretary."

"What? They have straight jackets? Now I'm worried."

"Look, we've got J. Edgar Hoover in our blood. I can handle any little criminal who gets out of line." She laughed, but her confidence was frightening. I couldn't decide if she was naïve, in denial, or just a hell of a lot stronger than me.

"I'm not touching Hoover," I cower. "You just keep yourself safe."

She took a sip of her drink. "Hey, how are your ovaries?"

"How's the baby?"

"Dette, you better be careful. Those fertility drugs float around in a body for a long long time. You could have quintuplets just looking at a guy."

"There's no man, so there's no problem. Pregnancy is impossible. That's the real reason I timed the egg donation with my divorce."

That night I dreamt I wore a fluorescent yellow straight jacket with wings coming out the back, and a Hoover G-man hat like our grandfather in all his FBI photographs. I flew above my sister's students singing Rock-a-bye Baby, tossing M&M-coated embryos onto the tops of their heads as they quietly deconstructed Ezra Pound's Cantos at their desks. But my hands were tied together at my side, tied with black satin ribbon. And the lullaby I sang was a version Mary invented when she was pregnant.

Rock-a-bye baby, on the tree top,
When the wind blows, the cradle will rock.
When the bough breaks, the cradle will fall,
And mom will catch baby, cradle and all.

I woke up with a strong urge to call Mary, to tell her not to take the teaching job. Some of those delinquent cradles were just too heavy to catch, especially if your hands were tied with ribbon. But Mary always did fall for that old wounded orphan shtick. Somehow, whenever we played in the fields, in the middle of two-foot high grass, Pinhead would spot the wounded frog or the bent-winged dragonfly. She'd find a shoe-box, pad it with oily rags and nurse her latest project right up until it died. We were getting pretty good at rodent funerals, and by the time Pinhead was four, we had tiny twig crosses all over our Texas backyard.

FIVE

*For I am the first and the last.
I am the honored one and the scorned one.*

Mary's been raising her daughter by herself and teaching the city's future death row inmates for three years now, while I've been burying myself in the library stacks and writing papers no one with a life would ever want to read. Since our divorces, we've both become rather cynical.

"There are only two kinds of people in the world," she says. "Me and my friends, and *ass*holes." Being her sister, I've never been too sure which category that puts me in. Staring at my computer screen, I decide, today, that I definitely belong in the asshole division. It's the proper classification for all of us who intermittently pretend we've committed altruism—the pure and noble act, the selfless and unconditional gift.

I put my head in my hands. Who was I kidding? I learned at Our Lady of Angels High School that there's no such thing as altruism. Father Charney swore to it in Religion class. Every single saint got a return on their suffering, he said. Every mystic, every martyr. I stopped drawing Guinevere in the margins of my notebook and scooted forward in my desk, the tips of my saddle shoes barely touching the floor.

"Even Jesus?" I cautiously pressed.

"Even Jesus," he smiled down at me.

I just looked at him. *Some* priest.

Then the bell rang and my virtuous dreams of being a missionary nun in Micronesia vanished into the linoleum where I kept my eyes. He's wrong, I told myself, baby-stepping to Latin class so I could think this through. Wasn't the Virgin Mary selfless? Wasn't Saint Veronica? So couldn't I be? Later, when I'm older?

And that's why I donated my eggs to Madeline. I thought it was time to prove that priest mistaken.

But back then, it made sense. My friend wanted babies, but her body was bereft of eggs. I did not want babies, but my body harbored the potential for billions. So I donated a few of my extras to her. Who needed all those dormant children anyway? She would have a little child, halo attached. And the halo would look just like mine. And I would get to visit every Christmas or so, watching from the shadows, never revealing who I was, because who was I? The mother? No, not the mother. I was the egg donor, the moron who spread-eagled herself to a team of fertility doctors, an average woman pretending to be a saint.

The child *had* a mother, Madeline. I thought I could be the quiet aunt. Or the distant godmother, some innocuous label. So enough already if she had my eyes, or my crooked smile, or my left eyebrow that arched more than the right. Pure coincidence. Dessert trivia. My consolation was the knowledge of her safety, what she did in school, what her heart longed for. Madeline agreed to tell me everything, for her whole life. We had a deal. It was the least I could do.

And as we lay there next to each other on our steel operating tables, the anesthesiologist poised with her needle, we held out our hands, clasped them together and shook on it, smiling deep into each other's eyes our secret: a secret of gift, gratitude and new life. She gave me the grandeur of altruism, and I gave her a child of God.

But it didn't work out that way. Now, three years of graduate-level religion classes later, Madeline doesn't have a child. And I surely have no honor.

So I'm sitting in my study, alone, talking to Isis, telling her about these things. Again. Asking her what she thinks. Again. But she doesn't answer. She never does. She's just a stretch of characters on my computer screen. She's Eve, Sophia, Epinoia, Mary Magdalen, Mother Mary, I could go on. She is the exemplary errant woman. She is the Thunder Perfect Mind. She is my dissertation topic.

"You just need a boooyfriend," my mother whines to me from her lakeside phone in Texas. "Someone to nurture. You're at that nesting age."

"Get more therapy," my sister quips with exasperation, "and not from one of your damn books. I'm talking about a live person you can talk to who will actually talk back." She lives near my mother. She's had a lot of therapy.

I push myself away from my scattered desk, for Isis can be no help to me now. And I've already tried therapy. It's obvious how much good that did me. No, I have to figure out this bald emptiness on my own.

I shuffle into my bedroom, get down on my hands and knees, and put my body to the floor, sliding my head under a disheveled bed, searching for my old journals. Exactly when did I start to change into…into *this*? A depressed graduate student who lives forever alone and swims, badly, in dust under her bed. I stop groping for the books and just lie there on the floor, half of me safe in this cobwebbed dark, my legs sticking out from under the frame like abandoned rubber pencils.

Altruism. What a crock. Why couldn't I have believed Father Charney and saved myself one hell of a lot of useless bloating. I cough on a dust ball and hit my head. God damn it, I'm scooting out from under here, it's so dirty, my t-shirt's black, forget those journals, I'm just wasting precious time. I'm going to the library. I've got to work.

But as I try to slide away, I wince in pain. My hair won't let me go—it's firmly entangled in the box spring coils. I try to unwrap it, carefully, for I like my hair, but even with my body twisted and strange, and my fingers attending gently, I know I'm caught for good. My left arm aches from supporting me and my right arm aches from working above my head, so I drop both arms the full nine inches to the floor. My body collapses, but my head still dangles in the air, chained like a ball to the underside of my bed.

The phone rings. Well, this is priceless. I reach up and grab the hair in my fist and pull hard, but nothing happens. The phone keeps ringing. I pull again, but no release, only pain. So I grit my teeth and rip it with all my strength and leave this space, leave these deeds, leave the strands of broken brown ribbon just dripping from the bars.

It's my sister. "You're going to the library now?" she yells. "On a Saturday night? Haven't you got a boyfriend yet?"

I knew I shouldn't have answered the damn phone. I should have stayed under the bed. "It's open till two," I yell back, with parallel fervor, yanking my backpack up onto the desk so I can fill it. This is going to be a short conversation, not only because I want to work, but mostly because I'm not in the mood for my sister's redundant diatribe about my lack of romance. To her, there's no point to a weekend if it isn't manned.

"Get a damn *date*," she whines.

"I'm not *lis*tening, Mary. Give it up."

"Why in god's name any human being would go to a library on a Saturday night is beyond me. I've already got Suzanna bathed and in bed and a completely buff guy I met at the gym is coming over in ten minutes. But no, you choose to throw away your last few years with a single chin huddling over some ancient narcissism crap."

"It's gnosticism, not narcissism." I ram some books into my bag. "And it's not a downer like you think. I'm on a roll with this research and I've got to keep going." I hear her sigh, but I don't stop. "Did you know that for the Gnostics, Eve was divine? Eve *is* the tree of knowledge and she was sent from the divine to breathe life into Adam. The whole rib and apple interpretation was devised by—"

"You *really* need a boyfriend," she interrupts.

"I *really* need to get to the library," I answer, deflated, rattling my keys near the mouthpiece. How come *no* one is interested in this stuff? Not my girlfriend Alice, not my sister, not even my advisor, although he does at least feign interest. But he has to, he's getting paid. In the end, however, this is why I'm alone—because I entertain my*self* so much better than I ever do anyone else.

"It's been over three years since you left the god-forsaken archangel," she reminds me, like I need reminding. "And he remarried light-years ago. So c'mon already. You don't even have to get a babysitter like I do, and I've dated tons of guys since Brad booted out: Larry, Tony, Spence, Duane, John, Scott, Keith, Ramsey."

I slip on my cowgirl boots and tuck my jeans inside. With every man she mentions, I feel my craving for the safety of the stacks increase, the rows and rows of bound ideas towering above me, holding me together on all sides, the feel of the volumes against my hand as I run my fingers across the spines while slowly walking down the aisles, the pleasure I'll feel when I stop, close my eyes, and pull out a book, any book, the worn cover or the faded title enticing me. Dropping my backpack, sitting down right there and opening it, an obscure treasure no one's checked out since 1928. And then an hour will vanish. Lost on a different plane, I'll pour over the text, reach up and pull down another volume, get lost again, pull down another, and another, any shelf will do. It's my own universe—fertile, soothing and safe.

Mary interrupts my reverie. "Can we say fun? Can we define it? Do we experience this concept at the library? Oh, I bet we do at the fucking computer, don't we."

"Wait, you know, you're right. Did you say you've dated about fifteen guys? At an average of about two hundred pounds each? You're looking at close to three thousand pounds of men there, sister." She doesn't say anything. I can't resist. "You see their maligned gender as slopmeat anyway, right? Think about it, a ton of raw meat. A ton."

"You're a nerd vegetarian," she starts to stutter.

I smile to myself, I have her.

"Listen," she folds, "Stop this. What about that Shane guy you mentioned?"

I cover the mouthpiece so she can't hear me laugh at her. Like changing the subject will diffuse her losing streak. I sling my backpack over my shoulder. "It's Sean."

"Yeah, him. You said he had good bone structure."

"No, not my type. Forget it." I ignore the involuntary flutter in my stomach. I knew I shouldn't have eaten those snow peas raw.

"You met him after your ballet recital?"

"Yeah."

"God girl, I could just beat you for not telling me you were going to perform. Suzanna and I would have flown up!"

"I didn't want anyone to know. It was just a fun thing I did for myself, no guests, too embarrassing."

"But it's *me*. And hey, I thought you swore you'd never do a recital again."

"Alice convinced me. And our teacher promised to choreograph us near the back of the stage, no direct lighting."

"You didn't invite us because you were afraid I'd take your place again. Admit it."

I bite my lip. She's not going to start gaining on me now. "I admit nothing."

"Ah ha! I heard your voice crack. I'm right. Damn, admit it."

"Look, I never told you to take my place. A ten year old doesn't possess such power. Mom did it. She was the commandant."

"She was *so* damn mad at you. I can still see her standing there, shaking her head. And that old Russian teacher, Madam Chomsky, on her knees, begging you to perform. 'Bernadette!' she's sobbing, 'your solo in five minutes. If you don't go on, my recital ruined! You must understand this, my Dettie. The music, I tape in sequence, and if you not dance, nothing on stage those minutes. The music play, but no Dettie. You understand, my little one? You must dance!'"

"There were tears in her eyes."

"Until Mom couldn't stand it anymore and yanks me by the elbow and says, 'Got a tutu that'll fit this one?'"

"And you did my solo without a hitch. In front of all those people."

"I'd watched you practice in the living room for months. C'mon, I knew it by heart."

"I can still see your tiny six year old body leaping and twirling around on that stage. And then you almost fell over doing the final curtsy. But you managed a good save, Pinhead, and the audience roared; gave you a standing ovation."

She doesn't say anything. And I can hear the clock ticking because I know what she's going to ask me, and I know I don't have the answer.

"Why wouldn't you dance, Dette?" she asks with a rare compassion for me. "You knew how."

I think of Alice standing in the wings right before we went on stage only days ago, smiling up at me, she was so short, telling me we were naturals, Balanchine's favorites, just for that night. "I danced last week," I said. "Finally. And I have to admit that regardless of how poorly I executed those pirouettes and arabesques, my ten year old soul in my eighty year old body felt bigger for simply doing it at all.

"And that's when you met the guy?"

"I don't know what he was doing there. But he walked up to me at the refreshment table, where Alice and I were toasting each other with fruit punch."

"Damn, I should have *been* there."

"You *should* have been there. It was incredible punch."

"Well, like, what he'd say to you?"

"He asked me if I lifted weights."

Mary bursts out laughing. "Jesus Christ, what a blatant pick-up."

"Yeah, Alice had to cover her mouth and walk away. But he backpedaled pretty quickly and said he really wanted to know if ballet dancers in *general* lifted, because that would tend to shorten the muscles that they might want lengthened."

"Go out with him."

"Oh come *on*."

"You're so goddam picky."

"I'm not picky. I'm just not interested."

"Then what about school? Aren't there any guys in your classes?"

"My classes? You should see the men in my classes. On one side of the room are the I-Can-Quote-Jaysus-Verse-Perfect Fundamentalists and on the other side sit the I'm-Holier-Than-Thou-Because-I-Meditate Pagans. They argue constantly, over every minute point. It's like religious wars without the heavy metal swords. I feel like I'm witnessing the Crusades first-hand sometimes, but in a bloodless window-free building. Go *out* with these people? Are you kidding?"

"Don't you have any damn *friends*?"

I plop down on the edge of the sofa, exasperated. "Mary, I've done both the grad, and the professor, party circuit. I did it with Mikhail for years and I did it here for one. Beer kegs in the basement on Friday night, I wear ripped jeans. Beaujolais on the veranda on Saturday, I wear a black dress. It's old. Now I play the piano, do my work, and sometimes Alice and I hit a movie or something together. It's a full enough life. Trust me."

"Shit. Your ballet buddy?"

"Who? Alice? Yeah, but she's in the sciences." I stand up to leave. "Look, I've got to get going."

"So you have, uh, like a lot in common, right? Jesus and DNA?"

My backpack is turning into dead weight. "We have our priorities in common. She's older, she's been married before, she's not into the student scene." Why am I defending myself? Alice and I may not connect on the strongest of levels, but we both appreciate relaxed ballet instruction for the aged, and a good cup of mocha at the coffee house afterwards.

"You're never going to meet a guy in a ballet class, you do know that. Call the bone structure. Tonight. Maybe he's into narcissism, who knows? I bet he would love to listen to you."

Okay, I give up. I quit. This is a pointless conversation. "Mary, I've really got to get to the stacks. I'll call you tomorrow, okay? When will you be in?"

She doesn't answer.

"Mary?"

"Brad called."

"Excuse me?"

"I said Brad called."

"Brad. He lives? How unfortunate."

"Bernadette, he...he wants Suzanna."

I drop my backpack onto the floor. "What? He can't do that. He hasn't seen her in years!" She doesn't say anything. "Mary, he gave you full custody, he wanted nothing to do with her." There is still no answer. "Mary? Mary?"

"I just needed to tell you," she says quietly.

SIX

Give heed to me.
For I am knowledge and I am ignorance.

Mary Catherine was dragging the pastry knife through Prince Eric's head on the Little Mermaid birthday cake when Brad phoned. No one had heard of him since their quick no-fault divorce, so the call was a repellent surprise. He asked Mary to meet him in a public place to discuss visitation. She banged down the phone, placed an extra rose on Suzanna's sea-blue frosting, and made a mental note to get an unlisted number. She split the Prince with Mom.

Within the week, however, a letter arrived from Brad's attorney stating the inevitable: It lies within a father's rights to see his child, even if he left when she was born. Mary put a can of mace in her purse and met him at Wendy's.

"Tell me, tell me." I beg, unusual behavior for an elder. I even push my chair away from the computer and focus on what she's saying. It's okay Grace, I say to my muse, this is gossip I can break for.

"He's a pig," she growls.

"True, true."

"I mean he's gained weight—about fifty pounds, all in the gut. He sat there and inhaled two double cheeseburgers, jumbo fries and two shakes, barely taking a breath."

"And you watched?"

"He wanted to eat before we talked, how nauseating. He burped so loud the teenagers behind the counter doubled over laughing. Have you called Sean back?"

Though I haven't seen my sister in a few years, I can imagine the scene fairly well. She'd be draped in some fashionably dark gray Voguesque *crêpe de chine*, every strand of her long auburn hair neatly brushed back into a bow, her face flawless. She'd bite her tongue to keep from revealing her embarrassment at being seen with an irresponsible slouch like Brad, but it would come through her long mauve nails drumming the table top as he crammed in the cow flesh.

"What will you do?"

"Dad's going to find me an attorney, the best in Miami, so I'm not worried. Brad's not taking her, not after three years of silence. Maybe I'll let him see her when we go to the park on Sundays. If he's fucking lucky." I hear her take a gulp of her immortal iced tea. She always glues a glass to her hand, even when she teaches. I think she's diabetic. "Did you go hiking with Sean in those Blue Ridge Mountains of yours?" she asks nonchalantly. "You better not have turned him down. You're so stupid."

"I don't like mountains."

"Right. And those fertility drugs you took when you *wisely* left Mikhail years ago may still be floating around in your system. Better be careful. Better not go on a date."

I tell her I have to go, to get to class, a lie. Seminars aren't offered at night. Usually I wave off her crises, but the idea of Brad coming back scares me. I stare at my blank monitor. More information is required, and from someone who isn't so casual.

I dial Mom's number, though I'm not sure why. She'll be victimized with one of her migraines and won't be any help, but maybe she knows something. A quiet mournful hello, like the bleat of a sick lamb, answers my call.

"Mom, you sound awful. Have you got a headache?"

"Oh, it's so bad. I put an icepack on it. I went to my doctor, then I went to the acupuncturist. And I got a deep-tissue massage about an hour ago. Maybe I'll make an appointment with my chiropractor. This mess with your sister."

"Did Dad talk to the attorney?" I interrupt.

"Oh, I don't know." She gives a little moan. "He thinks Brad will get Suzanna. I need to lie down." Another low bleat.

"Mom, Suzanna doesn't even know Brad. No judge rules that way. Never."

"I have to go, Bernadette. I talked to Dr. Tuley-Cashwell this morning." Bleat.

"How is your shrink going to help Suzanna and Mary?" Mom exasperates every last shred of equanimity.

"She said I need to take care of myself. I am the one I need to worry about. Mary will work things out. I'm going to lie down now."

"No, wait Mom. What are we going to do? Mom?"

When my sister turned five, our mother let her go down to the creek with us. That's when Mary Catherine discovered an entire new group of animals to mother: tadpoles, fish, newts. But the salamanders fascinated Pinhead the most. She loved wading into the water, lifting up the rocks, and fishing out those slimy little black snakes with legs. She petted them even, giving each one a name, a family history, a story.

One Saturday Pinhead decided that a certain family of salamanders she'd been naively torturing needed warmth; the creek water being a wee bit cold that morning. So when our mother called us in for lunch, Mary Catherine put two adults and four babies in a box, petted them, and set the box out on the front porch. The month was July. The hour was noon. We still lived in Texas.

"No Pinhead, you're doing it all wrong," Todd scolded from across the kitchen table. "Squish the bread like this, in a circle, like a frisbee. Hurry, before Mom sees."

"I can't do it right," Mary Catherine whined.

"Todd, she doesn't know what a frisbee is," I said, flattening out a Wonderbread and Velveeta sandwich between the palms of my hands. "And she *likes* Mom."

"Yeah, yeah, okay." He laid his sandwich on the table and whammed it with the flat side of his fist. "Hey Pinhead, where'd you hide those salamanders?"

Mary Catherine put down her mangled bread and squinted at the ceiling. "I don't remember," she shrugged.

"How can you not remember?" Todd yells. "It was ten minutes ago."

She looked like she was going to cry. "Oh, yeah," she brightens up, smiling proudly. "On the porch."

Todd and I looked at each other in disbelief and jumped up from the table.

"Sit right back down," Mom bellowed. She dropped an armful of lettuce and carrots onto the kitchen counter. "You're not going anywhere until you've finished your…WHAT have you done to your lunch?"

"Mom, please. It's life or death," we cried in unison. We were well-versed in this excuse.

Unmoved, she dunked a head of lettuce into the sink water and held it there. "Finish your plate. Period."

"But Mom, Pinhead's killed more babies!"

Mom let go of the lettuce, which bobbed up and splattered water all over the counter, the floor, and the embroidered apron Aunt Grace sent her from Damascus. We saw our chance, bolted for the front door and threw it open.

The salamanders were cooked, a shriveled family of burnt black french fries with heads. Huddled together in a corner of the box, it was obvious they sought cover, the smaller ones lying beneath their parents, but every one of them dried out like a cornflake. Todd and I snickered with miserly horror, but Pinhead bawled for an hour. Dad even offered her a much coveted Coca Cola straight from the green glass bottle, but her anguish and guilt would not allow her to enjoy such pleasure. Returning the bottle to the fridge, I thought I heard Dad mumble something about one more damn cross to mow around, but I could be wrong. When it came to my sister and death, he was usually quite accommodating.

The court awarded Brad full visitation rights. Though a stranger, he was to parent Suzanna overnight every other weekend.

SEVEN

*I am the mother of my father
and the sister of my husband,
and he is my offspring.
I am the slave of him who prepared me.*

I throw the *Gospel of Thomas* across the room. The worst-case scenario is never supposed to play out. It's but a backup, a contingency we invent to make the lighter result less harsh. But for my sister, the backup played out in spades. A judge forces a child to stay with a man she doesn't know? A court makes such a decision?

I pace from end to end of my study, stomping over papers and files and half-finished theories about the Gnostics. Martyring children to assuage guilt, who deals in such waste? I keep walking, keep stepping over confusion. Anger often sends me ideas, so maybe now I'll think of a solution to this stipulation. I continue to pace. But soon the monotony of the back and forth quiets my passion. Take a breath, Bernadette. Everything has a better way.

I bend down and gather up my disarray of notes on *The Thunder, Perfect Mind* and try to straighten them. And all at once I feel my crimped shoulders soften: in the entire collection of gnostic writings, *The Thunder* remains my favorite. The speaker is female, the ideas are riddled with paradox, and the rhythm of the words sounds like a hymn from High Mass. In this work live the fascinating aretologies of my Egyptian Isis, the shadowy darkness of my Hindu Kali, the androgynous spiritual perfection found in the Old Testament, and the omniscient wisdom of gnostic Sophia.

My great Aunt Grace might even be proud. I've never been to Egypt in body, but I've traveled in gnostic spirit. She looks down at me from the black and white photograph still taped to my monitor. She's sitting atop a camel, alone in the desert, wide open and barren on all sides. A pyramid looms in the background, the only hint of anything other than her striking solitary pose. She's smiling, though, her lips pressed together and the laugh lines on the ends of her eyes lending a wise sensibility. Loose strands of long gray hair fly about her face. This one woman's unchained autonomy, this captured image of her expansive spirit, inspires me to write, pushes me to continue the deserted gnostic search.

But I check my growing satisfaction with the world when I remember what I'm should be thinking about: my sister. She even bought Suzanna a Barbie suitcase, trying to make visitation sound like a vacation, a big treat. But the kid wasn't fooled. One look at Brad in the parking lot and she dropped the Barbie suitcase and started screaming. Brad's new wife tried to take Suzanna by force, but Mary met the task, kicked her in the shin and ran to the car, clutching Suzanna to her chest. The expletives followed, but Mary put pedal to floor and left the wife diving for the door handle. Brad stood there like a slug, watching the whole scene from behind his slouch.

He took Mary back to court. Now Suzanna is exchanged inside the lobby of the local police station. Monitored, protected. The judge said that since they couldn't trade Suzanna on their own, they'd have to do it in a legally chaperoned environment. Officers of the law, with batons and guns strapped to their thick black belts, now guard Suzanna's passage from the arms of her mother into the arms of a stranger.

I put down my papers and rest on my knees. *Once more the storm is howling, and half hid /Under this cradle-hood and coverlid / My child sleeps on.* "Prayer for My Daughter" resounds in my brain, pounding, over and over, like thunder. I should call Alice, see if she wants to see the new

French flick at the University Union. I should put on my ballet shoes and practice my jétés. I should sit at my old piano and pound out a good rock song, Dylan, Joni, anything.

But I can't move. Yeats, the police, they scare me now. But what would the Egyptian Thunder, my mentor, my ancient friend, what would she say about my sister? That it's time to go there? To help her? I vacillate between intention and passivity. I never used to. I always went straight for what I wanted, always knew what it was. But now I am confused, uncertain of any action. Should I act at all, I often wonder. Or should I wait, just wait, like ol' Siddhartha? Should I should anything? I look around the incessant clutter for my datebook. Hell, what would the Thunder say about this mess in my study?

"Be glad you never had a baby," She whispers. "Think of how wretched that poor child's room would be."

"Think of how she would only have this ragged mother to protect her."

I sit down on the floor, scooting away another pile of Isis notes. It's raining outside, full, steady. There's too much rain in Virginia—it clouds out the Blue Ridge mountains. In the night, the cruelest blanket, I go to the university library. There are no windows, so I'm not reminded of what I can't see. But in the early evening like now, when it is not the night but the incessant rain that obscures the mountains, the sky's veil is doubly cruel. *And for an hour I have walked and prayed / Because of the great gloom that is in my mind.* I can't stare out my window and lean on their layered shades of vaporous blue. In the night, like right now in this fog, I cannot find blue anywhere.

Mikhail's been remarried for a long time, but I've heard no rumors about children. *May she be granted beauty.* Jasmine, his wife, has brown hair like mine, or so Madeline said when she ran into them kissing in the antiquarian bookstore. But she's not beautiful like you, she said. Lying consolation. Ripping edge. Little does she know that I know that she went unconscious on the operating table before she could finish the most important part of the verse: *and yet not / Beauty to make a stranger's eye distraught.* But that is far past me now, that knifing phone call, that shattering information. I don't even know where Madeline is anymore.

And Mikhail, well, he married Jasmine six months to the day after I left, six months being the legal requirement one must wait after separation. If we had children, he would have had to wait a year.

Our children, they would have looked like me. Even if they someday come from Jasmine's body, they will still look like me—straight-shouldered tall and golden brunette and slender and full of hope, just like that girl the day she got in my car and drove away.

The rain starts coming in through the windows now, slowly at first, then more. *I have walked and prayed for this young child an hour.* More rain, too much rain. *And heard the sea-wind scream upon the tower.* It's coming through all the holes in my study ceiling now, streaming down faster and faster in hundreds of thin but gushing waterfalls. The wands with the hollow needles are moving in the sky, the fertility doctors guiding the flow, and the water, it's soaking me, making images of my children in the puddles and on the walls. *Imagining in excited reverie / That the future years had come*, images of children with my face. Not Mikhail's, not Madeline's, not Bob's, only my face. *Dancing to a frenzied drum.*

But the faces are not beautiful. They're distorted. And the children are not tall, they're hunched, not slender, but anorexic, not full of hope, but drenched in virgin despair. I cover my eyes with my fists and grit my teeth. No, no, no, I lost nothing. Nothing! I grab the ankle-high notes on Isis and with both hands I throw them up to the ceiling to stop the rain.

My shoulders drop down to my knees, my face down to the vapor, to the steam that rises off my floor. So this is it, the truth, the center, that he is still only, only—only very much everything. I think I cannot breathe, but I do, I think I cannot cry and I don't. I can't. I won't. I *won't.* I refuse.

I spread my arms out beside me, my legs bent and weighted beneath my body. I prostrate this soul to Mecca, to the Bodhi tree, to Calvary, and offer up the whole mess to the Thunder and She takes it all to her temples, scatters all of us to the ten thousand winds where we live as sound, as word, as Logos only, never in human form again, woven with the enchantment of all my unborn children. And here I fall, dripping with denial, down into the only real peace I ever know anymore, the velvet metta of drowning sleep.

Two hours later, I wake up completely dry. My Isis notes lie in a neat pile on the floor by my head, and my arm muscles ache from their lengthy stretch. I pull them in and glance at the ceiling for holes. Just to check in, such Irish histrionics. I must have really needed a nap. I unwrap my cramped body and remember my sister.

It is, indeed, time for this daughter of herself to make the drive to Texas. Visit the family. Picket that bad judge's castle. Classes are off-session anyway, so I have the space to travel. And maybe I've grown tired of spending every night in the musty library stacks, breathing in spores, avoiding the glances of equally tired bespectacled men. Maybe I only hang out there because all the words and chairs are organized, and it's warm, and there aren't any windows.

I look up for the clock above my bookshelf. Yes, yes, yes, I still have a few hours before the library closes. I need to research the Albigensians, a French outpost of supposed Gnostics around the Middle Ages, also massacred. I jump up and feel my jeans slide down around my hips. I pull them back up and look around for my belt. I find it behind the printer and as I'm lacing it through the loops I think my sister may be right about boyfriends. So maybe tonight, maybe I won't avoid those four-eyed glances. Maybe I'll try really hard to glance back, smile even.

I stagger to the linen closet to search out a brush.

EIGHT

I am strength and I am fear.

I hike the short distance across campus, intent upon my work, forgetting the secondary goal which occasioned the hair brush. The ground is wet, mushing beneath my boots, so the sidewalks become more sensible. I count the cracks like Bible verses until I see the lights of the main library shine upon my legs.

Mindlessly running up the stone steps, my eyes on the ground, my backpack over my shoulder, my body suddenly slams right into a rock. Knocked straight out of my gnostic reverie, I begin to fall, the weight of my pack pulling me down onto the steps, my senses confused and chaotic. But a strong hand grabs my arm and pulls me back to the present.

"Bernadette," he says, bending down to pick up my backpack while still holding on to me. "Are you okay?"

Fighting my bewilderment and the darkness of the night, I try to bring this person, this voice, into focus. It's ballet recital Sean. What's he doing here? I quickly brush the hair off my face and straighten my cloisonné comb. "Uh, I'm fine," I stutter. He slings my pack over his shoulder and takes me by the elbow.

"Come," he says with such serene authority, "let's get you inside." We move into the lobby of the library and he walks me to a corner far from the late-night bustle. "Are you just getting here?" he asks sincerely. "This late?"

"Well, I...there's only one thing I wanted to look up."

He smiles down at me. "How are you?" he beams.

I feel completely awkward. And guilty as all hell for never returning any of his phone calls. "Fine, and you?" I shrug.

"Hey, you never called about hiking in the mountains," he says playfully.

I reach out for my backpack. "Sean, I just have so much work. I mean, it's that time of year, you know? In fact, this library closes pretty soon. I should get started." But he pulls away, laughing.

"I'm used to rejection, Bernadette," he continues to smile. "I get it all the time in my work."

Okay, now I blush with shame. "Your work?" I ask with an attempt at concern in my eyes, realizing I don't even know what he does. "What do you do?"

"Investments," he says with some modicum of seriousness. "I come up with investment plans, try to get people with money involved, and then manage the investment."

"Oh," I hesitate, wondering why he's at the university library.

"It's something like what you do," he continues. "I sell ideas."

"Oh yeah, similar," I mumble, trying to be polite, trying not to look into his eyes, for I definitely do not want to know what color they are. "Well, it was nice to see you." I lift my pack from his shoulder and he lets me, disappointment showing in his well-defined jaw. I walk away, towards the stairs, turning to wave goodbye. He's just standing there, his arms out in front of him, palms up, his head to one side, like he's pleading, like he's saying, "Oh c'mon, give me a chance here." But he doesn't say anything. He just waves goodbye with his lower lip stuck out in a mock pout.

I push past undergrads socializing in the stairwell, climb until I get to the reference room and find an empty table. I pull out the chair and stifle the slight disappointment bending it's way into my bones. Why couldn't I just flirt for once? Where's the harm? He seems like a nice enough man, and so peaceful, what's my problem?

I pull out my legal pad of notes and begin to read. But I can't. All I can do is stare at the words and think of how I felt when I met him a few weeks ago after the recital, how he poured all his attention into my face, how almost luscious that tasted, but how unnerving it felt when he did it again tonight. I rub my temples and wince. No, no, no, I've got work to do. But then I feel the breath on my neck.

"I've got an idea," it whispers. I startle and turn to see Sean beside me, down on one knee, he's a Cheshire cat grin. "I'll help you with whatever you need to find," he says, "and then you let me buy you carrot juice at the student union."

I have to smile, such persistence. "Oh, you're nice," I give in. "But it's really, uh, obscure stuff. Very boring. No one is interested, I mean, I am, but, well, that hardly counts in most situations."

He moves a stray strand of hair from my eyes. "Try me," he says.

I turn away and fumble with my notes. "It's gnostic," I stutter.

"I bet I'd like it," he interrupts, and he pulls a small volume of Theravadan Buddhist essays from his jacket pocket. "See, I like the obscure."

Hmm, I think. Maybe something does skulk about behind the strong jaw and the lines that issue forth from it. "Okay," the traitor inside me says out loud. "But it's got to be mocha."

"Mocha."

"From the coffee house on Fifth."

"From the coffee house on Fifth."

I tear off a piece of paper from my notes and hand it to him. "If you can find this reference for me, we'll leave."

He walks away and I go back to my words, but I can barely breathe. He's so forward, he doesn't even know me. And there's no way he'll ever find that reference. I've been searching for it for days.

Thirty minutes later we're looking for a table at the crowded artsy coffee house. He sits down across from me. "This way I can see your face," he winks. I ignore him.

"You study Buddhism?" I ask, annoyed. "Is that why you were at the library?" He was probably there to read the baseball scores in the newspaper room.

"I meditate," he says. "And sometimes I find interesting essays, but I'm really only interested in technique. The scholarly stuff doesn't do anything for me." I scald my tongue on the mocha and think, well, *this* conversation isn't going very far.

He reaches across the small table and touches my shoulder lightly. "Bernadette, I know you study these things. I don't mean to denigrate the work you do. But frankly, most religions bore me—all the trappings, the rituals, the piles of books."

I pull away. "I know, I know. Religions are a clichéd concordium of rules devised by control-fixated men hundreds to thousands of years ago."

He shrugs his shoulders. "So why do people in this century still follow this stuff? Doesn't everyone know by now that these men only imposed structure on themselves and others because they couldn't grasp the simplicity of God, and, more importantly, they didn't want to?"

I raise an eyebrow. "Not in my religion department."

He raises both his. "And not in the suburbs."

I laugh with him for the first time and notice his eyes are a pale shade of blue. He takes a sip of carrot juice and I narrow my own to study him. The strands of gray throughout his dark hair give him a dignified look, prominent cheekbones, that jaw—must be some Navajo blood in there. He's older than me, though probably not by much. But more importantly, he's hit one of my favorite nerves and I lean forward.

"The real answers wouldn't have fit with their political and financial agendas," I say, "because the real answers wouldn't have fit with their desperate need to invalidate everything feminine, the ultimate source of power."

He clears his throat, possibly in a derisive manner, I can't tell. "Excuse me?" he says. "The ultimate source of power?"

"The feminine can create," I say firmly. "And that's threatening." This little diatribe of mine is followed by the stereotypically awkward first-date silence. I bet he hates anything that even suggests feminism. I put down my mocha. Time to leave.

He pushes the plate of dark chocolate and french bread towards me. "So," he asks in a clear voice, untainted by derision, "what religion exactly do you study?"

My flight response vanishes and I go for the food. "Many of them, actually," I say, slathering the chocolate onto a slice of bread. "I study their histories: Buddhism, Christianity, Zoroastrianism, you name it. But it's Gnosticism I love."

"You do know that old joke where God says, 'I have the truth,' and Satan says, 'Here, let me organize it for you.'"

I lean forward across the table and look right into those eyes. I've got a captive audience and I've got chocolate. It's time to unload.

"But not Gnosticism," I blurt out. "That's why it's so interesting. 'Gnosis' means 'to know,' and one thing all the variations of Gnostics believed was that the divine was within. Organized or not, a gnostic didn't need an institution or a Church Father to know God. A gnostic simply looked inside."

"So, uh, you're a Gnostic?"

"No such thing anymore, except for some new-agers. They were all massacred by the fourth century. And it was precisely because the Gnostic Christians didn't need the organized church that they didn't last."

"I don't get it."

"Sean, if a Christian believed heaven was inside his own soul, not inside the lining of the bishops' pockets, then how could The Holy Church become a powerful institution right in the middle of the Roman Empire?"

"Political and financial agendas decided where God was."

"And Gnostic Christians didn't aid those agendas, so they were heretics; hence, murdered."

I feel like bouncing up and down in my seat. He's actually listening. I can barely stand it. Pinhead was right. I have to remember not to tell her.

"In 1945," I continue with rapture, "near Nag Hammadi, Egypt—which, by the way, is where my very cool Great Aunt Grace lived—a peasant looking for fertilizer found a large jar near a cliff of caves. He was about to break it open when he became fearful that a dangerous jinn might dwell within, a spirit he didn't want to leash upon himself or the world. But then he thought the jar might contain gold, so he shattered it with his ax. And there fell at his feet both his fear and his desire, a once-dangerous spirit and ideas of priceless worth: fifty-two gnostic writings from before, during, and after the time of Christ, writings secretly written, gathered and buried almost two millennium ago."

He leans forward, close to my face. "And it's these writings you study?"

"They've only recently been in the hands of the public. Ideas about Jesus, women, transcendence. It's...it's the perfect answer for my dissertation—heresy and feminism all in one space."

He straightens his back and lightly slams his open palms on the table. "Whew, Bernadette, I can see why this fires you up. Pretty exciting stuff." He runs his fingers over his likable chin and looks off to the right. "Now, I get the heresy part, but where does the feminine come in?" I smooth some more chocolate onto bread and hand it to him, but he waves it off. "I bought it for you," he says.

I take a huge bite. "In Gnosticism," I slur, "unlike most religions, the feminine is not seen as other. The Muslim and Hindu traditions, for example, have justified the subjugation of women for thousands of years."

"And the Judeo-Christian tradition?"

"It's ludicrous!" I throw up my hands and my bread goes flying over to another table. The occupant, an abused punker, hands it back to me. Hell if I'm going to eat it now.

"Can't you just imagine some angry old man," I continue, not missing a beat, using the bread as a writing utensil, "thwarted by women, who became a scribe or a priest to seek his revenge. There he sits, the typical church father, writing by candlelight with a wry smile, thinking he's doing the right thing as he mythologizes countless generations of women to come into subservience."

A sort of shadowy gaze passes over Sean's face. His shoulders back up and he just stares. "Bernadette," he says with a firmness that surprises and unnerves me, "you know *he's* your enemy, not men at large."

All of a sudden, I feel stupid. I've been talking nonstop. I have totally dominated this conversation, and I've been way out of control with my rabid eagerness. You'd think I was desperate. I look around the coffee house and notice how vacant it's become. I push back my empty cup and stand up. This isn't fun anymore. I want to go home.

"It's late," I stammer. "We should go."

He doesn't move. "Hey," he says, "it's okay." Like he's read my mind. Like it isn't obvious that I've just migrated, in one quick breath, from mindless cheerleader to paranoid schizophrenic. "It isn't closing up yet. Really."

"No, no, I mean, I've got to get an early start tomorrow." I pick up my backpack, but he practically leaps out of his chair and takes it from me.

"Sure," he says. "But what's tomorrow?"

"I'm driving to Texas," I say, holding the door open for him, amazed that I've decided to go to Dallas, just like that, tomorrow even. "To see my sister."

He leans against the door until I walk out first. It's raining lightly now, and the air has become chilly, so we walk quickly down the side streets, from the row of shops to the university. Sean takes off his jacket and lays it over my head. "No, really," I protest. "You wear it. It's cold!" And I try to take if off, but he pulls it back over my hair.

"I like it this way," he says, and I acquiesce rather than argue. Sometimes it's better to just go along with an idea, no matter how abhorrent or against one's principles. It's less trouble than dignifying it with discussion.

"Your sister," he says, walking too close by my side. "Why are you going to see her?"

"Custody issues with her ex," I say with extreme brevity.

"And you can help by going down?"

"Of course. Why not? I'm her sister."

We stop in front of the darkened library steps and I look up wistfully. He stares at the side of my face. "You like this place, don't you?"

I turn away. "Yeah, I like this place."

"But how will you do your research if you drive to Texas?"

"The library closes for much of Spring Break, so now's the time to go." I pull his jacket off my head. The campus is empty and he's soaking wet, his hair plastered to his scalp. His shirt clings to his skin and the strength of the body beneath is unmitigated. No doubt this boy's a lifter of great weight. I feel guilty for his rained-upon condition, but he does look good, and I'm grateful for this rare opportunity to have my eyes entertained. It is a strain to turn away.

"Thanks for the mocha, Sean," I smile, handing him the jacket. "Your company was nice."

"Hey Bernadette," he calls as I walk away, "let me drive you home."

I turn and walk backwards. "Thanks," I wave. "But it's not fair, I mean far."

He runs up after me. "If it's close, I may as well go. You mind?"

I shake my head. I don't mind. I may even like it. But we walk in silence for the rest of the way, only two blocks, and I start to get nervous as we near my apartment. He's still clutching his jacket in his hand and I'm not looking at his chest. I swear I'm not looking. It's a body, that's all, nothing but a shell. That's what the Gnostics believed and I'm trying to assimilate my studies.

When we get to my door, I keep my backpack clutched to my chest. Hunkified as Sean is, he isn't going where I fear he thinks he's going. I put the key into the lock as fast as I can and say goodbye as politely as these situations allow.

He puts his hand out to stop the door as I'm closing it. "Wait!" he says. "What about when you get back?"

"I'll call?"

He starts jumping up and down, his hands stuffed into his front jean pockets, like a little kid. "No you won't, Bernadette! Admit it, you won't." He's got those ornery pleading eyes again.

I lean against the doorframe and laugh. "Okay," I give in. "I promise."
He points at me as he backs away. "You promise."
I nod and smile and close the door.

Texas
1990 A.D.

NINE

I am the whore and the holy one.
I am the wife and the virgin.
I am {the mother} and the daughter.
I am the members of my mother.

After two days driving, I arrive on Mom and Dad's doorstep and dump a black dufflebag onto my pink twin bed. Within fifteen minutes, I've trashed the room, clothes and makeup everywhere. But I don't have to share with my anal sister anymore, so I'm allowed this wretched anarchy. I survey my ghetto: a variation on the graduate student uniform—depressed black leggings, black shirts, black skirts—every shade of night now dripping over pale pink bedspreads and peachy pink chairs. I pick up an ancient Chanel No. 5 sitting atop the white vanity, and I spray it on the pink rose in the Tiffany vase. My gray beaded necklace hangs from one of the thorns, mature darkness slumming with the pastel pink of youth.

"I bought you a jumper for the hot weather," Mom calls from the kitchen. "It's hanging in the closet."

This should be good. Let's see. Is it pink? I slide back the white louvered doors and there it hangs, sleeveless, belted, the color of tongue. I sigh. What can I do? She just doesn't get it. It's not her fault.

"Thanks, Mom," I exclaim with the same voice I used in high school when she'd do me "favors," favors like the newspaper clippings she'd leave by my cereal bowl every morning, reports of girls who were murdered or molested because they didn't ask for help. Like the young woman who left her baby in the apartment while she went to look for a job. She couldn't afford a babysitter, thought the German Shepherd could do it. He did. No need for a sitter after that.

Twenty years later, I still jerk at the story, and remember jumping off my bike on the way to school to vomit on the sidewalk. "You've got to learn to ask for help," Mom would say. "That's why I give you these articles. Because you always want to learn the hard way."

"Have you tried the jumper on, honey?" she calls. Damn. I leap off the bed with some unexplained fear and yank the pink clo (singular for clothes, coined by Pinhead) from the hanger. Where *is* my sister? I need her for protection. She said she'd pick up Suzanna and come over right after teaching. *Hurry.*

Two hours later, we're all at the butcher-block table eating Buddha's Delight off paper plates. My first night here and my mother orders Chinese take-out—such a welcome. I sit there, in between Mary and Dad, separating out those fake little corn things and moving them to the side of my soaked paper plate when I feel that familiar urge to get out of the house.

Mary and Mom gab about children, and I ask myself what exactly it is that I don't like about this place. Is it the kitchen counter tops, olive green and dated? The yellow and white wallpaper with the print of teapots swinging on ribbons? Maybe it's this country kitchen in general— the way the den and the kitchen flow into one big room so Dad can watch the news while we eat. And what's this style got to do with the country, anyway? What kind of interior architecture is it? She could fix this place up if she wanted, modernize it, paint all the walls white and hang up actual art instead of pale blue wooden ducks with bonnets.

I fish out a snow pea and dip it in the duck sauce. Ducks, I'm surrounded by ducks. In high school, I'd bolt for my bike as soon as I could escape dinner and take off for anywhere that wasn't home. I'd try so hard to get lost, knowing full well that I couldn't, that I was just riding in suburban circles, going nowhere, like no-aware I'd think, but grateful, after each night ride, that my illusion was dissipating, that I was, at least, finding out faster.

"I lost my sunglasses," I sort of burst out. "Anybody want to drive to the mall?"

"I do," squeals Suzanna, climbing out of her booster seat and running over to her black patent-leather Mary Jane's. I watch her. She's putting them on the wrong feet and I wonder why children making mistakes is so adorable. Why isn't it adorable when adults make mistakes? I walk over to help her and trip on the dog.

"Damn you, Mugs," I curse, grabbing onto the LaZboy before I fall on my face. But as I straighten, I find myself looking right into Suzanna's bewildered eyes. "Oops, sorry Suzanna. I said a bad word."

"Aunt Berndette," she asks, "why when big people get hurt they get mad, and when we get hurt, we cry?" I get down on the floor and buckle her shoes. Is the kid psychic? Was I not recently posing a similar question?

"Hmmm," I muse, "maybe it's because—"

"Mommy, I want a new dress at the mall. A black one like Aunt Berndette's."

Okay, so it was a rhetorical question. Meanwhile, the kid's barely three and my Cosmo sister's got her trained for Lord and Taylors.

"Bernadette likes being in the big city," Dad says with pride. "Wants to go to the big-city mall." He pushes his chair back from the table and heads over to the TV. Now that he's retired, he's home all the time driving Mom crazy with his satellite dish of sports channels. It's like he's making up for lost time, all those football games he missed when trying to keep our growing family in a decent ranchhouse.

"No seriously. With all this sun, I really need a pair of glasses."

"Well, we usually drive over to the nursing home to see Lon after dinner," Dad says as he clicks on Brokaw. Mom doesn't make a peep, just starts clearing the table really fast, like it's a race or they're late or something.

"Yeah," Mary Catherine rolls her eyes, "visiting Grandpa is always a treat."

I stop clearing dishes for a moment. "Actually," I muse, "I wouldn't mind talking to him. It would be fun to ask him about his FBI days with Hoover."

"Oh no you don't," Dad yells as Mom glares at me and then runs back to her bedroom.

"What? What?" I ask, ignoring the obvious.

"Told you," Mary says, "can't mention Hoover or he'll freak."

"Oh c'mon, you guys are paranoid."

Dad clicks off the TV and starts locking up the patio doors. "You can talk to him after the first of the year."

"The first of the year? Why then?"

Mary Catherine interrupts. "That's when he gifts out all our money, you idiot. Isn't that what you're living on? If you upset him, he'll have a stroke and die and then the money STOPS." She puts her hands up to my throat, like she's going to play-strangle me. "The money stops. And the money doesn't want to stop. I need that money!"

"What do you mean the money stops? Money just doesn't stop. He dies and the money's still there and all the relatives get it. It's now or then, what's the difference?"

"His trust is all fouled up," Dad says, shaking his head. "Look Bernadette, just don't say Hoover." He leans his gray head into the hallway. "Rachel, Let's go."

Mary and I take my Honda since hers smells like spoiled milk. "Hey, I thought you lost your sunglasses," she says, holding up the RayBans on the dash.

"You can never have too many."

"It's been a mere two hours since you arrived and you're ready to get out. I live here. How do you think I feel?"

The unlikely fusion of luxury and urine keeps our visit to Lon's palatial nursing home short. Shriveled ol' Grandpa barely looks up from his wheelchair when we walk into his elegant private room. The TV news is blaring, but he's not interested. He's staring at a photograph on the wall—a picture of himself in a red sweater surrounded by Grandma, her sister Grace and some questionable FBI-types.

"Lon, Lon," Dad yells into his good ear. "Damn. He's turned the hearing aid off again." Dad fools with the plastic inside Lon's ear. Lon ignores him, turning his small wrinkled head to look up at me. He points to the photograph.

"The Chief Man is putting on his sheepskin coat and I'm helping him," he mutters. "We're interviewing people in a cattle car…it's the Polar Expedition." His eyes wander from me to the photo. "We were told not to give any attention to the Polar experience. We were liquidated. It was high-class. Our departure from this political state. We drove in automobiles."

I turn to Mary Catherine as Grandpa continues to mumble. "What in the hell is he talking about?" I whisper. "He's never been this bad. Does he always do this now?"

"Hell yes," she says, unwrapping the cellophane from the small box of mints she brought him. "Babble, cryptic babble." She pops two in her mouth and holds the box out to me. "Just play along."

Something stabs at my arm as I reach for a mint. It's Lon, trying to grab me. I move closer to his wheelchair. "What Grandpa?" I yell.

"His satchel. Break him. Incidentally, I'll have Rocky Road." He points again to the photo. "That man in the red sweater—I've lost track of him. I've forgotten his name. I suspect it was Grace."

I put my hand over my mouth and lean towards Mary. "Do I tell him the guy in the red sweater is *him*? Huh?" But before she can answer, Lon yanks me down closer to his face.

"I am…I am…I am devoid of any memory of the FBI or Hoover," he says clearly and slowly.

"Jesus H. Christ, Bernadette," Dad swears from across the room where Mom is huddled in a Queen Anne chair in the corner, Suzanna on her lap, playing with a troll. "I told you not to get him all worked up." But I tune him out because all I can think of is yeah right Grandpa. I'll just bet you don't remember anything about Hoover. You're ninety-six and drooling in your mashed peas, but you're still lying like a rug.

Dad doesn't let up. "Keep it zipped over there."

I whip around to defend myself. "I didn't say anything! I never even mentioned Hoover." I turn to Mary. "Did I say Hoover? I didn't say Hoover!"

"There, you said it again!" Dad cries, pointing.

"But wait. This isn't fair. He said it first."

Mary Catherine grabs my arm. "We're going shopping, guys. Bye! Say goodbye, Dette." She pulls me down the hall, past nurses and wheelchairs and IVs. "Forget it," she says. "They're all hyper. Just forget it." She pushes me out the French doors. "Switch it to glasses, girl."

We wander from store to store in a stucco mall, a paean to western hemisphere pagans. If only the Pharaohs could see this. But as we dodge indoor trees and fountains and fat people, a subtle paranoia begins to build.

"You keep looking around," Mary says. "What is it?"

"Mom in the nursing home. Gave me the creeps."

"Yeah, she hates going there," she answers, stopping to look at a silk scarf. "That whole business with her sister. Mom will never forgive Grandpa, ever."

"Do you *blame* her?"

"No."

"So nobody ever says Hoover or FBI."

"Look, he'll kick the bucket soon enough, regardless of who mentions whom."

"I don't know. Did you see his face when the nurse brought in the ice cream? He lit up like an elf. Anybody that interested in dessert isn't looking to die."

"Yeah, well, he knows he's not getting any in hell."

I pick up a boot. "I used to own a pair like these in high school."

"Yeah," she brightens, "that Christmas it actually got cold—we could finally wear our hip suede boots. Remember?"

I quickly return it to the display. "No."

She laughs. "You're not too transparent. It was Midnight Mass, with Todd and Jackson. You were so excited. You blushed twelve shades of red when you had to take his hand for the Our Father."

I keep my eyes on a pair of black pumps, feigning disinterest. She sighs too loudly. "Jackson had plenty of girls swooning over him."

"Exactly," I interrupt. "The track star."

"But," she commands, pointing the spiked heel of a red dancing shoe at my face, "he asked you out constantly and you'd never go."

"Constantly? Oh, not constantly. Definitely not constantly."

She flips the shoe over in her hand, like it's a baton. "Chicken then. Chicken now. Just like with that Shane or Sean or whatever guy. You won't change."

I grit my teeth to argue when suddenly I hear a noise that doesn't sound like the blur of bustling shoppers. I turn around, immaturely grateful for any distraction. At first I don't see anything unusual, but then I hear the sound again. It's like something, or someone, is hitting a wall. Then I hear a young voice plead, "I promise! I promise!"

I move quickly out of the store to see a man banging the side of his fist against the wall of the store next to us. Mary is close behind me.

"What's going on?" I ask, pointing to a boy, maybe eight or nine years old, lying on the floor nearby, sort of in an empty inset between the stores. Two men in dirty clothes hover over him, the boy's hands cover his face. One man begins to draw back his arm.

"Go, get security, now," Mary yells as she runs to the boy.

But I just congeal. Mary is a small woman. Do I go to help her, or do I go to a phone? I feel frozen in my sandals. I can only stare at her as she kneels on the floor by the boy. One hand is gently on the young boy's shoulder, while her other hand is stretched out straight and hard, pointing at the men. They yell at her, but I can't make out their words. Suddenly I feel a curious shopper jolt past me and I wake up. I run to a kiosk and yell at the cashier to call security, and as she reaches for the phone, I run to Mary Catherine. She's standing up now, standing between the boy and the two men twice her size. She's pointing her finger, firmly telling them to move away from the boy, while the men are swearing at her, threatening her, raising their arms again.

"C'mon Mary," I yell. "Let's go!" But she doesn't hear me. She's deep in that Artemis archetype again and I don't stand a chance. I reach out for her arm when from behind me step two security guards.

Walking to our car, Mary is still on fire. "The cops won't do a damn thing," she fumes. "Those gorillas will lie like hell and get that boy back home and beat him for getting them in trouble." She swings her purse and hits the hood of the car. "And all those damn scarf-necked hairdos who just walked by without even trying to help him. Do you believe that?" I look around as I unlock the doors.

"You could have been really hurt, Mary."

"Bullshit," she snaps. "I should've maced the bastards."

TEN

*And do not look upon me when I am cast out among those who
are disgraced and in the least places,
nor laugh at me.
And do not cast me out among those who are slain in violence.*

"Bernadette," Dad chimes first thing the next morning, "Go with your sister to the police station." He stares at the sports page while he talks. "The Bucs are on ESPN at one. Give old Pop a break."

"Sure. I'll get Mom to come, too."

"Mother of Christ! Are you kiddin?" He bangs his open hand on the kitchen table, laughing. "Gives your mother headaches just thinkin' about it. She'd be on the doctor's couch for a week."

When Mary prances in an hour later in her ironed Guess jeans and pedicure, Mom whisks Suzanna back to her bedroom for a visitation present. "Where's *my* present?" Mary whispers to me as she steals my orange juice.

I point to her toes. "Icy mauve?"

She points to mine. "Sandpaper?"

I take back my orange juice. "I'll go with you for the switch, okay?"

"Great. You'll get to see Brad and meet the witch." She turns her hands into claws, lifts her shoulders and cackles. "Can't wait, huh?"

Then she picks up a toast triangle that Dad's enveloped in butter. "Jesus," she says, squishing the bread until the fat streams onto his plate. "You playing tennis today, Dad?" she winks, sticking out her stomach and patting it. How does she get away with this?

In the car, thumbing through an old Protestant hymn book of my grandmother's, some remnant Mom had on the bottom shelf of her bookcase, I ask Mary if trading Suzanna at the police station helps.

"Well, she still cries. It's the same every week."

I read the inscription inside the front cover. 'To my sweetheart Lon, Love Millicent.'

"So Brad doesn't see her get upset?" Suzanna's in the back seat singing the ABC song, thinks we're going to Kmart. And this car really does smell like rotten milk. I'm so glad I don't have children.

"He sees. But his WendyJo is there." Sitting at a red light, she turns to me. "You do know there're only two kinds of people in the world, don't you?"

I close the book. "You've been asking me this question for ten years. But go ahead and answer it again because I know you want to." I point to her face. "I can tell by the sneer forming in your upper right lip and nostril."

"Two kinds of people" she continues, turning right. "Me and my friends...and eeeevil."

"So where do Brad and WendyJo fall?"

"Called Sean back yet? And what the hell ancient book you got there?"

"Grandma's. Thought I might find something heretical for an essay."

She grabs it out of my hand while she's driving and looks at the cover. "It's a hymn book, Dette," and she tosses it onto my lap.

I just look at her. "Really?"

She flicks my shoulder, pulling into a small brown building with an American flag up the pole in front. She lifts Suzanna out of her car seat while I grab the suitcase and walk ahead to open the door.

Inside, the lobby is small and dim, but I see Brad, slumped way back on a bench in a dark corner and looking sheepish as hell. A cop lazily reads a newspaper, and I suspect the new wife is the redneck with the perm, tapping her high heel.

"Hi Brad," I say, trying to be civil, but really wishing I could slap this hymn book up the side of his head.

"Hey Bernadette. Long time, no see." He slumps even more, if that's possible.

I put the Barbie suitcase down next to him on the bench and turn to Mary. Suzanna winds her arms around Mary's neck and buries her head. My sister turns pale, her eyes become rigid. She looks straight ahead into blank space, into no one.

But nothing prepares me for what happens next. Not phone calls, nor images, nor Mom's headaches have allowed me room for what I witness: a mother, my sister, trying to hand over her child to a man the child does not want to know. The child, my niece, Suzanna, refusing to let go of her mother's neck. One pulls away, one clings. Both are desperate.

"Please, Mommy, please, Mommy, don't give me away!"

Mary tries to unwrap Suzanna's arms from her neck, whispering short, gasping words to her that I can't hear.

"Please, Mommy. I don't want to go. No, Mommy, no!"

Brad stands up and slouches in front of my sister. You can tell he doesn't know what to say or do. But the wife is right behind him, her hands on her hips, and a scowl on her face. "Take her, Brad," she commands. "Just take her. This is ridiculous."

"No, Mommy, no, don't give me away. No, no!" Suzanna begs, as Mary, reluctantly stronger, pulls her thrashing child away from her own body, Suzanna's shiny brown curls wet and stringy around her puffy tear-soaked face. Trying to hide her own tears, Mary hangs her head as she forcefully hands her daughter, flailing and screaming, to Brad.

But in the passing of the sobbing child, I see the swirl of a soft pink dress and dampened yellow bows desperately fighting free of a father's hands, dropping to the floor, dashing back to the mother, wrapping small strong arms around the mother's knees, gasping for breath in between sobs, choking on her own hysterical appeals, "No, no!"

I throw myself up to the police desk. "You can't stand here and witness this. You're sanctioning child abuse. You're here to protect!"

"Ma'am. Now Ma'am," this overweight uniform leans across the counter, "Ma'am, we're just supposta make sure the two adult parties don't fight, ma'am. And they ain't fightin. Now the judge says that baby's gotta go to her father avery Saturday."

Someone takes me by the elbow. I yank myself loose and whirl around, ready to strike. Mary Catherine takes my arm again and pulls me out the door.

I remember waking up on a Saturday morning, when I was ten, to the sobs of my little sister. Her legs were still under her sheets, but the top half of her body hugged the metal hamster cage that sat on a small table between our twin beds. The cage was home to Fritz, the hamster she dressed in Barbie clothes.

Every night after Mom turned out the lights and closed the door to our pink room, my sister and I would remove the bread we'd hidden under our pillows and open up our bakery. We'd squish the bread flat, tear it into strips and roll up each strip like a danish. Then we'd sell our goods to Fritz. He'd pay us in cedar chips, which we'd store under our pillows where the bread had been, stupidly hoping we'd get an even stupider tooth fairy mistaking the chips for teeth. It never worked. But it was always fun to watch Fritz gnaw and nibble at our creations, lulling us to sleep with his quiet chewing.

But that night we must have rolled one too many buns for Fritz. For that morning, I sat up in bed to Pinhead's sobs and saw Fritz on his back in Barbie's best evening gown, his four furry little paws straight up and stiff. His eyes bulged open and this tiny pink tongue hung out one side of his mouth. I didn't even know hamsters had tongues.

"Is he dead?" Pinhead asks me in between gasping sobs.

"No, Mary, he's stretching," I smirk. "Just open the cage and shake him a little. He'll come out of it. Really."

So she did. My six-year-old sister actually reached into that fetid cage and picked up that stone-stiff rodent and started shaking him like a maraca.

"But he's so cold," she moaned.

"Then rub him," I answered, wishing my brother was here to witness this.

So Pinhead rubbed and rubbed that corpse until its tongue started lopping back and forth from side to side and I could bear the torture no longer.

"It's dead, Pinhead, dead! Put it down, will you?"

Fritz was not only dead, but bloated. I think the gown was too slim, and when Fritz ballooned up from the white bread expanding in his stomach after he drank his water, the waistline of the dress didn't expand with it. But the more Mary rubbed, the smaller Fritz became, and a curious odor filled the air. When Mom came in to check on all the crying, she sniffed and knew what happened. Sympathy showed on her weary face, but it disappeared when she pointed to the tell-tale signs of pastry gluttony that lay all around Fritz's Barbie bed in the corner of his cage.

"Bernadette, what is going on here? What? "

"Fritz is dead, Mom."

"Don't be smart with me, I can see that. Mary, put that hamster down and go wash your..." She took Mary by the wrist. "Put it down!"

"No," Pinhead sobbed, shaking. "I can't, I can't!"

"She's squeezing it, Mom. Get her!"

"Here, give me that," she commanded as she tried to pry the hamster out of her hands, Pinhead gripping that dead animal with all her might, the muscles in her neck sticking out like jail bars.

"No, no, stop!"

But Mom was stronger and meaner, and Pinhead, empty-handed, ran from the room screaming.

Mom turned to me, the mangled corpse in one hand, the other pointing to the cage. "Bernadette, you know I'm referring to the bread crumbs. What have you been doing? Tell me now. One, two..."

I took a deep breath. "We had a bakery, we fed the donuts to Fritz, he ate too many, he croaked."

"Does she get grounded, Mom, or does she get the belt? Want me to go wake up Dad? Huh?" It was that punk brother of mine, born six weeks premature and still trying to accumulate power. I'd get him back for this later. Meanwhile, I kept my eyes on the carpet and hoped for grounding. I liked to read.

Mom just looked at me. "Get your father," she said to him. "Then go help your little sister find some twigs in the backyard."

ELEVEN

I am the ruler of my offspring.
But he is the one who [begot me] before the time
on a birthday.
And whatever he wills happens to me.

Mary and I sit in silence for the drive home from the police station. And all I can see are Pinhead's dying animal babies, her Florence Nightingale black thumb, how the twig crosses she hammered into the dirt were just preparations, miniature rehearsals for the weekly death she'd later have to endure with her own frightened child, never knowing for sure why she cries, what happens to her, or if she's safe. My sister is a strong woman, but being a strong woman doesn't mean you're protected from darkness, especially the darkness in those who think they're doing the right thing.

She pulls into Mom's driveway, but doesn't turn off the engine. "Let's go to a movie tonight, Mary. How about, maybe, a comedy?"

She keeps her eyes on the windshield. "I've got to go back," she says. "A stack of papers need grading and I need to sleep."

It's that don't-beg tone, so I just get out. "Call if you change your mind. I'll be right here, lounging with ma and pa." My cheerleader tone is nauseating. Today, I definitely fit into the asshole category. She shifts into reverse as I ever so gently close the car door, still smiling like a stewardess.

Mom has dinner waiting. Baked potatoes and hot frozen vegetables. "Your sister's not staying for dinner?" she asks.

I plop into a chair and stare at my plate. There's a lonely wrinkled potato sitting in the middle of it. Looks like a friendless brown rock. "Not tonight."

"Bernadette," she sort of gasps. I jump. "It's Saturday night!"

I slouch back to my plate, spearing my spud with Dad's steak knife. So this is special? A Saturday night? "She wants to be alone, Mom. I don't blame her."

"We shouldn't leave her alone. Here. Fix it up," she commands, setting a plastic tub of fake butter before me. "Maybe your father and you could drive over and check on her."

I pick up the potato in my hand and take a bite out of the pointed end. "Look," I mumble, chewing on the bland and depressing, "between teaching doped-up teenagers and single-mothering a three year old, sleep is a luxury. Let the girl sleep."

I stop chewing. There's a song in my head, one I haven't heard in awhile, one I used to play over and over around the time I was ending my marriage. My mother talks, but I'm staring at the ceiling, trying to listen to the song. There's something about glass, cut glass.

I remember, it's Dylan, and I flash to our best wedding present—sixth row seats to the Budokan tour—the concert where he played the soul-pinching violin version of "Tangled Up in Blue." Mikhail tried to find it on subsequent albums, bootlegs even, but Dylan never recorded it. I can't believe he remarried in only six months. I wonder if their wedding blushed as beautifully as ours. My mother's voice drones on. The song in my head continues. Glass is everywhere.

But glass from what? A woman, she's crawling, without a sound…, shards of it all about the floor she moves, I wince and cringe, watching her in a yellow silk dress, *crawling across cut glass to make a deal*, blood stains spreading upon her knees.

"Glass? Where's the broken glass?"

I startle from my reverie to find Dad standing at the table yelling into my face.

"Oh, sorry," I stutter. "I must have been thinking out loud." He keeps looking at me. I look back at him and widen my eyes in exasperation. "No glass, Dad, no glass. Sit!"

He pulls out a chair. "So, big sister got to see the police station extravaganza, eh? A little upsetting?"

"Don't joke. It's brutal."

"Who's joking?" he says. "I see it every other weekend. Your mother stays home and takes a nap."

My irritability subsides and I suddenly feel sadness for these two. They really are doing the best they can. I lean towards Dad. "I know it helps Mary that you go," I reassure him. But he's already focused on mashing his potato with peas and butter.

"*Saint Death IV* is on at 8 o'clock tonight," he announces. "You'd like it, Bernadette. Lots of suspense."

"I'm sure I would, Dad."

After cleaning up the kitchen while Dad watches the news, Mom brings out her nail kit. "Here honey, let's do our nails. Mary told me a very nice man has been calling you."

I put my hands behind my back. "I never do my nails. My nails are fine."

"Oh, it's not fancy stuff, just sit here and I'll show you. What's his name?"

I sit. "Sean. And it's nothing." She lets out a defeated sigh. "Mom, did a judge…?"

"Your father and the attorney will handle everything," she interrupts. "Here, put this on first. Makes them stronger. See how long mine are getting?"

I look down at ten of the stubbiest nubs for fingers I have ever seen. The nails are, at best, a fraction of what they should be. Mom has bitten them so far down that the fact that they are no longer bleeding is considered, by her, progress.

"Looking good, Mom."

"Oh, I know I bite them too much. Dr. Tuley-Cashwell is always remarking about it."

"The shrink?"

"I'm thinking of ending my sessions," she answers with a sort of twitch to her upper lip. "I never have anything to say when I go in there."

I slip with the miniature paint brush and coat my knuckle. Nothing to say? You've got to be kidding. I try to hide my cynicism with a polite probe. "What about dreams?"

"You're supposed to do your cuticles before applying the base coat," she says, handing me the nail polish remover and a cotton ball. "And I don't have dreams," she adds with an unfortunately questionable finality.

"Everyone dreams, Mom. Sometimes we don't remember them, that's all."

"Oh...well...we talk about my dad, I guess...and my sister."

There. The cat's out. I knew she could do it.

"I noticed you hung Londa's picture on the wall. She looks a lot like you."

I stare at the Olan Mills portrait of a girl of maybe nine or ten. It isn't like the portraits of my sister or me when we were that age, tanned and excited, gaps in our toothy smiles, eyes full of cotton candy circuses and wrestling puppies. In contrast, Londa's face is somber, and the edges of her face are vaporous, like there's no definition between her skin and the space around it. Her hair is auburn, wavy beneath two languid lavender bows. The smile is slight, her expression soft, as if someone has just told her how much they love her and she feels sadness for that.

"I may take it down. I don't like it."

"Why?"

She shrugs, looking away from Londa's portrait.

"Well, if you ever want to lose it, I'd love to have it."

She doesn't answer. She gets up, like she's forgotten to serve the ice cream and Vienna Fingers, and she goes over to the sink and starts rinsing the pans she's already cleaned, running them under the faucet water over and over again. I push at my cuticles with that little wooden stick and watch her. I'm still hoping for dessert myself, but it becomes clear that isn't on her agenda. She's on some mission, in some far away country.

It reminds me of how she'd stand in the driveway holding the hose out in front of her, two or three times a day, and just let the water run. We kids could never figure it out. What was she watering? It was asphalt. My brother and I would make fun of her, Dad too sometimes, but she never stopped. She'd just stand there in the hot sun watering the driveway.

"You want to go to a what?" her father yelled across the dimly-lit living room in November of 1941. "Did I hear that girl correctly, Millicent?" He turned to his wife. "Did I hear her say she wants to go to a football game?"

"Lon, maybe..."

"Shutup!"

He turned back to the girl. "Speak up when you are spoken to, Rachel Jane," he commanded. "Answer me!" She didn't. He whirled around, grabbed the stem of the floor lamp and threw it to the ground, the light bulb shattering, the fringed shade ripped and bent. He slammed the back of his fist against the stack of books on the marble coffee table, and sent them flying across the room. He took an angry step towards Rachel Jane, his arm held high, when, from the corner of his eye, he saw the minister pause from putting on his dark gray coat. Lon froze mid-flight, glaring at his daughter, his breath still forceful and mean. This girl of fourteen was a disgrace. "A football game," he growled. "You actually want to go to a football game at a time like this."

Standing in the kitchen doorway, her sister's favorite doll dangling from one hand, her new black coat dangling from the other, she softly replied. "Sarah's mother said she would drive us. It's Homecoming...I think."

Lon threw his hat to the floor. The minister fumbled with his gloves. Grace folded her hands on her lap and Millicent pulled her wool scarf tighter around her neck. "How dare you treat your parents this way. You ungrateful child." her father screamed. "How dare you do this to us on the day of your sister's funeral. How dare you."

"Mom. Mom." I stand next to her at the faucet.

"Let her go, Mary Catherine."

"I'm Bernadette."

"She likes to wash 'em again. She'll be okay. Come watch ESPN."

I put my hand on her shoulder. She turns to me quickly. "Mom, let's finish our nails. These pans are clean enough." I turn off the water, and lead her back to the table. "I don't need the picture."

She rubs her temples. "No, you can have it. I hate looking at it. I hate it." She's digging into her own scalp now. "He killed her. I can't, I can't stand it."

"Who?"

"My father."

"But Mom, I thought Lon doted on her. You told me once that Hoover almost fired grandpa because he spent too much time with her in the hospital." I begin to apply the clear base coat, very sensitive.

"It doesn't matter. My sister chose to die."

"She chose to die? She died of cystic fibrosis."

"We could have moved to Tucson, where she would have lived. She needed the desert air. The doctors all warned him. But he wouldn't leave D.C., no, he couldn't leave the Bureau."

"So she died because of the humid Washington D.C. air, because she couldn't live in the dry Tucson air, not because she chose to die."

She leans right into my face. "He wouldn't move to Tucson, so my sister *chose* to die."

I get up to make tea. "Okay, fine."

"Bernadette! While you're up, bring your father some of that ice cream in the freezer, the butter pecan, two scoops, big ones."

Digging into the overly frozen carton, I tell myself that a religion major should be more accepting of various belief systems, completely misled as some may be.

"Well Mom, what about Millicent? She was educated for her generation, but subservient. With a Mistress Degree in hand, why didn't she just take Londa herself? Leave the guy."

She stops rubbing her head. "She had a what?"

"Femspeak. Nevermind."

"Bernadette, it's hard for you to understand her generation. There was little choice, divorce was the end of the world. I often heard her say that to Mrs. Vixyboxy."

"Well there you go, she talked about divorce with Mrs. Vixyboxy. At least she thought of it."

She returns to the manicure session, a shift for which I'm grateful. She's pushing back her own cuticles now, sort of absent-mindedly, like she's in a fog. "It's hard for you to understand because you walked away from your marriage when you felt like it. You grabbed your checkbook, got in the car, and left. But honey, you were extroverted since birth. I'd watch you when you were little, and feel such gratitude that you were so full of yourself, so fearless. Remember the time you pushed that girl off the stage at your ballet recital? You were annoyed that she wouldn't move, that she just stood there, afraid. You were three. That's when I knew life would be easy for you. I knew you'd never be like my mother."

I ignore the bully reference and dig around the box for black polish, grateful that she's forgotten the Madam Chomsky affair. "Grandma could have taken care of herself. She could have taken off to Egypt with her sister. She had her teaching degree."

She puts down her cuticle stick and stares at her hands. "Bernadette, you should know that degrees aren't even half of it."

Wait. I thought degrees were all of it.

"My father was cruel. Told her to shutup all the time, embarrass her in front of her friends. And then there was Grace. I think that embarrassed Mom the most."

"Did Aunt Grace ever defend her?"

"No, her sister wouldn't say anything, but she'd get a real sad look on her face."

It was a bit curious that Mom could talk so easily about her mother, or about me...but not about her youngest daughter, and not about herself.

"I'll bet Grace never canned a tomato in her entire life, not a one."

"Well, that was easily a source of tension between them. Grace definitely became the more self-centered sister, and more fun. She'd bring back hundreds of slides and pictures from her travels to the Middle East, while Mom slaved in the kitchen and not too happy about it. She resented Grace's freedom to come and go."

"You know that black and white photo of Grace is taped to my monitor."

Mom's eyes perk up. "Where she's on a camel? Pyramids behind her? Maybe it's time to give you something, Bernadette." She stands and goes in to her bedroom, comes out carrying a large white box. "These are Millicent's diaries. She wrote everything down, just like you, honey. Take them home to Virginia. I don't want them in my house anymore. The picture, too. I'm going to bed, I'm sick." She walks away, holding her head.

I sit there and stare at Londa again, turn away and pack up the nail kit, trying to figure out how to maneuver past Dad without getting the old invitation to watch the movie. I decide to just leave all the lights on and wait for a loud, violent scene, and then tiptoe by. I hear explosives and make my move.

"Hey! Can't go to bed yet. Jesus H. Christ, your mother snuck off, didn't she? I'm gonna get her."

Damn.

"Listen, here's what's happened so far..."

"Dad, I'm really tired. Been a pretty rough day."

"Half an hour. That's all that's left. You'll just stay in your room and read all your damn books anyway. C'mon in. Sit there on the big sofa. Okay, here's the scoop. There's this guy in Nam, escaped from a POW camp and on his own in the jungle..."

When I finally do curl up in my old twin bed with my grandmother's diaries, I feel like I'm back in the stacks of the library. I turn over page after yellowed page, eager to analyze every grammatically correct sentence, like I'm researching a gnostic tractate. But I soon meet with disappointment, for grandma's script is minute and clean, free of secret and emotion. Unlike *The Thunder*, there are no half-finished thoughts, no ambiguity, no ellipses, paradox or confusion.

We were up at 5:30am. I thought it was 6:30. The rug was not dirty, but I swept it out and washed two dresses, the chambrae and the print. The humidity is so high that I do not think they will dry quickly. We drove to town and went to two stores. I bought a piece of material half-price for chairs. We bought oranges. I mailed two letters from the mailbox. Worked on my washcloth pot holders. We had canned meat for dinner. There was a program at Church at 7pm. I could not get supper and dishes and cleanup in time. Retired at 8.

Curses. I'm here to search for some dead and gone drama, some rich Victorian angst that is, by birthright, mine alone to peruse. I want to immerse myself in some ancient juice and there is none. Instead, I get an account of every bar of lye soap boiled in the basement.

But who am I to be critical. I doubt my grandmother had that kind of personality before she knew her husband, before she knew her daughter, before she watched one turn into a tyrant, before she watched one die. So her mind-numbing diary belies her life. Filling your mind with the tedious and petty can serve a purpose, for it leaves no room for the unbearable. My grandmother knew how to contract pain. Maybe I should take note.

I reach over to turn out the light. But as I do so, one of the diaries slides back into the carton on the floor, revealing a small wooden box near the bottom. I pull it out, but it's locked, no key. Then I notice the lock has already been carefully pried open, so skillfully in fact that at first glance, it appears intact. I open slowly to find a cache of letters and loose diary pages obviously torn from their original book.

Washington, D.C.
1926 A.D.

TWELVE

*And now give heed to me, my children,
concerning the things which I saw during my time of penitance,
concerning the seven spirits of deceit.*

Testament of Reuben 2:1
from The OT Pseudepigrapha

"Millicent, you can't marry him. He doesn't look honest in that photograph."

"I am marrying him." She yanked the scarlet embroidery thread through the indigo silk and made a severe knot. "Saturday."

"Father agrees with me."

"Your stitching is crooked."

Grace leaned over closer. "Travel with me instead—Egypt, Greece—every place in the Bible. We can—"

"And how do you think we'll pay for these adventures?" She snipped a wayward black thread.

"We'll minister to those who need us. With my nursing and your teaching degree, we'll be in such demand. Every city has hospitals and schools. I've been reading up on -"

"I know," Millicent interrupted, holding her square to the light, "That's all you do."

"Think of the pyramids, the temples, the holy places Father has told us of since—"

"Since we were children."

Grace resumed her embroidery, hushed by the stubborn rejection, the disdain that ran between them like course thread moving through burlap. Millicent coughed and Grace told her hands to choose the amber patch now. So she moved the quilt and began sewing a different corner, noting that if only the rational could reach her sister, then the rational she must adopt. She put down her needle.

"You met this man by mail," Grace continued. "You don't know what life with him will be like. It's an uncertain path."

"I know all I need to know," she replied quickly. "He's a hard worker with an accounting degree from Columbia. He's mannerly. I need nothing else of a husband."

"You said he was a barnstormer. Is that not illegal?" She slowly smoothed out a triangle of golden velvet upon her lap, biting her lip to keep from grinning. Millicent could not possibly argue.

"Lon never flew in the war. He trained to fly in France, but we signed the armistice. He simply applied an inactive skill in a creative manner."

"Well, if he's honest, why can't he tell the people at his job that he's coming out here to marry? You don't even get a honeymoon, all such a, such a…secret." She folded her hands across the velvet and looked toward the fading window light, her face softening with the approaching dusk. Her sister was lost to her now. She knew that. Her voice dropped to a whisper. "I guess one might view it as mysterious, as mysterious or exotic or—"

"His boss doesn't want his agents to be married," Millicent answered, completely unaware that her sister wasn't listening, but was, instead, walking up the steps of some Egyptian temple, alone. "Lon must send him a Western Union telegram at every stop. He must tell him all his activities, including where, how, why and with whom. If he doesn't, he'll be fired. That's why the marriage is a secret. Lon has a very important job and his boss is a very important man."

"Who is he?" Grace asked with an unnoticed indifference.

"His name is J. Edgar Hoover."

Grace dug her hand into the sand and let it sift through her fingers. "I've never heard of him."

"Lon says you will. He says the whole world will."

Hoover didn't know about the unlogged trip or the covert marriage until eight months later when he called Lon into his office. Lon staggered in late that night, looked at his wife's pregnant stomach, turned and walked out. He took nothing with him. He was gone for six days and never said where.

THIRTEEN

*Do not devote your attention
to the beauty of women, my children,
nor occupy your minds with their activities.
But live in integrity of heart in the fear of the Lord...*

Testament of Reuben 4:1

My Dearest Sister,

So she is a girl, perfectly healthy, how blessed you are. Do not concern yourself with Lon's disappointment. All men want boys, how silly they can be at times.

And you've named her Rachel Jane. How pretty. Is Londa happy to have a new sister? So close in age, they will be close in life.

You have done well. Do not regard Lon's edicts. He will come around.

I found the most unusual baby rattle in Lebanon and will send it next post.
all my love,
Grace

FOURTEEN

*Beware, my children, of those who hate,
because it leads to lawlessness
against the Lord himself...*

Testament of Gad 4:1

My Dearest Sister,
 How I wish you were here. I know I say this in every letter, but to share my travels with you by my side all these years would have been my greatest joy.
 Finally we come to Egypt, a land unlike any I have ever read or dreamed of. Floating down the Nile transcends even the furthest flights of my imagination, and the strength of the pyramids fills my soul to such an extent I find I am sometimes unable to breathe.
 Enclosed is a photograph of my adventures upon the back of a contrary camel. I envision you upon this camel and laugh at how you would scold him for his unruly manners.
 And now I must be serious. Get Londa to Tucson, Millicent. Go there now. Get on a train, a bus, whatever it takes, delay no longer. Rachel Jane can travel with you, helping with Londa's medicine. She has a way with Londa, so able she is to make her smile. I'm enclosing money for tickets for the three of you. Wait until Lon is away on a case. Do not allow his tyranny to impede your daughter's health. To all of you I send my blessing, Grace

FIFTEEN

Hatred is evil,
since it continually consorts with lying,
speaking against the truth;
it makes small things big,
turns light into darkness,
says that the sweet is bitter...

Testament of Gad 5:1

Millicent stood at the sink peeling cucumbers, a new tear falling with each strip of waxy green skin. The raw rabbit lay next to the rim, angled so the blood would drip away from the counter's edge. She didn't feel the tug at her apron.

"Mommy?"

No answer.

"Mommy, Londa's coughing again."

She kept peeling.

"Why are you crying? I can peel the vegetables. I can do it."

"Bring her into the kitchen."

Rachel Jane ran up the stairs, two at a time, to help her sister up off the floor. "Here, take Martha," she said as she pressed the doll close to Londa's chest, as if to stop the heaving. "C'mon, hold on to my shoulder."

Londa clung to Rachel Jane, suppressing the cough for as many steps as she could. But the convulsions always burst forth and Rachel had to let go of the banister and hold her sister around the waist with both arms, her own frail frame jerking with each renewed spasm. Then she grabbed the railing so they wouldn't fall down the next step. She had to choose, every time she had to choose, between holding onto the railing and holding onto her sister.

Millicent stood at the bottom of the stairs with blood on her hands. She wiped it on her apron, untied it, and let it drop to the floor. She ran up to the landing and took Londa upon her shoulder, carrying her the rest of the way down.

"Rachel, move the books off the chair so I can sit her down. You know where to put them so your father can't tell I...well, hurry."

Rushing to remove the leather-bound editions of Dickinson and Tennyson and Hawthorne, Rachel tripped over the footstool and the books flew across the carpet. Millicent said nothing as she cradled Londa in her arms, rocking her, singing a lullaby. Rachel pulled herself up off the floor and returned the books to their proper place on the shelf. That's when she saw the letters scattered on the table. She scooped them up and ran back to the living room.

"Mom, may I read Aunt Grace's letters? I can read them to Londa."

Millicent stopped singing and looked away. "Those letters need to be burned."

SIXTEEN

*So understand, my children,
that two spirits await an opportunity with humanity:
the spirit of truth
and the sprit of error.
In between is the conscience of the mind
which inclines as it will.*

Testament of Judah 20:1

EXCERPT FROM *MY MEMOIR, LON TAFT,* 1908

I was using the 22 caliber rifle, maybe 8 years old. At butchering time I was detailed to do the shooting, a bullet between the eyes. No compassion when it was a steer or a hog, but maybe some when it was a horse or dog or cat. For a hog, knives were sharpened on the grindstone, two big kettles were hung on a pole over an open fire for heating water with which to scald the hog. There was the big black iron kettle and the brass kettle. When the water was boiling it was time for the rifle between the eyes, followed by "sticking" to bleed the hog. This was a strong hickory stick called a gambrel that was placed between the hog's hind legs. A barrel was half filled with scalding water, a rope and pulley were made fast up in a hickory tree, and with all hands helping, the hog was hoisted, then lowered into the scalding water.

Trapping and hunting of animals was an important part of my life; I was fascinated by it and made some money from it. Dad taught me how to skin skunks without getting the stink on me; he showed me the glands which made the liquid that the skunk sprayed when frightened. I liked to shove a steel trap in a hole, then plug the entrance so the creature could not get out. When I caught one, I sold his pelt to a fur buyer and it brought .25. It was not very much but it would have bought a pound of chocolate drops at the grocery store. I bought a nickels worth at a time.

SEVENTEEN

*So I tell you, my children,
flee from the evil of Beliar,
because he offers a sword to those who obey him.
And the sword is the mother of the seven evils.*

Testament of Benjamin 7:1

"Mom, I need material to make a dress for the Spring Dance."

"We're walking away from her grave and you're thinking about a dance?"

"I remembered, I remembered making dresses for her dolls, while we were standing there."

"Well, you'll have to sit on his lap. You know that."

"Mom, I'm nineteen."

Millicent rinsed canning jars at the sink while Rachel stood at the living room doorway. He was reading the Wall Street Journal in his Queen Anne chair, but he looked up and smiled, opening his arms. She sat as far out on his knees as she could, but he was short, so this never helped. He'd just put his feet up on the stool and she'd slide down onto his lap.

"Are you going with a boy?" he asked.

"Yes."

"Are you shacking up with this boy?"

"No."

"Is this the Catholic boy your mother told me about? Is this what I send you to college for?"

She was sweating. She hated him. "He was in the Navy before school."

"Oh, the Navy," he said. "A Catholic and a sailor."

She tried to get up, but he pinned her arms to her sides. "What kind of dress will you make with this material your Daddy buys you?

"I haven't found a, a pattern, but—"

"A dress your Catholic boy will like? I know what kind of dresses sailor boys like, Rachel Jane. Shall I tell you what soldier boys…"

Rachel leapt out of his lap and ran past her mother, out the back door, down the porch steps, across the field and into the raspberry vines behind the shed, right to the spot where she used to run and hide with Londa. She covered her ears, but she could still hear him screaming out the back door.

"You forget that Catholic boy business or you forget school. Do you hear me? You won't get a dime out of me for college! You'll never be a nurse. You'll be out. You hear me? Out on the street!"

Millicent leaned her elbows on the edge of the sink and held her hands together under the running water.

Without the fabric, Rachel returned to college and finished the semester. At dinner on her first night home for Christmas break, she announced her June wedding plans. And before Lon's reddening face could spew squirrel stew, she walked out the front door, retrieved the bags she'd hidden under the boxwoods and walked to the end of the snow-laced street. There she phoned a taxi, found the downtown YWCA and asked for the bed in which she slept for the next six months, supporting herself as a cashier at the corner Woolworth's.

EIGHTEEN

The first is moral corruption,
the second is destruction,
the third is oppression,
the fourth is captivity
the fifth is want,
the sixth is turmoil,
the seventh is desolation.

Testament of Benjamin 7:2

My dearest sister,
Religious wars surround us in this part of the world. Fighting over the same God. All the rich history of great men and women, yet few can coexist because their religions have different names. And now it is so with your family. So he's a Catholic! You and I know the foolishness of the boundaries we invent. Rachel is getting married and you will watch her walk down the aisle for both of us. Lon will not allow you to go? You will go.
How he angers me! I wonder if Hoover has made all his men into the oppressor Lon has become. Or maybe he was able to spot the men who already had such blood running in their veins, and his talent was to lech it out a little, stir in more darkness of

his own, and reinject it to get the perfect investigative agent, the perfect beast.

I read the excerpt from his memoir, enclosed herein. I see the single bullet between the eyes, the sticking, the skinning, all without emotion, an eight year old boy. But Millicent, there are many men who come up straight with farm work, the killing for food a necessity. However, it appears that some who walk the path of the steel trap continue to set it for the rest of their lives, long after the need is gone. Lon holds tight to that gambrel. And though initially I know you would never have thought such a thing of your husband, I bet Hoover counts on it, and builds his empire upon its promise.

Enclosed is the money for a bus ticket to Rachel's wedding. Please give her all my love, Grace

NINETEEN

*The deliberations of the good man
are not in the control of the deceitful spirit,
for the angel of peace guides his life.*

Testament of Benjamin 6:1

<u>My Memoir, Lon Taft</u>

I recall with most immediacy the bay mare incident: I rode her bare back, as usual, into the yard near the kitchen. Something scared her making her jump to one side and throwing me off. The fall was so hard that I could not get my breath at first, but when I did, I grabbed a board bigger than a ball bat and belted it across the mare's ribs with all the might I could muster. Mother, seeing the performance, yelled, "If you don't learn to control your temper you can never do anything."

I still think the mare should have had ten belts instead of one.

Texas
1990 A.D.

TWENTY

Why have you hated me in your counsels?
For I shall be silent among those who are silent,
and I shall appear and speak.

I am the one before whom you have been ashamed,
and you have been shameless to me.

"**B**ernadette, Mother of Saints!" cries that familiar voice from the kitchen. "I hear you in there, I know you're up. Church starts in fifteen minutes, are you ready?"

Just like high school. I slowly unwind the quilt clutched beneath my chin, determined to forget why I fell asleep gripping it like a garlic braid. The mountain of monotonous diaries and telling letters are splayed on top of me, and as I slip out I'm reminded that a woman can see the difficulty of her sister's path, yet possess no power to change it. Sometimes she can only watch. But how could two sisters, born of the same mother's womb, sleeping side by side for years, be so different.

Standing between the pink twin beds, folding up the quilt, I wonder about the two of us, exchanging breath and sleep night after night. Now I watch her, she watches me, nothing changes, seventy years later we're still begging for the whirlwind to stop, but it keeps on coming no matter what we say to each other. Sisters weaving side by side, choosing different velvet, different ways to stitch it together, I don't think we've learned anything from our mother's mothers.

I stop to hold the quilt close one more time. The velvet and silk, the intricate embroidery, some pieces stitched with such uniformity while some with such waywardness, so easy to see which square was woven by the precise hands of Millicent, which circlet by the wandering hands of Grace.

I struggle out into the kitchen, still wearing the old blue bathrobe that's been hanging in the closet since college. Dad looks up from the sports page. "You better hurry," he laughs, knowing I'm not going to church, knowing I haven't gone with him for fifteen years. But sadly, I hear a little hope in his voice.

"Dad, you pray for me, okay?" I mumble, shuffling towards the pantry. "Ten Hail Marys."

"Father Joe still asks about you. He says, 'Where's Bernie?'"

"He'll never understand why I wouldn't dress in pale blue sheets and play the Madonna at Midnight Mass." I search among the cereal boxes for something healthy. *Fudge Frosted Flakes?* I never did like Father Joe calling me Bernie. *CocoaChunks?* I thought he did it because the word Bernadette was too difficult to pronounce with a thick Irish brogue. A saint even. *PopTart Spoonfuls?* Time for toast.

"You should have played her, no big deal, eh? Remember he wanted Chip's friend to be Joseph, what was his name? Jackson?" He dips a hunk of danish into his coffee and crams it in his mouth. I'm surprised there's any left. Mom always buys it for Sunday breakfast, then finishes it off before anyone else wakes up. But maybe even pastry didn't interest her after *last* night. I pull out a chair and sit down at the table.

"Dad, it was bad enough I never had any dates in high school, but if I would have crept up the aisle of church as the Virgin Mary, my fate of home-alone would have been sealed forever." I shudder. The real reason I wouldn't do it was the horror of my nerd self playing meek virgin bride to the ever popular Jackson. All the girls loved him. I didn't even know how to kiss.

"That God-forsaken Michigan thinks they got away with something yesterday," he mutters as he folds up the sports section. "Ohio State will show 'em. Rachel, let's go!"

Mom appears in a silk dress, still rubbing her temples raw. "I've got a headache."

"Just get in the car. Church will make you feel better." He holds his palms above his head. "Hallelujah, hallelujah!" he cries to the ceiling. Then he resumes his businessman stance and jingles the permanent change in his pocket. "Hold down the fort, Bernadette, and don't forget to let the dog out."

Ever since Mom's little dip in the pool a few years ago, Dad's always trying to find ways to make her laugh, but I don't think he's found the key. Like it's his responsibility.

Mom doesn't even say goodbye. She is just so *out* of it sometimes, not that I blame her today. I run to the phone and tell Mary to hurry over.

"Hey," she says glumly when she walks in. "Let's sit out by the pool." I agree, but only because she looks so depressed I'm thinking the sun might help. She opens the fridge and pours herself an iced tea from the permanent pitcher she's kept in there for years.

"Mary," I say once we're in our little lounge chairs, sipping our drinks, how lush we have it, "Mom gave me some letters between Grace and Grandma."

"Yep," she snaps. "Pretty sick shit."

I stare at the deep end.

"Her dad was a total douche to her," she says. "You know he told her she had the personality of a dog, right? A dog."

"Tell me again, was it Dad who pulled her out or was it Chip?"

She leans her face up to the sun. "The ankle weights she used were Chip's. But Dad found her at the bottom. He heard the splash during the eleven o'clock news and thought it was the dog. Ironic, huh."

I wince. "Jesus, where *was* I when that happened?"

"*You* were off prostrating yourself at the feet of Mikhail, throwing him a graduation party or something."

"Oh yeah, I remember feeling sort of bad about that. I wasn't much help."

"No one could help. The D.C. cousins had every right to call and say they were done taking care of Grandpa. Regardless of Mom's feelings about him, it was her turn to play nursemaid. And she just couldn't handle it." She slams down her tea, like she's mad at Mom for having had an abusive childhood.

"Well, we all knew she'd have to face the bastard *one* day, sooner or later."

"Later would have been preferable, say, at the viewing of the casket."

I pull the bathrobe up around my knees to get some sun on my legs. "So Dad saved the day, as usual."

"With Mom coughing up chlorine in his arms, he knew he better do something fast, before Lon's plane arrived. He'd made fun of her being afraid of an old geezer in diapers before, but all of a sudden it wasn't so funny."

"So she never even saw Grandpa when he arrived."

"Nope. Dad drove him straight from the airport to the nursing home."

I stretch my arms out to the sun. "I wish Grandma had been the one to live so long, not Grandpa."

Pinhead's voice softens. "Grandma was quiet and cool. I miss her."

Growing up, we only knew our grandmother. She actually took the bus to visit when I was born, me the tiny crucible of mediation, no one knows how she got away. But every summer after that, there she was, the bearer of tortuously boring gifts: flannel pajamas sewn by hand (Texas), jars of pickled cucumbers grown in her garden, misshapen bars of lye soap potioned in her basement. It was understood we were never to talk about our grandfather, and when Grandma died of a stroke, Mom refused to go to the funeral because he would be there.

"Did you know that Grandma secretly bought a bus ticket to Mom's wedding, but Grandpa found out?"

"Yeah, Grace told me. Grace sent her the cash. But who's surprised? I mean, he was rather skilled at reconnaissance. He told Grandma if she got on that bus, she better never come back."

Mary bolts up in her chair. "You remember telling me in high school? We were sitting in the orange tree and you were saying how Aunt Grace begged her to move to Jerusalem, to leave Lon."

"But Grandma refused to divorce him."

"And Mom overheard us and she *blew*—threw that hose down on the asphalt and started shaking her finger. 'You put that out of your mind,' she yelled up into the tree. 'You hear me? Don't you ever speak of it again!' Then she stalked back to her hose to water the parts of the driveway she'd missed."

I want to laugh, but it probably isn't that funny. Mary leans back in her chair. "You were always close with Grace. You two had some kind of connection."

"Her letters were filled with Isis. And she sent cool presents."

"I remember. I enjoyed drawing on them."

"God, I promised her I'd come. Told her I'd do what Grandma wouldn't."

"You mean go to Jerusalem and live with her?"

"We'd roam the deserts of Mary Magdalen and J.C. together, the ancient cites, the barren, the magnificent. Right after senior year."

"What a perfect time to go."

"We planned it all out. I was so excited to ride a camel."

"So why didn't you ever do it?"

I don't say anything.

"Oh for the love of God, how pathetic."

"Yes."

"You got married instead. To the snot." She shakes her head and pounds her feet against the cement. "You knew better than to get hitched right after college. What were you thinking?"

"I really disappointed her."

"And now she's dead. Up there with Grandma, watching us makes fools of ourselves on an hourly basis."

"Mikhail was studying for his orals while I outlined his notes. I couldn't concentrate. I knew something dark was happening."

"Oh please."

"You know the week before Mom made her poolside vault, she sent me all the things Grace had ever given me? She had each item neatly wrapped in tissue paper, all together in a box."

"You used to sleep with that crap under your pillow. A cross, a rosary, a palm leaf for Christ's sake, and a jar of holy water. My crayon wouldn't work on the holy water. Oh yeah, and that Bible."

"You slept with wounded frogs in a box."

"The Bible had a wood cover. You'd wake up with dents in your face."

"Anyway, the timing of the mail was not coincidental."

Mary looks off. "When people tie up loose ends like that, it usually means they're pretty serious about the deed." She shoots off the chaise, leaving her iced tea on the pavement. "Gotta go. Before they get back from Church."

"Stay," I whine. "They'll do errands, load up on Mom's prescriptions at the drug store, won't be back for hours. Really."

But she keeps walking. "No," she yells over her shoulder. "Suzanna's coming home. See ya."

Worried, I watch her go into the house. But before I can lift my lazy body off the lounge chair to beg her to stay, I hear the car pull out of the driveway.

And then I remember Dad's one request: fish out the tumor-ridden mass of fleas or he'll pee on the carpet. I look under sofas, under beds, and behind curtains for a tiny gray terrier who can't see, can't smell, and can barely walk.

I find him huddled behind Mom's stash of shoes in a corner of her crammed closet. I drag his arthritic self out by his tacky rhinestone collar and carry him outside. I set him in the grass and he just stands there, his back legs shaking, his face looking up at me, like I can squeeze it out of him.

"It's all up to you," I bend down and whisper. He moans. I roll my eyes and put my hands on my hips, hands aching for my piano, hips longing for an arabesque. I've got research to do, papers to write, and libraries to call Mother. I can't help Mary Catherine, I don't have the tranqs to help Mom, and Dad's living in Buckeye lala land.

I pick up Mugs and notice pee still drips from the rear. I try shaking him a little but it doesn't stop. He turns his small fuzzy head around and gives me another look. Why does Mom clip this dog's hair? It sticks out in clumps. He looks deranged.

I put him back on the grass and sit down myself, two feet from him at least, and survey the gardens and glittery lake. I must admit there's beauty here, shades of green, effortless palm trees, big sky sun. All this I lean towards, my eyes closed, my face held high. I absorb it fully now, free of satire, knowing I'm returning to forgotten religions and gnostic tractates. *The Thunder*, she prays me to her perfect mind, back to her chaos that doesn't confuse, back to first-century Alexandria or Damascus or Greece, lands and ideas I invent and control because no one can tell me I'm wrong. I've studied *The Thunder* in such depth that my advisor claims I understand more about the subject than anyone on the planet. The compliment is spoken with kindness, although we both know that Dr. MacLeish from Harvard comprehended more, but died of heart failure a few months ago. So I stand first in line due to death more than skill. I advise myself of this fact because it forces me to study harder, pushes me through that extra hour in the library stacks when most of the other lookers have sailed home to hot cocoa and down comforters.

I lie back on the grass and reach my hand out to pet Mugs. But my hand, searching for the errant dog, meets only grass. I open my eyes. There's no Mugs. Jumping to my feet, I scan the deep end of the pool. No, he can't be that feeble.

If I've lost the dog, it'll be the end. The belts have retired, Dad gave those up when I left for college, but Catholic guilt never dies. He wouldn't admonish me, he'd just get the abandoned look. *My god, my god, why hast thou forsaken me.* I will now burn in a serious Judeo-Christian hell, on one of Dante's really low levels. I cup my hands around my mouth and start calling. Then I remember. The dog is deaf. I head out to the road.

I find him five houses down the street, peeing on Worthingtin's front porch. And I imagine the relief on my father's face, his nod in my favor. There is something so gratifying about being someone's child and learning to set things right when you screw up.

I sit down on the grass, my finger looped through Mugsly's collar. Tonight I'll pack, say goodbye to my sister, watch some TV with Dad, and pull out first thing in the morning.

Virginia
1990 A.D.

TWENTY-ONE

I am she who is weak,
and I am well in a pleasant place.
I am senseless and I am wise.

Seven messages from Sean on my machine. I could have presumed the point with one, but I am somewhat flattered by his tenacity. I toss my bag onto the bed and start to unpack.

I'm not calling him. Dementia on many levels prevented any reading in Texas, so I don't wish to play now. But within the hour, the phone rings and I know it's not my mother.

"Bernadette, you have to be back because classes started. I want to hear about your trip, your sister. Mocha? Tonight? After the library? I'll meet you on the steps, ten o'clock. Ciao."

I flop down on the bed and stare at the ceiling. Damn it, I want to work at the library and be left alone. I hug my stomach, I need to burrow.

And how presumptuous—ten o'clock, ciao. How does he know I'm home anyway? He's going to be standing on those steps a long time.

I turn on my side, stretching out my lower back. That drive from Texas kills. It rode so much easier when Mikhail and I drove it together, singing to Dylan, or reading short stories aloud to keep each other awake. I close my eyes and rub my neck. Everything hurts.

So there, forget the research. I won't be able to stay awake tonight, so I may as well meet him. I sit up and make a face in the mirror. I am so scraggly, there's no way he could find me attractive. I resemble the dog.

The sky watches every crack I step on as we walk to the coffee house. But how intriguing that I'm actually pleased to see Sean. He's so cleared out, so unhindered by crisis. After living with my family for a week, his energy resonates calm.

I tell him of Mary's ex and the police station, and like a good date, he listens without comment. But as we turn the corner, he interrupts me with a surprising tone of irritation. "Come on, Bernadette. She's got your parents living down the street. How bad can it be?"

I look at him from the corner of my eye. He's not smiling, which could be a clue that he's actually serious. So I decide to be the same. "My mother's completely incapable," I say firmly. "That's why I drove down." I sneak another look at the side of his face. It's furrowed. This could get shadowy.

"So what's with your mother?" he asks with that same hint of hostility.

I muse about where I should take this. If the evening is going to be argumentative, I'm doing a u-turn to the stacks. They don't talk back and I'm always right.

I decide to go with humor, a technique that can usually salvage any wreck. "My mother's problems started when she was born a girl. Her parents already had one."

He leaps into my boat, such a chameleon already. "They were Chinese?"

I wrinkle my nose at him, so proud of myself for quickly converting his cynicism. "Yeah, that's why I am."

We're standing at the coffeehouse now and I notice it's not so crowded tonight. Probably because everyone else is doing research. He pulls out my chair. "So girls aren't a good thing in your family?" he continues, smoothing my hair quickly and sitting across from me. God, he's forward. But maybe that's what I deserve.

"No, they just didn't have a girl name." I put my hair behind my ears, grateful that I conditioned it. "Each of Lon's brothers had a daughter named after himself. Brother John named his daughter Jhonda. Brother Ron, Rhonda. Brother Lon, Londa."

"You're kidding me now."

"But my grandmother, that rebel, has a second baby girl. So what are they going to do for a name? Mrs. Vixyboxy, the neighbor, suggests Rachel."

"Why didn't they use a form of her mother's name?"

"Yeah, like Millicentonda? If it did occur to grandma, she kept quiet."

"Because she was Chinese."

"Because her husband was an agent for J. Edgar Hoover. You don't argue with these people. Especially if they live with you."

"Hoover? No, really, your grandfather?" He stands up. "Edgar was wrapped pretty tight. Still mocha?"

"Yeah," I smile, reaching into my jeans for money. But when I look up, he's already at the counter. I turn away and think how nice he is, and how rotten it must have been to be my mother. I picture the entry Lon might have written when she was born:

LOG: **September 14, 1929**
    5:45am: Arose.
    6:03am: Ate breakfast.
    8:16am: Had second girl baby. Named her Millicentonda.

And I think, no, this would not have worked. J. Edgar would not have been happy. He would have to speak to Lon in his office. He would say things Lon could never repeat, words that would make him shake and gag and fall out of his wheelchair at the Cedar Hills Nursing Home sixty-two years later. I've seen this. But sometimes the shaking is precipitated by what my mother whispers in his ear. I never hear what she whispers.

"Where'd the wry smile go?" Sean asks, setting down a tray. "You look so somber all of a sudden." He unloads the pastries onto my side of the table.

"Sean, really. I can't eat all this."

"You lost too much weight in Texas. Need to get it back." And I'm thinking, well, I got rid of his wrinkled brow, but how does he know what

I look like under the intentionally baggy clothes? Then it hits me—that damn ballet recital. He's seen me in a spandex leotard, under bright lights no less. "Now," he says, leaning forward in his seat, "you have to tell me about Hoover."

I shudder. No, no, I don't want to go there. I was just *at* that nursing home where my grandfather drools. I was just standing in front of my mother when that name came up. "I talk too much, Sean. *You* talk. Tell me how your work is going."

"Bernadette," he says. "Please. The last thing I want to talk about is work, especially after I've been doing it all day. I want to escape."

"Well, what about your family? Any siblings? Parents live where?"

He clears his throat. "I'm an only child," he says. "Waited upon and spoiled."

"And parents?"

"Dead, last year. My father a stroke, my mother cancer."

I drop the lemon bar back down on the doily. "Oh God," I stutter, so socially inept, always stumbling into the wrong river. "I'm sorry."

He looks up and smiles, such a genuine concern for my discomfort. "Impermanence," he says. "Everything moves on." I just look at him. "No really, don't worry. It's okay. You know the concept of upekka?"

I narrow my eyes. "Equanimity."

"Yes," he lights up, enchanted by the suggestion of a bond, lifting his carrot juice in a mock toast. "To equanimity."

"To equanimity," I reply with some semblance of grace, clinking our cups, intrigued with how peaceful he is for such a huge loss. I can expound upon these Buddhist concepts in a seminar, but this man embodies them. In the middle of a loud coffee house, he can speak of his orphaned status like it's the check. I want to be this tranquil, to accept consequence without a twitch.

"You can do this with everything?" I tentatively ask. "Observe the emotion, watch it dissipate, change to something else? You have developed upekka?"

"No," he winks. "I haven't. My ex lives in town and she's the most manipulative manic-depressive known to man. Well, actually, to a whole lot of men."

"Okay then, that's *some*thing," I say, grateful that this boddhisatva has an Achilles' heel after all. "You can tell me about *her*."

He grips the sides of the table and the veins on his neck stand out like jail bars. "No, don't make me. We've been separated for months and she's still calling me, asking to come over, sobbing for money."

"Oh. But that's pretty normal, isn't it?"

"Today she said that I should pay for her plane ticket to visit her parents."

"Should you?"

"She says I should...because my parents are dead."

I want to burst out laughing, but it's not funny. "I don't get it. Are you paraphrasing, or are you quoting?"

"Direct quote. Her mantra is 'Who made the rules' so what can I say?"

"Well there ya go. What can you say?"

He stands halfway out of his chair. "Tell me about your grandfather, tell me about Hoover, anything, please, I'm *begging* you."

I lean back and stare at the busy baristas. His request seems innocuous enough, and it might feel good to relax into a drama that's only a tale, that's not my home, my life. Or his questionable ex-wife. "Well," I muse, "there is the Mom in her pedal pushers mystery."

"Pedal pushers? I like pedal pushers. Go with pedal pushers."

I grin with delicious pleasure at all this attention. "The first time I heard the word Hoover, my mother was pointing at the TV and screaming, 'Hoover did this, Hoover did this!' She was so pretty in her tight blue pedal pushers, furious in the middle of the braided rug."

"Sounds just like *my* mother."

"Dad was hunched over at the end of the naugahyde davenport, his head down in his hands. Mom spun around. 'Lon's been saying for years it's just a matter of time. My own father predicted this. Him and Hoover and all the rest of them, villains, every one. And why?' she yelled. 'Why? Because he's Catholic?'"

"Hoover was Catholic?

"Dad stood up and put his hand on her shoulder, but she jerked away and pointed to the TV again. 'This is an evil place, Bill. They hate Catholics and they hate blacks. We've got to get out of Dallas. These Texans hate everyone who isn't them.'"

"Man, was she right?"

"Hell if I knew. I just saw us packing up the car, so I jumped up from behind the La-Z-boy to wail out my protest: 'We're not moving *again!*'"

Sean shakes his head. "Somehow I picture you doing that."

"I was four, thought I was in charge."

"Bernadette, you *are* in charge."

I just look at him. "So Dad's carrying me back to my room and I ask if someone from *The World Turns* died. But he doesn't say anything, just tucks me into bed and sits on the edge.

'I came home early for the parade,' he says real slow, like his voice is stuck. And it was a big deal, I mean, he traveled most of the time."

"An absentee father?"

I bang my fist. "Do you want to hear this or do you want to play Freud?"

"Would a lengthy couch be involved?"

"Excuse me?"

"Nevermind. Tell about the parade, really. I promise not to interrupt."

"So I ask him if he saw the President wave at me. Which was really important. I'd prayed all morning for it to stop raining so that the top of their car would be down. And then he could see me, right?" I tap my chest. "It was all about me. The leader of the free world... seeing me."

"So he just chuckles, 'Right at you,' he says, patting my foot, not saying a word about the ballet shoes I'm still wearing. Major venial sin."

Sean leans back in his chair and laughs. And I remember wriggling in contentment beneath my blanket. I had made my dad smile. And when I could make him smile, the world was mine.

"But then he puts his head back down in his hands and rubs it, so I'm thinking he's caught one of Mom's headaches.

'Well,' he says, 'he's been hurt.'

That's it, all he said. But after he leaves, I know there's something more, like who's Hoover and what's a villain. And what did my grandpa do? So I slide out of bed and inch my way back down the hall on all fours. I had to find out. And I see them both in there, glued to the TV.

Then I sneezed and she caught me. So those pedal pushers marched me straight back to my room and locked the door. And the fire-ant takes my ballet shoes with her."

"She didn't tell you he'd been killed?"

"No, she didn't. But later that afternoon, while we're playing in the yard, kids on the school bus were leaning out the windows *cheering*."

"Children were cheering about the President's assassination?"

"Mom throws the potatoes she's peeling, bowl and all, straight down on the front porch and goes running across our lawn. Her arms are waving in the air, her hands clenched into fists. But she's so angry she can't even yell at those kids, she's just running like a maniac."

"And you still had no idea what was going on."

"She chased that bus half way down the street."

He narrows his eyes, sits back, like he's piecing this all together.

"I figured it out at Mass. Chip and I were picking at each other's fingernails when she gave us the final warning to stop fidgeting."

"Chip?"

"Brother. Anyway, after two warnings, you were hauled outside to the Church steps and got your ass cracked, so I scooted away and sat on my hands, waiting for Communion when the women walked down the aisle in their lace mantillas."

Sean smiles. "I remember scoping the communion scene. The only reason to go to Mass—the *women*."

"They mesmerized me. Watching them coming towards my pew, I'd always choose the woman I wanted to be—red lipstick, tight dress, blonde hair with dark roots."

"Exactly," Sean winks. "So the priest said it. That's how you found out he was killed."

"No. No. They were crying. All the women I wanted to be, they were crying."

I hold my cup to my lips, but I don't drink. I feel small all of a sudden, like I did then, looking up at the cross. I smell the incense thick around me. I hear the priest sing in a low voice, songs in a language I'd never paid any attention to before. Mass is crowded, but I become completely alone in that pew, sitting on my hands, my shoulders hunched and my eyes open wide, watching the sobbing women in black, one by one, slide into the pew in front of us, then looking up at the crucifixion, the blood on his hands and feet, the rip in his side.

I put down my coffee. "It was so quiet, I mean, this eerie silence, but I could see the tears running down their faces. No sound, just tears. A line of women coming back from communion, their black mantillas covering their faces, every face the same.

And I look up at my father, and his face is covered in tears, and when he sees me watching, he wipes them away, but he leans down and says, 'This is Good Friday.'

And I don't know what the hell Good Friday is, because I thought we went to Church on Sundays, but I'm thinking whatever, my grandfather did this. He killed my President. He made all the beautiful women cry. And now he's made my father cry."

"You were just a kid," Sean says, stepping over things. "You were too young."

I see the white handkerchief Grace sent me from Damascus, how I knelt next to my bed that night, tilted my head back and laid it over my face, pressed it to my forehead, begged God please the next time I cry, please let it be quiet.

"My little play-world changed at that Mass," I say. "The whole place, the energy, it was like an archetypal grief."

He runs his fingers lightly down the top of my forearm. "Embodied in the Arthurian death of one handsome public man."

"Yep," I smile, shedding the whole business by standing up. I push in my chair so two black-clad women from my department can scoot by without spilling their lattes. "Be right back."

He grabs my wrist as I slip by. "Go out with me Saturday night, Bernadette. I'll take you to dinner. That's it. Or a movie. Or both. Whatever you want."

Such a switch already. "If I get my paper done," I shrug. "Then maybe I could go."

"Maybe?" He lets go of my arm.

"I'm whipped, Sean. I really need to head back."

"Right, right," he says hurriedly. "Let's get you to the library."

And so we walk, or in my case, slog. I attempt to change the subject. "So, you grew up in Newark?"

"Yes sir. And in a fight every day."

"What? You in a fight? That's impossible."

"It was a pretty rough neighborhood."

"But you're so calm. I can't even imagine you angry."

"Bernadette, if you knew how many times I was suspended for fighting."

"Oh, c'mon."

"No, really. All my old buddies are either in jail or politics."

"But you ended up the Buddhist meditator."

"I've taught meditation courses in prisons, just to feel at home."

I stop here; we're at the library. I can take a breath now, I'm safe.

"Bernadette, I am so sorry." He sounds like he's about to cry.

"Sean, are you serious? Why would you apologize for that?"

He bends down in front of me, trying to look in my eyes. "The library," he says, "It's closed. You wanted to work. And it's my fault you can't."

I look up and see all the lights are off. Damn, all my papers are in there. My entire backpack. "I'll just have to get here when it opens."

He laughs. "You're actually excited about that, aren't you?"

I look around campus, how quiet now, only a few students meandering through the darkness, undergrads kissing on the steps. I take a breath. "Sean, I find serious amusement burrowing deep into those stacks."

"Bernadette the burrower."

"I walk down the aisles, pulling out fat and moldy books, written by fat and moldy men. It's fun."

Now he's staring at me, thinking something way too serious for the moment. His scuba watch ticks really loudly without an ocean to muffle it. "But what's the real reason you dig, Bernadette? It's not just to criticize. And it's not only for fun. Most people hate research. But you seem to thrive on it."

The massive locked doors beam down at us and I wonder whether or not to tell him, to go that far. Our easy banter's a balm, so please no solemn intent, no analysis now. Maybe it's his face, all that attention pouring in again, waiting so patiently for an answer, such a peaceful man. I decide to risk it.

"I dig because of a vague hope that someday I'll find something that sounds…, I mean something that will, I don't know." I stop. I can't finish the sentence. I don't know how. And he's looking at me with way too much passion all of a sudden. I take a step back.

He reaches out his hand and puts it lightly on my shoulder. And he begins to pull me towards him, it's the slightest of pressure, I may even be imagining it, but I let him.

TWENTY-TWO

I am she who does not keep festival,
and I am she whose festivals are many.

For weeks after JFK was killed, my mother and I argued about Eve and the garden of Eden. I'd be playing in the dirt in the backyard, near all these tiny twig crosses, and I'd have funerals for JFK.

Every day I'd lay fresh pink portulaca on a grave, cover my head with a black lace mantilla, and kneel down in the dirt and pray for him. My mother would yell at me from the kitchen window, "Stop stealing the portulaca!"

She didn't get it. "I have to, they're for the funeral!"

"No you don't! Flowers are a waste on a grave!"

To make her mad, I'd stomp back into the house screaming, "I hate Eve. She ruined it for all of us by eating that apple."

"Stop saying that," she'd cry, banging a pan on the stove and glaring at me.

"I hate Eve!"

"That's blasphemy!"

"Well, my legs hurt," I'd cry, getting down on my knees and walking around the kitchen, holding on to chair legs, moaning. This'd really piss her off.

"Then you're quitting ballet and we're going to the doctor and he'll give you shots in your knees. Big ones. Get in the car!"

Sean walks into the bedroom. "Bernadette? Have you seen my blue shirt?"

I roll over on the bed. "Eve messed up everything."

"Eve who."

"Genesis Eve, in the garden. My mother and I used to argue about her."

"She's been calling you again?"

I throw a pillow at him. "No, when I was little."

"You argued about the Biblical Eve when you were a kid."

"You know if that tart hadn't eaten that apple, we'd be frolicking in the woods right now." I stuff another pillow under my head. "Instead, we suffer."

He throws the pillow back at me. "Well, I've got a garden we can frolic in. Arrived from Boston today. Remember the starving artist friend of my ex?"

"The guy she wanted to move in with you so she could, quote, service you both?"

"Right. That guy. He sent us some stuff."

"Stuff? Wait. This is her dealer, Sean. What are you talking about?"

"It's a gift."

"Are you a bedlamite?"

"Bernadette, his stuff is so good she would lick it off the floor."

"I don't care if she licked it off a cross of Jesus, it's no gift."

He leaps onto the bed and tries to tickle me behind the knees. It works every time and he knows it. "I'll do whatever you want," he says, "but think about it this way: wouldn't your FBI grandfather leap from his wheelchair if he knew? He'd be jumping up and down like that garden snake."

I'm gyrating with all my strength, trying to get him to give up. "That's. Not. Funny. Stop. Tickling. Me."

"Okay, okay," he relaxes, putting his hands in the air. Then he lies down next to me, slides in real close. But now I'm mad, in a funk. And he can tell.

"He was pretty rough, wasn't he?"

"I think so," I say, uneasy with this topic. "I'm told he had a reputation in the agency."

He leans over. I lean back.

"Agency meaning FBI?"

"Quick confessions. He obtained any confession Hoover wanted. In five minutes."

"Five minutes? There's no way."

"Hence my mother screaming at the TV in her pedal pushers."

"Jesus Bernadette, how does a man get a confession from anyone, much less a criminal or a cold-blooded killer, in only *five* minutes?"

"I don't want to imagine," I whisper, embarrassed by my dysfunctional ancestry. "All I know is that this is the man who raised my mother."

He shakes his head "And this is the woman who raised you," he muses, rubbing his prominent chin.

A cringe rides up my spine. Wait, this isn't exactly the angle I would choose. "She was a good mom," I defend, propping myself up on my elbow. "I mean, in my few and far between more compassionate moments, I can see that she was doing the best she could."

He sits up, too. "I'm sorry, I'm sure she was," he says, but I can read in a heartbeat the subtext of psychoanalysis and pity.

"She hated Dallas. I heard Dad tell her his boss called her 'the Yankee wife,' and that she needed to 'be quiet.'"

"What was she saying?"

"Well, Richardson was the boondocks back then, pretty much a small town, so what you said got around. Apparently she objected to the neighborhood rule that 'the blacks' walk down the alley behind our house, never out front."

"What a rebel."

"Dad came home one night with his tie cut off. Mom was upset because, you know, we weren't rich, and ties cost money. Apparently he walked into work and his boss walks up to him with a scissors in his hand and the guy says, 'This is what we do here, Boy.' And Dad says, 'Do what?'

And the boss grabs his tie and cuts it off. So Dad never asked her to be quiet, I think she just figured it out on her own.

"The good old boy network."

"That's why she was always asking him if we could move back up north. I heard her say 'Dallas is a sick place to live.'"

Sean moves his hand up my arm, down again, over my hand. I pull it away. My mother was a smart woman, she saw more, she knew more back then.

"She didn't do anything wrong," Sean says.

I close my eyes, I remember her running across the lawn, I see her running across the lawn, I see her running and running across the lawn, my mom, she couldn't have been much more than 27 or 28, so young, so isolated in that God-forsaken hell, she was such a good person, in the middle of so much evil, running across the lawn, waving her arms.

"Bernadette, Bernadette, stop stop, it's okay, come here, it's okay." And I realize I've been talking out loud and Sean is wiping my cheeks with his hands. But all I can think of is if Eve had just been a little more patient, if she hadn't wanted more, there'd be no confusion or loneliness or doubt and we'd all still be living in Paradise. If only she knew upekka, if only she knew that what she had was enough.

TWENTY-THREE

I, I am godless,
                     and I am the one whose God is great.

The phone only rings after I've fallen asleep.

"Dette, wake up. It's me!"

I turn on the light, shielding my eyes. It's one o'clock in the morning and I have a seminar at eight. Moreover, Sean kept me up until midnight preaching the benefits of a strict adherence to two hours of meditation a day. "What *is* it?" I groan. "Why are you calling so late? And why are you so happy?"

"We're getting married!"

I turn the light back off. So that's news? I get critical REM interruption for a wedding announcement? I fall back down to the pillow. When my sister called a few months ago to say she'd met an Ohio State basketball player who was so tall he had to duck through doorways, *I* knew they were getting married.

"Dette? Are you there?"

"Oh, sorry. That's great, really great," I garble. "Uh, when?"

"Tomorrow!" she laughs. "And you and Sean will get hitched with us."

"Tomorrow?"

"Well, we can't wait, so we're going down to the courthouse. We'll have a real wedding sometime when you can come to Texas, if you ever do. It's been so long, so get down here already. Why don't you ever visit me anymore? It's because of muscle man Sean, I know, I know, he keeps you a happy girl."

I roll over and lean on my elbow. Pinhead is looped. And it isn't because this guy's dreamy. She'd gone out with beautiful men before. No, this boy made the final cut for one reason only: he could beat the hell out of Brad.

"What about a honeymoon?" I ask sleepily.

Her voice drops. "I don't want to leave Suzanna. I'm really careful. And Curtis wants to build her a playhouse right away."

I sit up and turn on the light. "Look, since Brad came back into the picture, you've never had a date over to your house, you've never gone out of town, you've never even visited me. Brad wouldn't lay out any threats over a honeymoon, would he?"

"I don't want to tell him I'm getting married. It's been pretty smooth with visitation, so I don't want to rock the boat. But listen, you and Sean get married with us. Hop a plane."

"His redneck wife piercing Suzanna's ears with a sewing needle is not smooth."

She doesn't answer. Damn, she's so positive and I bring up smut. "Oh look," I apologize, "forget what I said. You guys know what you're doing. So hey, congratulations. Send me pictures?"

Now Curtis Stepdad the Giant supervises the visitation trades. And I visualize myself as Gregor Samsa on the police station wall when Brad and WendyJo have to crane their little red necks further and further back just to look up at his firm face.

"Dette," Mary laughs. "They just stand there. They don't know what to do. And for once, the perm doesn't say a word, zero harassment. But she barks at Brad all the way to their car, tugging the leash."

"So what does Curtis do while you're giving Suzanna to Brad?"

"I don't anymore. Curtis and Suzanna devised their own little plan. He carries her into the lobby and they talk. He's coaching her, he says. Then when she's ready, he puts her down and she walks over to Brad by herself."

"No tears?"

"No tears."

The safety Suzanna must feel to do that, the ease with which her mother can speak of it. "The three of us," she says, "we fit. Sometimes I feel we've been sharing meals and doing laundry together for years."

The timer goes off, so I pull the miso-kale casserole out of the oven. "Isn't there anything he does that bugs you? Everybody's got some flaw, some nuisance, like Sean's aversion to showering because it removes the *good* bacteria?"

She slowly conjures a defect. "Well, he isn't used to kid mess, you know, toys around, crusty cornflakes stuck to the table. But I'm trying to be neater."

"You couldn't get any neater."

"Oh yeah, I forgot, I'm talking to *you*—the one whose corners are never lonely."

"Me? A slob? You've been saying that since high school, it's not true."

"Give me a break. One night I went to sleep before you and I couldn't believe the crap on your bed. Poetry books, ballet shoes, cassette tapes. I decided to stay awake until you came in so I could witness what you'd do. Would you put everything away? Or would you just shove it all to the floor? Well, were we in for a surprise. You walked in, looked at the pile, and eureka! You just slid under the covers and fell asleep. Instantly. You were out cold. I sat up in bed and couldn't believe it." She launches into hysterics. "I could have blackmailed you with a photograph of that landfill moving up and down on top of your snoring body. Could have threatened to sell it to Jackson."

She continues to laugh as I observe the lack of floor and desk space around me. Sean is not allowed in my study, which really ticks him off. He stands in the doorway and notes that the trashcan is the only place free of the proverbial heap of papers and books. Some semblance of a path winds from my chair to the door, but even that's narrowing.

"You remember too much from high school."

"Well," she begins in a somber voice, "I remember you."

I'm a little taken aback by her sudden seriousness. Is she serious? "Younger sisters are always looking at the older sister," I say, sweeping it away. "It's that birth-order chicanery."

"Girl," she says with a country singer twang, "I've been left standing in the rain, but never by you."

I hesitate. I don't know if she's kidding or not. I'm not sure how to respond.

"Don't you remember all the fun we had here?" she asks, laughing. "Don't you remember that hot summer before you sprinted off to college?"

"No."

"C'mon! The orange trees, the alligators? The guy in the ice cream truck? Now you've got to remember *him*. The brunt of our bedlamite sister years? Our sweetest high?"

My memory knows of all these things, but they are weighted down under the scratchy blankets of later more important scenes. Nothing is light, not like she suggests, not like that.

"Jackson and the alligators?" she probes, reaching under my bed, swimming merrily amid my journals and dust. "What's wrong with you?"

I lean back in my chair and I remember one thing: I remember that laugh of hers, from deep within, honest and clear. Safety resides in that laughter and years have crossed over us since I've heard her sing it. This must be it, this safe place: she has found love. And I remember how it can be so very generous. Even with the most frightened and fragile among us.

TWENTY-FOUR

For why do you despise my fear
and curse my pride?
But I am she who exists in all fears
and strength in trembling.

In our formative years I ignored my sister—she belonged to the category of gnat or flea, a pestilence not worth noticing. But one summer I'd been reading a gothic romance about an Irish missionary and I felt charitable. I turned to stare at her as she watched *Bullwinkle* and decided that she didn't look quite so useless. There were two chips and a few crumbs left in my Pringles can so I held it in front of her face and with that magnanimous gesture our bonding began. And just in time, too, as Watergate had started, and Mom and her ironing board monopolized the TV for the rest of the summer.

Mary Catherine and I defined festive after that day of conjoined Pringles. In fact, we were inseparable. While normal teenagers were getting drunk, learning how to smoke pot, or fumbling with sex beneath football bleachers, my sister and I were swimming straight and sober in our two-alligator lake. We never saw the alligators, but Jackson told us their eyes stuck out of the reeds when he was fishing. She didn't believe him, but I did. I'd been given enough newspaper clippings to believe anything. Mary never got clippings. Mom said she didn't need them because she already knew when to ask for help. I suspect it has something to do with being the youngest. Those kids are always whining.

Whenever Jackson's alligator rumors got me scared, we'd run away from his fishing boat mockery to climb the orange trees in the front yard, throw fruit at the telephone pole and listen for the music. Once hidden in the camouflaging branches of the tree, I became look-out while Mary turned her shirt around backwards, pulled her hair half way out of her ponytail and formed saliva in the corners of her mouth. Once the ice cream truck pulled in front of us, we dropped to the grass and Mary began a running limp towards it yelling, "Ez Crem, Ez Crem" in a drunken slur, waving a dime, the spit flying. I ran after her, "Mary, wait. Wait!" Her shaking head cocked to one side, she banged on the side of the truck with her crimped arm, screaming, "Now, now!"

The vendor, reminiscent of Abby Hoffman, tried to run his shaking fingers through his light brown afro, sort of like he had a twitch. But his fingers always got stuck about half way and he'd have to start over at his brow.

He rarely spoke. The only word we actually ever heard him say was "out," referring, usually, to the popular Nutty Buddy, but suggesting to us his own current status inside the truck. He was unconditionally stoned. And this sad condition prompted my sister and me to take advantage of him. Daily.

"Please sir, we forgot the medication," I'd say, quickly handing him two dimes for two fudgesicles as my sister began kicking his tires or trying to eat the dream bars painted on the side. He gave me the ice cream with a wet and shaking hand, his forehead sweating, his dilated eyes filled with fear, my greatest reward.

I'd pull Mary away from the truck, but invariably she'd prove too strong and I'd end up falling onto the sidewalk, or worse yet, into the gathering of little kids. "C'mon," I'd plead, slowly walking backwards, holding the bars out in front of me. "Doctors say never take your eyes off her," I'd yell to him as he stare at the scene with gaping jaw.

Mary would begin the chase, limping and tripping over her own crooked legs as I turned and ran for the house. On especially cruel days, I'd slam the front door in her face and lock it. Abandoned and hungry, she'd turn to the truck. I watched from the window as she tore across the yard, back to her source of nourishment, gnashing her teeth, growling and tripping every sorry step of the way.

Then one day it ended. When our beloved stoner saw my sister raging towards his truck, he tossed all the ice cream to the group of kids, jumped in the driver's seat and peeled out. Pedal to floor, he left black tread marks in front of the house.

"Okay," I said from one branch higher, as it should be, than my sister's. "Now what can we do for fun? Afro brain is never coming back. We've got to accept that."

"I really wanted the dream bar."

"All the little kids hate us," I said, flicking a mosquito off a green-tinged orange.

"Don't flick bugs," Mary whined.

"It was a mosquito."

"You're always flicking something. What is it with you and flicking anyway?"

I flicked her arm and searched the branches for an idea. "What about Chip? He deserves something for all the karate kicks he practices two inches from my face."

"You know he drop-kicked Mom while she was washing the vegetables in the sink? Then he laughed. Looked like she was going to cry."

"He's not one of us. They switched him at the hospital." I threw an orange at the pole and missed. "God knows why Jackson hangs out with him."

"He watched from his front porch, you know. Saw the whole thing."

"Who? Jackson?" I gulp. "No, not the ice cream scene, no, he didn't"

"He folded the biceps across the bare chest. Probably just came in from the lake."

"And?"

"He laughed his head off."

"Oh God, let's go inside."

"He can't see you in this tree, idiot. Took off in his car anyway." She started to climb down. "Let's put Chanel No. 5 on Chip's karate uniform."

"No, I get into too much trouble. We've got to be more creative."

Mary assumed an operatic voice, "Baby heads!" and she leapt from the tree. So we went inside, tiptoeing behind Mom ironing. Mary grabbed a *McCalls* and began cutting out heads while I cut out bodies when I noticed the lowered sound of the TV and extra steam from the iron. I glanced back at Mary to find her already gathering up the magazines.

"We were just going outside, Mom!" I apologized, and we moved our findings to the lanai and began taping together odd heads with random bodies.

"Okay, we've got enough. Let's begin." We quietly made our way to Chip's room. "I can't believe they let him paste these sports magazine pictures all over his wall, it looks so stupid."

"That's why we're here. To make the stupid more stupid, which in the case of this room, may be impossible."

We taped our warped champions in obscure places among Chip's well-formed heroes. He was at football practice so he wouldn't notice for days. We'd be lying in bed late at night and hear him swear a mouthful as he got up to remove a mutation he'd just discovered. Then we gloated in our coup, awaiting some minor payback. However, I should have known we'd crossed the line when we taped that bald white baby head over the real head of Joe Namath as he ran for a touchdown.

We were writing in our diaries when he blew. Apparently, he found the head and tried to remove it, but the tape stuck and ripped half of Namath's face with it. Chip, fuming, wisely waited until the Dallas Cowboys half-time to tell Dad. My father appeared in the doorway of our bedroom with the belt in one hand and the dangling white baby head in the other. "Inexcusable," he bellowed, his face red, his fists clenched.

The Cowboys must be losing. "Holy Mother of God, this is god-damn inex*cuuuus*able!"

I dove into the closet, my usual indoor hideout, but Mary didn't move. Peering out from behind the clothes, I saw her sitting cross-legged on the twin bed, smiling. "Sorry, Daddy," she said without one shred of fear. And then it hit me—the pattern of her charm finally made it to my brain as I watched my father melt. His face resumed its Texas tan and the belt fell limp by his side. Relieved, I poked my head out from the closet. That's when his hands clenched up again as he turned to me. "Bernadette, I know *you* are the one behind this," he cursed. "Now get out of that."

"Hey Dad!" my brother called from the hallway, "Jackson's here to watch the game." Dad growled, hesitated, then turned and stalked from our room as the picture dropped from his hand, floating gracefully towards the pale pink carpet. Sitting in the closet, watching Namath and my heart rate go down, I was grateful that the game was more important to my brother than watching me get beat.

TWENTY-FIVE

And I am an alien and a citizen.
I am the substance and the one who has no substance.

I am peace,
and war has come because of me.

"Bernadette, call your sister."

My mother only phones when there's a crisis. "Mom, what's going on? I just talked to her a few days ago, she's fine."

"Call her."

"Spare me," I whisper, trying to sew up a hole in the heel of my pink tights while they're on my body, trying not to stab myself with the needle. Alice picks me up in ten minutes and my hair isn't even in a chignon.

"Mary Catherine's upset and humiliated and says she's not telling you a thing. I've got to lie down. Why did Sean answer the phone? Is he living there?"

"Just tell me what happened, Mom." My shoes, where are my shoes?

"She needs to tell you on her own. I'm not getting involved." Bleat.

Wait, I think I left them hanging by the ribbons on the front door so I wouldn't forget them. A knot begins to form in my thread. I pull it loose. But I'd bet anything Sean has taken them off the doorknob and put them back in my closet. He wants me to be more organized, to keep a day-timer even, no matter how many times I tell him it's not going to happen. His theory that the price I pay for forgetting things will somehow translate into remembering them is not working.

"Bernadette, call your sister. I'm hanging up now." Bleat.

"Ouch! Goddam it." I drop the needle, blood begins to ooze. Grabbing paper out of the printer, I stab at the spreading pool on my pastel Capezzios. It's all I can do not to scream at her through the phone. "Mom, don't make Mary live through it again by having to tell me. *You* tell me." Aren't *you* the mother?

"Why are you swearing, Bernadette? Is it Sean? You're so short-tempered these days. Why did he answer the phone?"

I tie the knot and cut the thread close to my leg. I want to throw these sewing scissors across the room. "Just get Dad."

She puts the phone down like she's dropped it, doesn't even say goodbye. Fine. If nothing else, I at least have time to formulate a suitable answer for the Sean situation.

Dad picks up. Gulp. Here comes the Irish inquisition, the probe about my pagan lifestyle with a man they've never met. I don't want to hear it. I can already guess what they think: on the one hand, Mikhail is, and always will be, my only husband, and any attempt at a replacement is sacrilege. But on the other hand, the fact that I'm single suggests I'm gay.

Which hand will they choose? I suspect the latter would be the greater evil, a horror beyond the pale, their eldest daughter a lesbian. And it is this fear that could be Sean's ally. Regardless of who he isn't, he *is* male.

But Dad says nothing, just sticks to the facts about Mary Catherine, typically avoiding, like he has his whole life, any subject which smacks of emotion. Well amen and hallelujah, I am excused from explanation once again, which is what I hoped for. Sean's nearby anyway, in the kitchen, and I don't want him to hear.

He sneaks up and grabs me around my waist after I say goodbye to Dad. "That family of yours got more problems?" he whispers into my ear.

"No, it's nothing," I whisper back. "But I think Alice is waiting for me outside."

"That she is," he bites my earlobe, "so your sexy legs better run." And he swings me around, kisses me hard on the cheek and lets me bolt out the door, the pale pink ribbons of my closet-found pointe shoes trailing.

Dad told me that when Suzanna returned from her weekend with Brad, everything appeared normal: she wore torn clothing and rouge was smeared on her cheeks. This routine stopped bothering Mary a long time ago, so she ignored it.

"Where's Daddy?" Suzanna asked when he wasn't home to greet her.

"He's out of town, remember?" Mary soothed, "It's you and me tonight and we're eating hotdogs for dinner, your favorite."

So they ate a quiet dinner alone, went through the usual bubble bath and stories for bedtime. Then, as Mary headed downstairs to do laundry, the doorbell rang. She didn't open it.

"Yes?" she called through the wood.

"Ms. Madison?"

"Who is it?"

"Julie Smith, a social worker from HRS. May I come in?"

"No."

"I need to speak with you, Ms. Madison. We've received a report this evening about your daughter, Suzanna."

Mary threw open the door, but still blocked the entrance. "I'd like to see some identification."

The social worker eyed Mary coldly, handing her a card. "I need to see your daughter."

"I need an explanation."

"Ms. Madison, we have reason to suspect child abuse. I'd like to see the child."

"Child abuse? What? It's 9:30 at night!"

"Is your husband in?"

Mary didn't answer. The woman persisted. "Is it true he's out of town?"

"Excuse me, but where did you get this information?"

"I need to see the child or I'll have to call the police." She tried to push the door open, but Mary Catherine held firm.

"She's sleeping!"

"I won't wake her. This will only take a few minutes." She took a notepad from her briefcase. "Have you noticed any marks on your daughter's face?"

Mary took a step back. "Yes," she said, shaking. "I did notice that." She checked the woman's I.D. again, let her into the foyer, wished Curtis was home. "I asked her about it when she came in tonight. She said she fell onto her plastic blocks at Brad's. I, I let it go. I don't know. I shouldn't have let it go."

"Can we tiptoe into her bedroom?" the woman asked, her hand moving up the staircase banister. Stunned, Mary acquiesced, leading her up the stairs where they found the child deep in slumber, her Barbies and bunnies standing guard around her canopy bed, her breathing deep, her face gently lit by a nightlight of moon and stars.

Julie Smith leaned over close to Suzanna's face. "I see the marks," she said, straightening, looking coldly at Mary. "Now Ms. Madison, I need you to lay your right hand, fingers spread apart like this, against her cheek."

"What?"

"I need you to do this for me, Ms. Madison."

"But why? Why me?"

"Because you're the one charged with child abuse. May I have your right hand?"

Mary held up her hand and spread apart her fingers. Smith took her by the wrist and laid her palm against the child's cheek, trying to fit the hand to the skin's indentations. "That's all I need for now ma'am. Don't let this upset you. I know raising children is a tough job."

After Mary's HRS debacle, I search for encouraging words. Brad isn't going to mar her glory if I can help it. I turn off my computer and dial the number.

"Mary, I heard."

"Did Mom fucking call you?" she asks with irritation.

"Look, you know Brad's only trying to knock you off balance. Don't let him succeed. He's probably jealous you got married, and now you're having a baby. And, well, you know that just seeing you glow at visitation grinds him. And, hey, Curtis is taller than Brad. That really pisses guys off. And if you look at—"

"Dette, the marks on Suzanna's face, I saw them."

I have to think fast. "Brad's a schmuck, Mary, but he'd never hurt his own child. Kids fall. C'mon." These need to be the right words, words that will move her forward, let it pass. But she doesn't answer.

"Listen," I continue, "he tried to humiliate you and he failed. HRS confirmed it."

A few weeks later Sean and I are eating quinoa kashi cereal on my balcony. He brews it in the crock pot every night so it's ready by breakfast, organic grains simmering in distilled water for eight hours. In the morning, cinnamon drifts into our bedroom before dawn, a comforting wake-up call. However, regardless of how much honey I add to my bowl, the vomit-like texture still makes me gag.

"You're dying for Grapenuts," he says, not looking up from his baseball magazine. "Admit it."

"Processed food?" I gasp. "Never."

"I already saw the box hidden behind the soymilk. I don't believe dry cereal needs to be refrigerated."

I get up to find a fresh bowl, scrapping my mush back into the crockpot. "Did I tell you what Curtis did at last week's trade?"

"Do you have to?"

"He waited for Brad outside the police station, in the parking lot."

"So your brother-in-law used his physical superiority to get what he wanted."

I plop the Grapenuts down right on top of Roger Clemons' head and kiss him on his cheek. "Some men have that ability."

He pulls me onto his lap and wraps his arms around my waist. "Praise be to Allah."

I lean away, my hands clasped behind his neck. "When the judge called them to her bench for the child abuse charge, she recognized Brad from his plethora of court appearances, and told him this back and forth business better stop or he'd be held in contempt."

"So the charge against Mary didn't hold?

"My father told Brad that any more of this courtroom crap would cost him."

"Your father, what a case."

I kiss him on the nose while pinching his cheek. "I love my father."

He bolts out of his chair, knocking it over, his strong arms clasping my derriere to his stomach, my legs wrapped behind him. "And I love you," he says, slobbering up my face with quinoa kashi kisses.

Sunday night, after Sean leaves, I phone Mary. "What's with your voice?" I ask. "Is pregnancy wearing you down, or is the HRS chicanery still bugging you? Look, you're off the hook. The judge recognized Brad, and you're a great mom. Just forget it."

"I don't know what's going on," she says listlessly. "What's my imagination and what's real."

"You're real, Brad's an illusion."

"He may be up to his old tricks. I'm looking over my shoulder all the time."

"Name a trick."

"We think they're stealing our mail. But I don't want to point a finger or Suzanna will come home from visitation with her nose pierced."

"I wonder how much of this mess belongs to Brad, and how much to the witch," I ponder aloud. "He never pulled any stunts before the perm came into the picture."

"He never even *knew* Suzanna before perm came into the picture."

"Well, there you go." There's no response on the other end. "Mary?"

"A strange woman named MaryBob keeps calling our real estate agent, wants to get into my old place."

"MaryBob? Please."

"She called when I was in the office. The agent put it on speaker phone and the voice sounded like WendyJo. But I can't believe she'd stoop to such a psychotic low. Mom told me Sean moved in."

"Mary, I think it's her."

"No, I'm just paranoid."

"I don't think so. Sounds like Sean's ex—always snooping around, calling, sneaky and weird."

"So you're shackin' up?"

"Don't get excited. He travels."

"You like him?"

"No, I can't stand him. That's why he lives here."

"Well, you just don't sound bubbly and chipper, that's all."

"He's teaching me to meditate. It calms me down, I think."

"Meditate, huh…well, I've got to go."

Ironically, the next day, Mary Catherine was called out of Fifth Period. A police officer monitored her class so she could report to the office.

"Mary, please sit down," said Dr. Vick, pulling back a leather chair. "I need to tell you something that may be rather unsettling. That's why Sergeant Scott Wright came over." Heads nod politely. "We're thinking that, since you're nearing your last trimester, you might want to take more time off."

"My pregnancy is fine," Mary said. "Is something wrong in my classroom?"

"No no, not at all."

"Then I don't understand." They exchange glances.

"Mary," Sgt. Wright began, "you simply seem tired. Why not take a couple of weeks off. Get some sleep. Go to—"

Dr. William Vick leaned back in his chair and folded his hands under his chin. He'd worked with Mary for several years, watched her at eligibility meetings defend the most delinquent of students with not only a fierce loyalty, but an articulate and sound reasoning. He'd always counted on her, in difficult or even crisis situations, to be steadfast and untiring. Over the last few months, however, he'd noticed strain in her face and a certain lack of confidence at meetings. At first he attributed it to the fatigue of pregnancy, but when she left confidential files on the office counter, he suspected more. Only a few weeks ago he asked if there was anything he could do, but she shrugged it off as simple ex-husband trouble. "Nothing like what my kids, I mean, my students, have suffered through their whole lives."

Now he had to make an administrative decision. He leaned his elbows on his desk. "Mary," he interrupted Wright, "we've been getting some strange phone calls. The first one came about a month ago, but I didn't want to tell you. Two weeks ago, another. But when one came this morning, I called Sergeant Wright and decided I had to let you in on this because you may want to pursue it with an attorney. You do have an attorney, don't you? For your ex-husband?"

She nodded. Sgt. Wright noticed she stiffened in her seat, rubbing her hands together in a frantic sort of way. He stepped closer, standing next to her chair.

"A woman's been calling, defining herself as an anonymous parent because she doesn't want harmful consequences for the students. We've been recording all incoming calls the last few weeks, so I have a tape of her voice.

"A tape? Can I have it?"

"I've given the tape to Sergeant Wright, but you may have it if you wish."

"Can I listen to it now?"

"Mary, I need to warn you. She says you alter grades."

"Alter grades? Why would I do that?"

"Well, she says you abuse drugs and offer them to your students in exchange for grades."

"My students couldn't care less about their grades. That's why they go here." Her voice trembled, her fingers gripped the edge of his desk.

He looked down and held his left hand up in the air, like he was taking an oath on the stand. "No, I know, I know. But there's more. The worst of it is you are, uh," He looked directly into her watery eyes. "Now we know it's not true, but today she said she has proof you are physically abusing your students. And legally, we have to take every accusation seriously."

Mary collapsed. Sitting on the edge of the chair, her head fell down on his desk and she burst into tears. "I can't take this any more," she whispered, her bent shoulders shaking. "They win, they win."

Dr. Vick put his head in his hands while Sgt. Wright could only stand close as the sobbing echoed out of the office and down the hall and onto the lawn of swaying palm trees and brilliant Texas sun.

TWENTY-SIX

Give heed to my poverty and my wealth.

Sean hands me a message as we crawl into bed. "Others rule," he says.

"Funny, I didn't hear it ring."

I lie back on my pillow and read his scrawl. Then I jump up and thrust the message in front of him. "What's going on? How long ago did I get this call?"

He just lays there with his hands folded behind his head.

I dial Dad's number. But Sean leans over and takes the phone away. "It's too late," he says. "He'll be asleep." He points to his scuba watch. "Look at the time."

I grab it back and dial again.

"Dad, Bernadette. I'm so sorry, I just got the message."

"There's no problem, no problem here," he mumbles, and I know I woke him up.

"But is it true? Suzanna never returned from visitation? Brad kept her? That's kidnapping."

"Don't worry," he says irritably. "I talked to Johnson. He says the judge will remember Brad and throw the bastard out of court tomorrow."

I relax, releasing my grip on the phone. "Thank God Mary's taking him to court." Sean throws his hands up in the air and leaves, shaking his head. I suspect he's going upstairs to meditate on my family's dysfunction.

"Hell no, Brad's taking *her* to court. Charging her with child abuse again. Jesus H. Christ." He doesn't sound sleepy anymore.

"What?"

"He got a court injunction, the judge gave him temporary full custody. So she's living with him! Now how in God's holy hell he managed to pull that one out of his ass, we'll never know, but by the time I get…"

"Dad, Dad, how will you get her back?" I yell into the phone, aware that he's getting exasperated with my questions, that his anger is building. But I feel completely negligent, I've been so self-absorbed.

"Johnson says Brad's been in there so many times that this will be his last straw. Always hauling Mary in for some full-a-shit reason. And it's that kind of back and forth crap that judges get sick of. He's dug his own grave this time. Mary'll have Suzanna home after court tomorrow and that'll be the end of it. But not for me. He's crossed the line. I'm finding out his drug history, criminal records, everything. I know he was doing coke. I know he was dealing coke. That motherfucking bastard. And then I'm gonna find WendyJo's records. That mean snake of a goddam motherfucking whore. Those files are open to the public and I'm going through 'em. Those two fucking sons of bitches are gonna think twice the next time they want to pull this goddamn bullshit. I've motherfucking had it. I'm gonna—"

"Okay, Dad, okay!" He continues the stream of obscenities, and I'm holding the phone six inches from my ear, calculating a way to hang up. "Okay, Dad, it'll work out!" But he doesn't stop, so there's only one thing to do. I hang up.

Tiptoeing to the bathroom so as not to annoy Sean's meditation, I recall the curious plaque on Dad's office wall years ago. A growling linebacker in a threatening stance says, "Beware the fury of a patient man." I always thought it might better read, "Beware the patience of a furious man."

But the attorney's words about the judge are reassuring. Brad's unwittingly turned the gun on himself, and this climactic attempt to wound Mary will be thwarted by his own chicanery. Maybe this is the best thing to happen after all. Tomorrow morning, the trailer park tyranny will finally be eradicated. With intention and release, I quietly floss my teeth.

TWENTY-SEVEN

*Do not be arrogant to me when I am cast out upon the earth,
[and] you will find me in [those that] are to come.*

The next night Sean's out of town, so I can phone Mary Catherine before I walk to the library in the dark. But the Voicemail responds yet again. I start speaking anyway, telling her how I can't wait to hear the courtroom drama, how I want to talk to Suzanna.

Curtis picks up. "Hey Dette. I was screening calls, in case it was them. But, uh, listen, you haven't talked to your parents yet?"

"Not tonight, no, why?"

"We don't have Suzanna."

"Well, when will she get there? Should I call later?"

"Dette, he gets to keep her. Brad's attorney pulled a fast one on the judge."

"What?" I don't understand this jagged song, this chaos fast descending. "Let me talk to Mary."

"She won't come to the phone, but I can tell you. Our attorney was really angry when we approached the bench. He told the judge he couldn't believe she signed papers for Brad to have temporary custody of Suzanna. He told her we'd been in here so many times that she had to remember these people. Well, the judge looked at Brad and then at Mary and then back to Brad, and her face went white. She was pretty upset. She stood up and bent down right into Brad's attorney's face, said she'd been tricked and now had to remove herself from the case. Then she walked out."

"That's absurd."

"The papers Brad's slimeball attorney got her to sign were irrevocable. Her hands were tied. She assigned the case to a different judge and now we've got to wait for a new court date."

"Can't Suzanna come home while you wait?"

"That's just it. The papers he fooled her into signing say she stays with Brad. But it gets worse. This new judge, whoever he is, he won't know Brad and all the trash they've pulled. They got exactly what they wanted."

"Let me talk to her, Curtis. Tell her please."

"Okay, I'll try, but she's pretty upset." I hear muted voices and shuffling, then a whisper of a hello.

"Mary, how are you doing?" What a stupid question. "Would you like me to come down for awhile? We could paint together or—" Did I just say 'paint?' Who paints? I'm pacing back and forth in my study and my hip hits the corner of my desk and takes my latest paper with it, pages flying.

"I'm fine…keeping busy…Curtis's here…I have to go to work."

Well, it's ten o'clock at night, so she doesn't have to go to work, but I let that pass and hunch down on my knees to gather up the paper.

"Those boys at the penitentiary weigh heavy. Why don't you take a few days off, rest, put your feet up. I know you get swollen ankles with the baby."

"Did I ever tell you that if Suzanna doesn't say, 'Mommy WendyJo, I love you,' when she gets into their van, she gets a spanking?"

"Mary, c'mon, they're spoiling her. They'll want her to *like* being there."

"I get to see her in four days. On Sunday."

"That's great," I almost shout, making myself sick.

"At Mom and Dad's house," she continues listlessly.

"Why Mom's house?"

"They're the court-ordered chaperones."

"Ex*cuse* me?"

"They have to be in our presence at all times, to make sure I don't hurt her."

The court report from Dad sounds so dreadful I don't know where to turn. In ballet class, I do plies when I'm supposed to be doing degages, and chane turns instead of pirouettes. Worse, the class runs over, so when I get home after six, Sean has already started meditating. I slip off my shoes and tiptoe into the bedroom, sliding onto my zafu without a twinge of noise. I close my eyes, grateful for this gift of serenity he's taught me. I need it right now, for my sister's deep in madness.

Fifty minutes later, at seven sharp, the timer on the dresser goes off. I wait for Sean to open his eyes. "They're lying about Mary," I say.

He stretches his arms into the air and I know he doesn't want to talk about this, but his recent nirvana might inspire him to apply active listening skills. "Today was court?"

I seize the rare moment of interest, uncross my aching legs and put my hands on his knees. "Sean."

"Look, I know what you're thinking," he says, pushing away my hands, unraveling his half-lotus. "Your presence is not the answer, don't even consider going there, okay? I'll start the kale."

He walks out. I pick up the phone and dial United. But after the second round of Pachelbel, I hang up. Maybe Sean's right.

He shakes his head at dinner. "Look, your parents are five minutes from her house. She's got her husband and your brother is nearby, too."

"Curtis as support, I can understand, but Chip is hardly consolation."

"He *is* her brother."

I resent the insinuation that he's not mine, even if I do agree. "It's akin to expecting comfort from Hannibal. He continually criticizes Mary for her 'overindulgence' with Suzanna."

He gulps down half his spinach onion juice. "Bernadette, you're judging again."

My lower lip protrudes. "I hate it when you accuse me of that," I pout. "We all know he was switched at birth."

The long and momentous pause follows as he scoots his chair back and puts both hands on the edge of the table. "Please, please," he says, patiently looking at the ground. "I've asked you before. *Don't* use the word 'hate.'"

TWENTY-EIGHT

I am the one whom they call Law,
and you have called Lawlessness.

But I, I am compassionate and I am cruel.

I've been staring at the monitor so long that the After Dark worms have gnawed my entire page on Eve into blackness. Screensavers have little to do with preservation. They're here to remind us we're slackers. Aunt Grace frowns down from her camel.

The phone rings. Thank you Jesus, I'm rescued from thought.

Mom wants my old recipe for Ezra Pound cake, a sad diversion. But since when does Mother bake? She only serves frozen desserts. I cradle the phone on my shoulder as I look up the recipe.

"Mom," I say, changing from the bland but safe, to the anxious but more interesting. "Mary isn't rallying. When I call her, she sounds drugged."

"Well, that's understandable. These forensic and ad litem interviews have been going on for months. It's draining and it's expensive."

"But I'm the sister, she tells me *every*thing. And now it's like there's something she's holding back."

"Oh, she's fine when she visits Suzanna. You should see her." Then she pauses and goes into a sort of crinkly whine. "She becomes upset, though, when she gives her back to Brad."

"Does Suzanna cry?"

"She always wears a nice dress when she visits. How's Sean? Are you going to marry him?"

"Mom, a dress? You go by the *dress*?"

"It's always new, and she's a child! She parades it for us. Turns this way and that."

"Mom."

"Brad and WendyJo keep canceling their interviews with Dr. Kreber, so the court can't set a date. It drags on and on. Mary thinks they're doing it on purpose."

"Sounds like them, but to what end? So they can keep Suzanna longer?" I continue to dig for the recipe. I could swear I saw it recently, even though I haven't done much baking. If there's sugar, Sean won't allow it.

"I don't think they want anyone to see the real situation, so they stall."

Soyloaf, spirulina shakes, quinoa salad, I'm tossing index cards all over the counter. "Meanwhile, Suzanna's living with *those* two." Did he pitch that card?

"And it's slowly killing Mary."

Eureka, it's still here. I relax against the counter. "Ah, but the Judeo-Christians agree with the Buddhists that patience is a virtue. Maybe I'll send her an essay I wrote on equanimity." I switch the phone to my other ear.

After I hang up I think hey, where's the headache? I sit down at my desk and try to recall the last time she mentioned one. Maybe therapy can heal some of us after all. I smile at Aunt Grace, flick the mouse, and watch my latest brilliance on *The Thunder, Perfect Mind* appear through the vanishing blackness of the worms.

The association of a feminine gnostic revealer-figure with the voice of the Thunder is perhaps the ultimate antithesis presented by this tractate. For the sound of the thunder had long been associated throughout the Levant with the anger of a male sky god. Recall I Samuel:

> *the adversaries of the Lord shall*
> *be broken to pieces;*
> *against them he will thunder in heaven. (19)*

It is interesting that our revealer would use "thunder," the very symbol of the feared Judaic God, as her own name. She strove, after all, to embody under that name many of the pagan goddess characteristics that Yahweh thundered against. Yet she does not thunder against morality, but against the OT, apocalyptic and Hellenistic notions of who is "good" and who "evil." Indeed, the use of...

I click off the screen, enough of this, time to floss. I don't know what I have or what I lack or the name of what it is I seek. Indeed, I'm going to bed.

But I lie there and toss. It's Friday, so Sean comes home tomorrow and I've cleaned up nothing. And he even invented a most pleasing filing system for all my papers. I have no excuse. I keep spacing out that the weekend's coming, that *he's* coming, like if I forget, it will stay a Tuesday or a Wednesday night in the stacks forever.

"Your sanity is measured by the amount of ambiguity you can handle," he says. He thinks my sister is crazy. He thinks she needs to go to a meditation retreat. Meditation retreat? Like it's helped him? I reach for the water on my nightstand and knock something to the floor. Leaning over the edge, into the shaft of moonlight from my open window, I see Grace's Bible. I bring the small book to me and feel the shame of my dissatisfaction. I feel the sins of arrogance, judgment and want, the venial sins assigned to my smaller self in a huge confessional so many years ago. Maybe pressing this book of youth to my chest will push in a better truth. Gnosticism should not be burdened by cynicism. Or narcissism.

I lie back on my pillow, still clutching the book. Sean *is* a good man. And I'm quite proud of myself for maintaining the relationship, for not bolting.

Who am I to judge whether he speaks with mockery or curiosity or uncertainty or truth? I know his heart is pure. And I admire his physical strength, his broad smile, his long graying hair pulled back in a ponytail. He doesn't just *study* meditation, he lives it.

Two weekends pass without incident. Sitting at the computer, I decide I'm proud of my decision to choose the positive view. He was annoyed with me only once, over the tempeh stir-fry that I put too much tamari in—salt in his diet slows down his seven-mile morning runs. I smile arrogantly at my resolve as I type on and on about Ishtar and the Thunder. Today I am Sophia, wise and omniscient. How I love it when I'm good.

But my reverie is interrupted by the phone. "Bernadette? It's Chip."

My brother has never called me. And I know something horrible has happened. I stand up from my desk with a jerk, knocking my chair over backwards. "Oh no," whispers from my mouth.

"Mary Catherine's lost it," he begins, in a sort of quiet haunted voice. "There's glass everywhere. I don't know what to do."

"What? What's happened? Tell me!"

"Plants thrown, dirt everywhere, glasses smashed. Those good ones you gave her, remember the glasses?" And he doesn't miss a beat, keeps right on with his list of cyclone destruction, like I'm not even here, talking faster and faster, perseverating, catching his breath when he can. "There's holes in the walls, holes in the walls, the phone's ripped out, pottery, all her pottery, Jesus Christ, there's there's—God, she's destroyed the house. I was at Dad's office when Curtis called and we got here as fast as we could, it took all three of us to hold her down, she was so strong, like those women you read about who run over a kid and lift up the car to pull them out. She kept kicking and screaming, 'Don't leave me, don't leave me!' Then 'Let me die, let me die!'"

"Chip, stop. Stop!" I command, my body rigid. "Where is she right now, at this very moment. Where is she?"

"On, on the sofa, she's face down on the sofa," he answers quickly. "I think she's, well, we think she's asleep. But listen, when she was screaming that, you know, she started hyperventilating and we all kept telling her it was okay, it's okay, no one's leaving, over and over, all three of us yelling it's okay! And gradually her breathing got better, but she was still, like shuddering. Then Dad slowly let go, and then Curtis had to get the door because the police showed up, so it was only her and me, on the kitchen floor. I just held her, you know, I just held her like a baby, and then she started sobbing and, like, she couldn't stop. She wasn't mad anymore, she was beat, and she was crying so hard she had to gasp for air. And then, God, Jesus, then I started crying, I couldn't help it. And Dad and Curtis and the cops are standing there on all the broken glass just, you know, looking at us, staring at us on the floor, me holding her, both of us crying."

He hesitates, but his breathing stays hard and fast. I'm speechless. I can't even form words. Then his voice turns to a sort of pleading, like a humble appeal that I have never heard from him, even as a child. "God, Bernadette," he whispers, "please come home. She needs you. You just gotta come home."

My knees weaken and I drop down to the floor. I sit there, my legs bent awkwardly beneath me, the phone dangling from my hand. And it all goes into a swirl inside my head. I see our grandmother at her sink, cleaning out canning jars and rinsing rabbit-gutting knives, soundless tears dripping into dishwater. I see our mother, her ankles weighted and sinking her beautiful body to the bottom of the pool. I see our sister, screaming madly, throwing glass and phones and anything her hands can grab.

And the images become transparent and layered, weaving in and out, like this is the same woman, the same helplessness, the same grief. Thousands of years of distress, from Ishtar and before, and all for this— ending up on broken glass, cut spiritless and deep.

Maybe the first "I am" statement in recorded history was the Old Testament God speaking to Abraham, God as thunder speaking through men, through the law. So this is the law still, so loud and destructive and unjust that women lose, like my sister is now lost. Mary Catherine is deep in a scene from *Locks versus The Law* with the Law still playing God, just as it has for four thousand years. It will bore the spirit out of women forever. My sister is without spirit. She has given up.

I wrap my fingers around the phone cord, listless and dazed, I hear my brother calling my name from Texas. A breeze runs in through my cathedral window and blows my Ishtar footnotes across the room. Aunt Grace flaps against the monitor.

And all of a sudden I know I'm wrong. This didn't happen to Grace. She never caved. She walked. She flew to Egypt.

Maybe my sister isn't giving up. Maybe my sister's doing what the Thunder did. She's fighting against the Law—fighting with her arms and her legs and her voice. Every generation gets stronger. I've got to get stronger.

I run down to the storage room to get my bags, run to the closet to get clothes, then the bathroom to grab make-up and shampoo. Unplug computer, turn off lights, snatch keys, wallet's in the car, I'm set. Saint Christopher hangs about my neck and anything I forget, Mom will have. I take one last look and lock the door behind me.

But ten minutes later, on the highway entrance ramp, I remember my books. Unfuckingbelievable to forget the books. I make a U-turn and head for home.

Once on the winding wooded road that leads to my apartment. I press on the gas. A rabbit crosses in front of my car, so I slam on the brakes but my back right tire thumps. Coming to a complete stop, hardening myself to the wincing pain that I have killed her, I grit my teeth and cautiously look in the rear view mirror. She's alive. Her hind legs are crushed and she's dragging herself across the road with her front paws, blood covering the lower half of her body, blood covering the road. Screaming into the windshield, I slam the gear shift into reverse to run over her again, to kill her before she makes it to the woods or she'll die slowly, deep in the brush, a fate even more cruel. I must end it now, close my eyes and floor the accelerator. Another pelting scream to force myself into action, I peel back maybe ten or twelve feet, slamming on the brakes again, peeking out my front windshield. Jesus Christ, I missed, she's still alive and dragging her bloody body, almost to the woods now, maybe only inches away. I fucking have to do this again, but no God there's no way. Then someone else takes over, someone sicker, and my right hand rips off the steering wheel, forcing the gear into forward, screaming and crying as I bear down on the gas pedal, aiming my car closer to the woods. The wheels thump. I've hit her.

In my rear view mirror, she's crumpled by the side of the road, quiet and soft. My better self steps out of the car and stands next to her, some sort of post-trauma communion, a request for mutual forgiveness, but instead, my consistently lower self finds my forehead on the steering wheel, crying.

Eventually I wipe away my tears and look around. No cars travel this back way, so I stay by the side of the road, feeling little, only numbness and open space, staring out the window to the trees, waiting for the twitches of my shaking body to subside. I start the car and move slowly down the road towards home.

Pulling into my parking space, a twitch goes up my spine, a slight fear, like I've forgotten to turn off the stove or something. I get out and open the trunk to make space for my books.

"Going somewhere?"

Sean walks across the parking lot.

"Oh! Sean, I didn't hear you pull up." Damn, I knew I forgot something. Something like *the weekend*. Something like the Burmese movie we were going to see tonight because he was flying into town early. But wait, that's not until seven o'clock, *hours* from now. My mind begins to whirl, there is too much to absorb here.

I don't want this.

He stops in the middle of the lot, about six feet away, and folds his arms across his tightening pecs. "You didn't see me because I arrived awhile ago. Your car wasn't here, so I waited under the sycamore. I knew you'd return."

"Awhile ago?" I ask, trying to smile. I should have left my books, not come back for them. We've had this Texas conversation far too often, but this time discussion is not an option.

"Missed you, Bernadette," he says, kicking some errant gravel with the toe of his boot. "But it looks like you're taking off. With a grad student? Or maybe you always bring luggage to the theater."

I laugh. No matter how high his level of annoyance, he always maintains a sense of humor. "Some, uh, room needed to be cleared, in the trunk, for, um, other things back in the apartment. That's when I was going to call to explain. But, hey, now you're here in person." I close the trunk and pocket the keys.

"With a road atlas in your hand?"

Damn. I toss it onto the top of the car.

"Bernadette, are you trying to leave me?" Great. He's even more paranoid than usual. His ex must be sobbing into his ear again.

"Sean, please don't say these things. My books were left inside." I walk over to him, smiling, but his feet stay in their cowboy spread. There's no revelation here, however, for this is typical behavior. More amazing is the fact that I walked out that door without a book. To have forgotten to call Sean is easily understandable, but to have forgotten my work?

"You have to go back in to get your books?" he smirks. "You're taking your books to the movie, too? Are we going to work on our dissertation in the lobby or in the aisles of the theater."

I hold out my hand. "Come on, you clown. I'll tell you what happened." But he thrusts his hands into his back pockets and walks ahead of me to the door. I feel the urge to turn around, run for my car, and peel out, but instead I search way down in my gut for lightness. He hasn't had much sympathy for Mary before, but situations change. She needs me, I can make him see this. So I get on the road a little later? What's an hour or so? I'll just stop less often. Or drive faster.

I unlock the door and let him go in first. This will be easy. A few words, a kiss, and I'll be off.

Texas
1990 A.D.

TWENTY-NINE

*Come forward to childhood,
and do not despise it because it is small.*

for the smallnesses are known from the greatnesses.

I did not leave with a few words and a kiss and I did not leave that night. In fact, I did not leave for days. Sean moved his flight back until Wednesday to allow us extra time to continue "processing" our "issues," namely my codependent ties with my family, and his security needs involving my loyalty to the primary relationship—him.

"Go put on more lipstick," he says, pushing off my back. I find my arms and convince them to lift my shoulders away from the cotton sheets, a girl push-up, my heavy legs still weighted to the bed. The mirror he carried in finds my face. I look sick.

"There's still some on," I slur. I don't want to get up again. I can't get up again.

"C'mon, more. Go." He whips back the sheet covering my ankles. "The red." He reaches for the smaller hand mirror on the nightstand and lays it on a pillow. "Then we'll do another one."

I'm standing by the end of the bed now, the only place on the floor where he hasn't rigged up a mirror, my hand pushing the long hair he begged me to curl off my face. "No," I sway. "No, I can't do any more. No."

He doesn't look up at me. He's making a perfects white snake, straight and thick, he's tapping the spoon. "Be happy," he grins. "Don't you want to be happier than you are?"

I turn away and feign a walk.

But the bathroom light's too strong. The lipstick won't go on right. My hands feel like Pink Floyd's two balloons. I turn on the water. I want to go down the drain like that, just like that.

"Can I watch?" he calls, giddy. I turn off the water and pick up the lipstick, finishing the curved red line on my face.

I hate him. I hate him. I hate him.

I look up and read, as I always do when I feel this way, the spiritual messages he's taped to the top of the mirror. A new one is taped up tonight:

> *Free your brother here, as I freed you.*
> *Give him the selfsame gift,*
> *nor look upon him with condemnation of any kind*
> *See him as guiltless... p. 424*

He's right. I know he's right. I roll down the lipstick tube and fluff up my curls and go back into the bedroom. He's sitting there, propped up by pillows, holding out the hand mirror, all ready, his face beaming, like a child he is so excited, so anxious.

"God, that's perfect," he gasps, scanning my face, my hair, my body, as I walk towards him. So happy right now, no anger at all, how can I disappoint him.

When I dropped him off at the airport, I made a left at the exit as if to go home (I knew he'd be watching from the terminal.), but then I circled around a suburb and sped my heart onto the freeway bound for Texas. I was the midnight rider at noon, a highway pirate robbing herself of the questionable integrity of significant-other loyalty. I was not sauntering home to my computer as promised. I was racing to hug my sister. Not only had I lied to my lover, I lied for six days straight, with ne'er a flinch. But to tell the truth, I think he knew. Or else he would have remembered that I never unpacked my trunk. Maybe he did, but couldn't bring himself to admit I would win in the end. Denial, I do love that excuse, when it's in my favor. Freud gave us an explanation for everything we can't quite *get*.

When I felt calm enough to pull over at a truck stop, I phoned Mary, but no answer. At my hotel it was the same. When Sean accidentally pulled the phone out of the wall on Saturday, I should have taken care of it. I shouldn't have let him convince me that this privacy was growthful.

"We can meditate for your sister," he'd said. "What good does a phone do? She needs help on a different plane."

"The plane of my presence. I'm driving there."

"No, you're too attached to the physical. You have to go deeper."

"I've *been* meditating."

"Work harder."

"I can't."

"You can, you will, because you are stronger than her manipulative pull. You're not equanimous enough."

"I can't sit here on this zafu any longer. I have to take action."

"The Buddha waited. This is how we succeed. We wait."

I closed my eyes. "I am more Gnostic than Buddhist. This means I know. I know what I must do."

He leapt out of the living room chair and pointed in my face. "You don't know."

I could tell he wanted another fight, but I was too worn out. I stayed on my cushion with as much upekkha as I could muster, looked away from his hand and whispered, "I do know.'

"You do know you're governed by your ego!"

I got up and said nothing.

"Don't walk away. Don't you walk away from me."

I kept going, headed for the kitchen, when the Upanishads came flying over my right shoulder. "Missed, honey."

"Come back here and work this out. You think you're going to run off like your Aunt Grace? Some ego-centered false notion of bravery and freedom when it's just escapist gypsy irresponsibility? Your grandmother stayed, she knew what she should do." I kept going. "Don't you dare walk out, Bernadette." I kept going. "You answer me!"

I heard a noise and turned around just in time to see the Raku lamp Mikhail had given me one Christmas come crashing to the floor, the pottery splintering like painted desert dirt across my Baluchi rug, Sean gripping the rice paper shade in his fist.

The second day of driving was worse. My brutalized senses finally stabilized enough to allow my mind to review, without editing, the endless week in meditation/drugs-in-the-mail prison. I shuddered with each flashback, and held on to the Saint Christopher medal still around my neck, how it kept me safe, a gift from my mother years ago.

At first I tried my best to be available for Sean, to listen without ego, to debate without criticism, but when he threw the watering can at my face, there was absolutely no manipulative guru coercion or bodhisattva apology that would bring me back. Though I kept a good cover through all his profuse apologies, he knew I was through.

At a rest stop, Curtis answered the phone. Mary began having contractions but hours after the police left. Labor was a thunderstorm, but by midnight their child was born. From the chaos came the angel Kristen, four weeks premature, but healthy and screaming.

Driving down I-40, I readily forgot my hell and thought only of Kristen, what her presence could do. I wanted so much to drive fast, weaving in and out of cars, and so I did. And I remembered back when I was a pretty short kid, driving on a trip to somewhere, asking my father about the first car leading all the other cars on the highway. He tried to explain that no one led, but I couldn't understand the concept that all the cars were just moving, that there were more roads than the one I was on, that no one car was first, that people were only going where they had to go.

Chip interjects. "Just tell her to shut up, Dad."

Mom told him to shutup and keep counting telephone poles.

"Okay," Dad says. "There is one car leading everyone else, a red Thunderbird with fins."

"Have you ever seen it?" I continued, relishing Chip's admonishment.

"Yes," he said, "and the owner keeps it in mint condition, very shiny." My mother slapped him lightly on the arm and actually smiled. "And if nobody has to go to the bathroom for the rest of the trip, we can catch up to it."

So that's the one, I smiled slyly, proud of myself for getting the real scoop out of Dad: a red car that looked like a bird, smelled like a mint and sounded like thunder. Satisfaction was mine. I stuck my tongue out at Chip, sat back in my seat, and stared out the window, ready to resume the telephone pole count myself.

Little did I know then that the key to living with kids lies in the acquiesce. Mary taught me you learn to parent when you not only give in to their perception of how things are, but when you learn to enjoy it. My father's frustration ended when he saw the road through my eyes and decided to go along. The trial then became the game and even my mother laughed.

As I pulled off the exit for gas, I decided that Kristen was our red T-bird. She would rescue my sister and lead her to safety, just like that red Thunderbird led our family to the Holiday Inn. Kristen would bring my sister back from across the river Styx, back from the madness that hopelessness creates, back to the promise she still had to keep.

Only days after her birth, I finally pulled my Honda into the driveway of the large white stucco house Mary so meticulously OCD landscaped. Walking up the slate path lined with red geraniums and pink azaleas, I felt this could be any year, any day. But the bland "come in" that echoed from inside seriously warned my cheerfulness.

Mary barely looks my way as I walk up to her on the couch, and her A-frame hug lacks even the slightest warmth. She's wearing my old blue bathrobe, frayed and worn, and the once flawless hair is scattered. She looks like a bag lady fresh from the landfill.

"Mary!" I chirp. "Where's Mom, you know, the *chap*erone?" My humor doesn't work. She doesn't even look at me.

"In the laundry room," she answers dryly, no movement but her lips. "Ironing."

"And Suzanna?" I probe, as if continually asking questions forces interaction. She doesn't answer.

"Is she playing hide-and-seek?" I sort of sing, still in denial that my sister may be certifiably nuts. Mary doesn't respond. I turn away, pretending to be looking for Suzanna, but in truth finding it unbearable to watch my sister in screensaver mode.

Then a new thought occurs to me—have I missed Suzanna's visitation? Or did Brad not bring her today? I even drove extra fast the last hour just to arrive at the right time. But it might explain Mary's dejected persona. Then I hear a giggle and the swish of taffeta.

"I bet she's hiding," I call out. "I'm going to find somebody quick!" And I round the corner to find her pressed against the wall, her hand over her mouth to suppress her grandfather's Irish grin. "You little munchkin," I say as I scoop her up. "How glorious it is to see you again."

"Aunt Berndette?" she says, gingerly pointing to my face. "What happened to your eye? There's some tiny purple over here."

"Silly me fell over right into a ballet bar," I laugh. "Boing! Do you ever do that?"

"Yeah, a big one sits on my leg. See?" She pulls up her dress to reveal a bruise, and pats it gently. "Do you want to see my new sister?"

She takes my hand and leads me back to Mary. We stop about three feet from the couch and Suzanna hesitates. "Can we see her, Mommy?"

Mary rises from the sofa without a word, goes into the bedroom and returns with a plastic baby basket. She sets it at my feet and I slowly get down on my knees to see the sleeping bundle. "She's only seven days old," Suzanna whispers.

"She's an altar," I whisper back, unfamiliar with babies, having not seen one in years. No one in academia appears with children, at least not in the classroom or stacks. I smile so uncontrollably I fear my enthusiasm might wake her up.

"Mommy, Mommy I'm hungry," Suzanna calls. I look at Mary. She's returned to her same spot on the couch, her eyes fixed on the TV.

"Then we'll just have some fun food," says the jovial aunt, and I reluctantly stand up and walk away from maybe the most wonderfull embodiment of breath I have ever been near. My knees are shaky as I go to the fridge and hunt for food. I scrounge around, land on peanut butter and fix a sandwich, carefully cutting off the crusts and sectioning the bread into those beloved triangles. Then I sit down by my sister.

"Smell that?" Mary asks, still glued to the TV.

"Smell what?" I say, checking my fingernails for peanut butter.

"That's how she smells whenever she comes for visitation. I give her baths, but it doesn't help. It's no accident. It's no accident."

"What do you mean?" I ask, confused. She sounds as cryptic as Lon in the nursing home.

"She shows Curtis and me a new pose every visit," Mary continues, "tells us she looks better naked, in front of a camera, black and white pictures best."

I stare at Mary's face and I can't believe these words, the ideas they suggest. I turn to look at my niece at the table. She's feeding her Beach Ball Barbie squished up parts of her sandwich, humming the Little Mermaid theme song.

But as I watch her, I feel each fiber holding together my playful persona start to fray. Reason, compassion, the excitement of reunion and resolution, they all vanish. In this one devastating instant, my determination to fix my sister's pain completely disintegrates. The resolve that grew stronger with every mile on the road has suddenly turned into ugly water down a gutter. Mary starts to talk.

"The attorney knows Brad's charges are lies, but he can't do anything. The forensic psychologist and the ad litum know Suzanna is a pawn in their control-game, but they can do nothing. If I file a counter-abuse charge with the HRS, they could throw up their hands and put her in a foster home and then I might never get her back. Until Brad and WendyJo's investigation is complete, nothing moves. Nothing. She lives with them. Nothing moves."

Here tone is deadpan. Her backbone never cringes. Her eyes never stray from the soundless images on the TV screen.

I stand up and turn to Suzanna. Then I start to move towards the TV. I want to turn it off. No, I want to smash it. I sway and sit back down, rubbing my forehead. Then I sit bolt upright and slide down the sofa to Mary's side. I put my determined hand on hers and whisper earnestly to the side of her frozen face.

"Run, Mary. We'll run together. I'll cover for you, just like with the ice cream vendor, remember? We'll hide out, like we did in the orange trees. They'll never find you. We'll go back to Texas, then Mexico, then further down, until we find a safe spot. We'll do what Grace did. We'll throw all this away. I'll get you set up..." My heartbeat is deafening and my breathing a jagged rhythm as I whisper these words with frenzy, racing with my sister and her child down a crooked road, police and pornographic cameras and yellow straight jackets with wings flying fast upon us. I can't stop, can't stop with the running, until I notice her face flinch in pain and look down to see I'm squeezing her hand so hard I've stopped the circulation.

She yanks her hand away as she turns to me, a hard stare in her eyes and a sneer on her lips. "Grow up," she snarls.

There's a tap on my leg. "Aunt Bernadette?"

I jerk my head around to see Suzanna looking up at me. "Will you read me a story? This one?" She's holding a Disney book in front of my face. God, has she heard me? How did she get from the table to here? I blush and laugh too loudly.

"Of course," I practically shout. "Now, now you just climb up here and snuggle in and we'll see what you've brought me to read." I take the book. "Oh my, the beatific Snow White, a codependent slave with a deadly fruit fixation." Suzanna smiles a bit too knowingly at my fairytale melodrama, ignoring my slant, burrowing into my side, wrapping her arm around my stomach as I begin to read. I turn each page, but I am so off-center and distracted, I can't hear my spoken words. They read like the Apostle's Creed at Mass, rote and monotone. Sentences and syllables blur as I hear myself speak of dwarves, but think instead only of the different hands we're all dealt, the car we'll take, the things we'll pack, the states we have to cross through.

A barely audible sound startles me back to the fairy tale. I hear a gurgle and Suzanna sits straight up. "Aunt Berndette, Kristin is awake!"

The baby lets out a wail and I look at Mary. She doesn't move. So I give the book to Suzanna, grateful for this opportunity, sad as it is, to rush to the baby myself.

"Don't."

Stooping to pick up the crying infant, I turn to the harsh command. My sister stares directly at me again, her lips tense, her eyes narrow and piercing. "Don't pick her up."

"What?"

"I said don't pick her up."

"I heard you, little sister. But maybe you can't hear her crying three feet from your lap." What a wasted bitch. The HRS and Brad are right—this chick is abusive. But then I pull back. Wait, Bernadette, don't leap to conclusions. Maybe there's some medical reason this baby can't be held, colic or something. Admit it, you know nothing of babies.

I move my hands away from Kristen, how it kills me to hear her cry, and I sit back on my calves. "Okay, I'm sorry. How can I help?"

She continues to just look at me, a stone this wench. "Leave her alone," she says.

I swallow my desire to scream and instead feign a graduate student's pose, pliant and subservient. "Leave her alone? But why? I don't get it." Kristen's cries are becoming more and more tragic, her tiny hiccups punctuating her tiny gasps.

Mary Catherine slowly turns back to the TV and her voice, though lower, remains harsh and firm. "It's *good* for babies to cry."

Without a breath, I forsake my submission and spin around to face my sister, rage steaming from my eyes. "Good to cry? She's seven days old for Christ's sake. It's the only way she can talk, you asshole. She needs to be fed or changed or held, you think? Could that be it?" My gut reaction is to slap the woman as I wait for her head to do a three sixty. But again I check myself. This deck is not full.

"Oh please, Mary, I don't have a baby," I brightly beg, giving her power, while searching still for some scrap of compassion within her cement skin. "Please, can I play with her for a little while?"

She doesn't answer. I take that as a yes, quickly scoop up Kristen before there's another command to stop, and bring her to the warmth of my body, holding her close, feeling her conform to my chest, melting all my righteous chaos.

We sit next to Suzanna on the sofa. "Let's sing her a song, Aunt Berndette," she says with a blameless smile. "It will make her stop crying, I know which one she'll like—Rock-a-Bye Baby, Mommy's version, okay?"

"Sure angel," I answer, cradling this treasure inches from my face, her beaming sister close by my side. "I bet you know it by heart."

"I even know it in parts," she says. "I mean, in rounds. We can do rounds. I'm first and you're next."

So we sing. And as harmony gathers us up, simple and soft, my newborn niece stops crying and opens her pink and puffy eyes to gaze around the edges of my face, focusing finally on my moving mouth. And then she slowly begins a ballet I have never seen before: her tiny legs stretch and pull, then come back into her, while her body turns gently towards mine, then languidly curves away. Black lashes flutter as she casually yawns, and her red and clenched fists open and move and gracefully grasp for the air, or for the shapes that only she can see, or maybe for the words and notes of the lullaby.

THIRTY

You have wounded me and you have had mercy.
Do not separate me from the first ones whom you have [known].
[And] do not cast anyone [out nor] turn anyone away.

After who knows how many rounds of Rock-a-Bye Baby, everyone's fallen asleep. Suzanna, Kristen, even my asshole sister on the other end of the sofa. Carefully maneuvering my stuck body off the couch, I leave Suzanna curled up against the armrest and snuggle Kristen down into the cotton blankets of her baby carrier. I tell myself, as I gaze at her, that I will pick her up every time she cries, cradle her in white linen wrapped around my shoulders, keep her close to my chest. Screw my lost sister. *I* will care for this child.

I stand up and take out my barrette, pulling my hair back tighter, refastening the clip with all strands intact. And who would have guessed. All those years I never gave a damn for a frog or a bird and here I am *burning* to mother my sister's daughter. I bend back down next to her, but in a flash sadness envelops my gaze. What am I thinking? This cannot be, it's not going to happen, she is not mine.

I stand abruptly and jerk my body towards the laundry room, and with each step I take away from Kristen, I feel a wave of loss course through. But as each step takes me closer and closer to my own mother, I feel the waves begin to curl with annoyance. She hasn't even come out to say hello. How does a mother go so long without holding her daughter in her arms? Now that I've beheld within myself the semblance of a mother's gaze, I know I could never do that. If I had a daughter, I would *never* stop hugging her.

I open the door slowly and there she is, her back to me, how fitting. She sits in the windowless room with the lights off. The glow of the open dryer bulb outlines her petite shape.

"Oh honey," she says, startled, standing up, arms open wide. "It's been such a long time. I've missed you so."

I stop dead in the doorway. "Mom, is it you?" And instead of the usual A-frame hug I've known for decades, she gives me a full body wrap, her arms holding tight, warm and full of love. God, this feels good. Forgetting who's actually hugging me, I begin to melt, but quickly recover and take a step back.

"You're different," I say, feeling dizzy, barely hiding my surprise.

"There's so much to tell," she says, "but we'll turn on the light."

"No, no, let's just sit here in the dark. It's restful."

So we sit on the bench together, my good side next to her. "Were you listening?" I ask. "Is that why you didn't come out?"

"How was the drive, honey?"

"Mom."

"I wanted to hear everything," she whispers, "because I wanted your reaction. I'm worried. This waiting has taken its toll."

She bends down to gather up a pile of white washcloths in a wicker basket at her feet and starts to fold them in her lap. "When her psychological interviews were done, she thought she'd get Suzanna back right away, but weeks and weeks pass and still no court date. She lost it, even with Curtis. And then the baby premature, labor was simply horrible." She shakes her head as she continues to fold. "She's not pulling out of it."

I help her with the washcloths and wonder how they can all be the same color. None of mine are, not a one. "Mom, I don't think that's everything. Sounds like Suzanna is abused."

She stops folding and closes her eyes.

"Didn't she tell you?" I gasp. I feel my nerves once more beginning to sweat. "What are we going to do?" Wait. Did I just ask Mom for help again?

"Honey," she hesitates, taking hold of my wrist. "I'm praying it's all in her mind."

"All in her mind?" Oh, this is just like Mom—priceless denial of anything dark.

"I called the forensic psychologist myself," she continues. "There's no indication of abuse from Brad and WendyJo. They're probably priming Suzanna to say the suggestive things she does because they know it will destroy Mary. They will do anything to make her upset so she'll seem paranoid and unfit for the psychological interviews. Well it won't work, because Mary's interviews are over. We've just got to keep her calm."

I drop my tense shoulders. Mom's version makes sense.

"There's more," she continues, releasing my wrist, patting my hand. "Curtis may get a transfer up north. He flew out today for a week of interviews. I want Mary to stay with us while he's away so we can help with the baby."

"That's perfect. Will she do it?"

"No."

"No?"

"I was hoping you could change her mind."

I start to fold again. Fat chance. Mom may have heard everything Mary Catherine said to me, but she obviously didn't see those dagger looks. "Doubtful," I say dryly.

She ignores me. "If Curtis can get transferred, the judge will be moved to let Suzanna go. And to tell you the truth, this has been dragging on for so long now, I think Brad's tired of parenting. He's letting Suzanna visit more often and he's actually nicer on the phone with your father."

I stop folding. "Are you suggesting that Brad might drop the charges and give Suzanna back?"

"That's what your father and I are counting on." Boy, does Mom sound in control. Doesn't she have to lie down?

"Once Mary Catherine gets on a plane to a new home, away from *here*, she'll get stronger." She stands up and walks to the light switch. I'm still whirling from the news, and frankly, from the refreshing coherency coming from my mother, so I just sit there, taking it all in. The light goes on.

"Bernadette?" She puts both hands to her cheeks and makes a leap towards me. "That's no closet door," she gasps, reaching out to touch my face. "Sean did this to you, didn't he. Tell me. Tell me!" She grabs me by both shoulders, but I back away.

"I can handle it, Mom. It's okay." But there's heat in my throat as I say it, and futility behind my eyes. She moves towards me again, taking my shoulders and holding on, like she's trying to stop my lies.

"Wait Mom, wait." I try to pull her hands away, but they're gripping me. "Mom? Stop it. This isn't like you." But she's got me tight and I just can't fight her. I don't have the strength to pry her loose and her breath on my face is so foreign. I give up, letting go of her wrists, closing my eyes, sinking into myself. Everything, all this, it is so much, I'm swimming.

"I never liked his voice on the phone," she whispers with anger, shaking me. "I never liked his tone. You get away from him. Do you hear?" Then she wraps her arms around me, pushing my head against her shoulder, and I start to cry a little, but then, suddenly, it all comes down and I just can't stop. My sister, my mother—all that pain and all this love. And as she's rocking me back and forth, smoothing my hair, whispering to me such kindness, I keep thinking I can't remember the last time I felt such warmth and love coming from someone else, coming towards me. Not since Mikhail, not since then.

"You're staying right here with us," she whispers. "Here with all of us. You and your sister and the baby, you're all coming back home and I'm taking care of you."

And we stand there rocking, calming down with each gentle word, the shudders subsiding. I sink into her body now, like I'm the one cradled in white linen around her shoulders, so tired from the drive, the research, the devastation of my sister, and the chaotic futility of being the equanimous girlfriend.

THIRTY-ONE

*In my weakness, do not forsake me,
and do not be afraid of my power.*

*I am the one whom you have scattered
and you have gathered me together.*

I did not implore Mary to move over to Mom's house. I just packed her bag, set it next to her on the sofa, and told her to get in the car. She didn't argue. She did go put on a clo, however, which was a relief. If she'd climbed into the car in that frazzled bathrobe, I'd have considered her certifiable. But if even a fraction of her fashion sense remained intact, there was hope for revival. Not that external trappings a sane human makes, but on some scanty level, it seemed to work for my sister.

Mom showed me how to put the baby to sleep. She walked us back and forth across the bedroom, holding Kristen against my shoulder and humming to her until she nodded off. It was the warmest fun I've ever had. Mom says its the nesting instinct. Can't hide from it in that library forever, she says. And for the first time, I don't contradict her. The thought of having a child, someone closer than the child of Madeline's I might have watched from the corner, appeals.

I lay Kristen down into the crib on her back, per Mom's instructions. She congratulates me as we walk out into the den, but stops mid-sentence to see that Mary has lumped herself on yet another sofa, her eyes transfixed on yet another TV. Same psychosis, different house.

Worse, she's dragged that old bathrobe with her and has it on again, *over* her clo. We both shrug our shoulders. Maybe she needs the mundane.

"Let me get you a snack," Mom says, opening the fridge.

I accept, looking around homeplate for the first time since I walked into the house. Mom's finally redecorated. I'm standing upon a Chinese silk rug, and Mary is stuffed into the corner of a burgundy Victorian sofa with a mahogany carved back. So where's the suburban kitsch?

"Did you see the tile counter tops?" she asks. "I did it myself."

Dad stands up and clicks off the TV. I have never seen him do that. He leaves it on when he goes to Church, or to water the grass, some kind of burglar scare. And he even has Pinhead, splotch that she is, to stare at it with today.

"I'm going to visit Lon," he says. Then he glances at Mary, mumbles an apology and quickly turns the set back on. "Anybody want to come?"

We all just look at him, even my sister. "Mugs'll go with you, Dad," I chuckle. "Mugs and Lon have a lot in common."

"Ah, now you're hurting Mugs' feelings."

"I bought extra bananas for him today." Mom says. "They're on the counter." Mom bought bananas for the dog?

"Do you know what he does with them?" Dad asks me. "He hides them, for Christ's sake."

That's impossible, I think as I look at the blind furball. He couldn't hide anything. Dad takes the bunch from Mom. "I figure he's eaten them and then I'll find one in his drawer, one under the bed, one behind his shoes."

I straighten. "Told you he and Mugs have a lot in—"

"I keep telling him no one's going to take the bananas," Dad continues, fixing the Dallas Cowboys hat on his head, smoothing his hair back on the sides, "but his eyes get real big and he starts looking over his shoulder, mumbling, '...the enemy... the enemy...' Then his voice trails off.'"

"Tell her about the photo," Mom says.

"I showed him a photo I'd found in his files, a shot of this estate with people out front," Dad says, jingling the change in his pocket like he always does on his way out the door, making sure he has a quarter for a phone call, forgetting he's had a car phone for years. "And Lon started yelling and coughing, 'Get that picture out of here. Get it out of here!'"

"So we don't show him anything anymore," Mom adds. "It upsets him too much." Wait, didn't they advise this years ago?

"And he knows everyone he put away is dead by now," Dad says, shaking his head. "He's been keeping track of each guy he ever got convicted, just waiting for them to die."

"Why would he keep track of criminals he put in jail?"

"So he can sleep at night. He thinks they're going to break out of the slammer, tracks him down to the Cedar Hills Nursing Homs and kill him."

"But if he knows they're all dead, why is he paranoid? I don't get it."

"No one gets it," Dad says, bending down to catch Mugs before he walks into the wall trying to follow Dad out the garage door.

Mom turns to me. "There's no reason for him to be afraid anymore. Nothing's left from those days to hurt him, but he continues his crazy talk anyway, like some stone remains unturned."

"I wonder what he thinks about all day, just sitting there."

"Your father asked him that very question. And you know what he said? He told him he was going over all his mistakes."

"All his mistakes? Well then he's going to live awhile longer." I turn to scratch my shoulder blade and see the diamond resting on Mary's limp hand. Damn, what a ring. I look down at my own barren hand, to the place where my wedding ring once wrapped me up. It was the thinnest sliver of silver I could find, more like a fairy ring than human, with just the smallest chip of a diamond set to the side. I hadn't wanted a ring, too much ownership in its history, but Mikhail begged—it goes on forever, he said, forever around you.

Sean was talking about rings a few days ago, a transparent ploy to make me stay. "When does that husband of yours get back from up north?" I ask Mary. She keeps her eyes glued to the set.

"Oh, you haven't met Curtis," Mom whispers close to me like it's a secret. "He is so sweet. All this time has passed and you haven't been down for a visit. I don't understand." She looks up from her nails. "Oh, I'm sorry. Does it hurt?"

"It's okay, Mom. He just never wants me out of his sight. The jealousy is…I mean, well, we can talk about it later." Mary Catherine looks right at my face, starts to say something, but back to the TV quickly.

"Does Dad visit Grandpa often?" I ask.

"Every day," she says. "Brings him all the magazines and newspapers he's read. Lon's face lights up when your father walks in his room. You'd think he was seeing Jesus himself walk through that door. Isn't that ironic?"

"Well, it may as well be Jesus he's seeing, because that's about only person who'd ever forgive him."

Mom smiles at me, pats my hand, my left hand no less, tapping the empty ring finger, like she still comforts my loss. She loved Mikhail. "There's nothing *to* forgive," she says quietly. "Not really."

"Nothing to forgive?" I ask in disbelief.

"Forgiveness suggests arrogance," she says, "a hierarchy, like you're better than the one you think needs forgiveness."

"Excuse me? We *are* talking about Grandpa?"

She looks away and twitches a little, like she's told a lie, or a confidence, something she wasn't supposed to let loose. "Your father feels sorry for him, that's all," she half whispers, apologetically.

"Or maybe he wants Lon to see that being Catholic isn't a total noose around the neck. Partial, yes, but not total." I touch Mary's diamond, checking to see if it's bigger than my thumb nail.

"I don't know. I think your father's learning. He's learning about powerful men being humbled by the way of things. Lon was such a forceful person most of his life and now he's a half-deaf shell strapped in a wheelchair." She sighs. "It's all right on time, though." I look up at the cuckoo clock in the kitchen. "But, I have to confess," she whispers. "I feel a little guilty about what I did to him."

I grit my teeth. I'd seen her in that nursing home a few years ago.

"I wrote a horrible letter," she continues. "Confessed exactly how I felt about him. But I never mailed it. I just practiced reading it in front of the mirror, when your father was at work." She giggles. I've never heard her giggle. And I don't see any guilt.

"Well, then I felt a little better about only visiting him every few weeks or so. But your dad, you know, he said Lon always asked where I was. So Dr. Tuley-Cashwell had an idea."

"You still go to her, Mom?"

"She said I should read the letter out loud to Lon." Mary's hand jerks beneath my touch.

"You didn't," I gasp.

"I did," she proudly smiles. "And your father was an accomplice."

"Dad?"

"Your father and I went in and said hi as if it was any other Sunday. Then I took off Lon's glasses, like I was going to clean them, and while your Dad was opening the newspaper on his lap, I took out his hearing aid and threw it in a drawer. Your father kept his attention with the stock page and I read my letter out loud. Well, actually, I screamed it. 'Pedophile!' I kept yelling at him. It felt so good. And I was standing behind him and I know he couldn't hear me because he's deaf without that hearing aid, but I swear he knew what was going on because he kept trying to turn around in his wheelchair and look at me, but he's strapped in, you know, so he won't fall out, and then your dad would yell, 'Here, Lon, look. AT&T is up!' so Lon would turn back to your Dad, then try to turn back to me, drool going everywhere, but just as I was about to really let him have it, the nurse opened the door and I had to stop, which was probably good, or I would have kept yelling 'Pedophile, pedophile,' for the, for the—Mary? Mary Catherine? Are you okay?"

I turn to see Mary doubled over, her head in her hands, her body in convulsions. I look at Mom and she looks at me and we don't know what to do. "Jesus, Mom, she's going to vomit."

"Oh my God, she's choking." Mom jumps up and kneels in front of Mary while I put my arms tightly around her shoulders to stop the shaking. I bend down close to her shivering face.

"Mary! Mary!" we yell, but she doesn't answer. I'm trying to hold her steady, but it does no good. She continues her epileptic fit, her body shuddering, her hands over her face.

"We've got to get an ambulance here, now, get her to the Emergency Room."

"I'm calling 911," Mom says as she jumps up from the floor.

But then Mary's hand reaches out from the folds of her clothes, and she shakes a finger at Mom, like she's trying to tell her no. Mom kneels back down, takes the hand into her own and puts it to her cheek. "We're trying to help, Mary. Tell us what to do."

"Wait," I say. "I don't think she's hurt."

Mary holds her other hand out to me and sits up just a hair, enough so we both can see she isn't going to vomit, she's not in a spasm, she's laughing. She's holding onto her sides and laughing so hard that even though her mouth gapes open, no sound issues forth. I pull her up and we hug, and then I start laughing, and then Mom starts laughing, and suddenly everything becomes so absurd: Mom yelling "pederast," at crumpled old Lon, Dad pointing to the stock page, trying so hard to be supportive, and maybe just the inanity of our human whining in general. Laughter so hard we make no sound, holding onto our sides and each other, our heads bobbing, tears falling down our faces. And as I laugh, I watch her out of the corners of my running squinted eyes and I'm absorbing as much of her laughter as I can, before she remembers, before she stops.

But no, I think as I bob, this isn't going to end. For it's too much like when we were young, too much like I remember her. She's been but a shadow of light for so long, and here she glows her brightest. Old Pinhead, full of mocking, swimming laughter, she's back. I squeeze her tight. I must work hard to keep her.

THIRTY-TWO

*I, I am sinless
and the root of sin derives from me.
I am lust in (outward) appearance,
and interior self-control exists within me.*

After we soak a small box of designer tissues, Mom gets up to make mint tea. Mary lifts her hand towards my face, but I jerk back. "Closet door, huh? You can do better than that."

I pull my long hair out from behind my ears and smooth it close to my face. But I know there is nothing I hide well.

"Get rid of him," she snaps. "I never liked his voice on the phone. Sort of stiff. No fun."

"Coming here was hard enough," I wince.

"You mean Sean's the reason you haven't visited in so long? Your own family?"

"You and Mom have been talking about this, haven't you? You're both carrying the same line. Look, he just never wants me to go anywhere."

"I'd cave and die with a guy like that," Mary says, picking nubs off the sleeve of her robe.

I hunch over my knees. "I do miss the stacks," I say wistfully.

"What? He doesn't want you going to the library? Your second home? Your womb? You left Mikhail for this?"

"I didn't leave Mikhail for this."

"The idea is to move up, sis. Not down."

"I'm doing my own work, work I love. I'm not supporting Sean like I did Mikhail. It's different."

"Dette, you do know how to tell if he's truly an *ass*hole, don't you? I mean, down to the bone? Not that it isn't fairly *ob*vious."

"Yeah, if he's my friend or not."

"Well, that too, but I've refined these distinctions. I'm referring to his perspective on high school. Did he just loooove high school?"

"He loved high school."

"I rest my case."

"Jackson loved high school, so your theory is blown. And anyway, Sean's fears are understandable. His wife had affairs."

"*So?*"

"She lied, wanted an open marriage, always manipulating him, telling him he wasn't forgiving enough, or that he drove her to do it."

"Twenty bucks says she's unattractive. Only ugly people want open marriages."

"Her motto was 'who made the rules?' She even suggested that since one of her boyfriends was a starving artist, he should move into their house so Sean could support him, too."

"Ah, the ol' like-your-Visa, but-don't-like-you, with a twist of Zen."

Mom hands us each a mug of hot tea. "So he thinks you'll do the same?"

I blow on the steam. "I tried to work with only women's groups, and ballet of course, but it didn't help. When I took a class that was predominantly male, that's when I got to see the real shadow."

Mary moves to the edge of the sofa. "Because of a class? Go fish."

"Some of the men were single."

"Oh my, that's terrible." She flips her hair and gives the effeminate wrist wave. "You slut."

"Whenever the teacher called about an assignment, he'd listen on the extension."

Mary points a finger at my face. "There were always tons of single grad students around your place when you were married to Mikhail. He'd bring half the department home every night. He was never jealous."

I shoot her one of those dagger looks. "Mikhail has nothing to do with this," I say.

"I think he does," she snaps.

"Look Pinhead, you were the one who pushed me to go out with him, remember?"

"Girls, girls," Mom interjects. "Please."

I shake my head. "It just is because it is."

"Like he just *is* listening on the damn extension."

"I told him I'd quit the class, but he said no, it made me happy. But then he'd say that the only reason I was happy was because I must be having an affair. He knew the signs from his ex-wife, I'm the same age she was when she started."

"How long have they been divorced?" Mom asks.

"About a year."

"That might explain," she muses. "He hasn't been separated long enough to work through his anger and hurt. So he's taking it out on you."

"Who cares what his reason is," Mary interrupts. "Get rid of him!"

Mom continues the analysis. She must have learned all this psych from that ol' Tuley-Cashwell, but I don't mind. She's fun to watch. "Do you know if he ever hit her?" she asks.

"No. Never. In fact, he never even raised his voice with her."

"Well, what a crock of shit," Mary sneers, throwing up her arms and falling back into the sofa.

I turn to her and plead. "If he ever got angry with her, she'd start sobbing on the floor that no one loved her. He feared she'd kill herself."

She bolts upright to the edge of the couch. "Great idea," she shouts, raising a fist to the air. "The planet is saved from yet another manipulative whiner. Get the rope. Stop global whining."

"Bernadette, honey," Mom says. "Sean needs help." Mary pretends to gag. "He needs time alone to work through his marriage."

"Why in God's name, ugh, Jesus, were you ever attracted to this guy?"

"He was outside the university, he wasn't an intellectual. He was into the physical part of life—the body, exercise, nutrition, sports -"

"Beatings."

I have to smile. I do love my sister. "And you just spoke of him in the past tense," she lights up. "A very good sign."

"Honey, didn't you say he was a meditator? That can be helpful."

"Well, since being around him and his ex-wife, I've learned that the meditating types are often the ones with the most anger. They're trying so hard to put on the guru persona that their shadow is not only right below the surface, it's seething." (Thank you, Psyche.)

"But it doesn't have to be that way."

Mary starts playing with her hair, trying to tame and braid it with her fingers. "This guy's a brown-breader, Dette. Forget all your gnostic stuff. You should change your dissertation to *Granola Warfare*."

I laugh, Mom laughs, but something's wrong. It isn't light, it isn't loose like the laughter we just knew.

"Really, he's never hit me before, ever."

The garage door slams hard. We all freeze. It's Dad.

"Your mother said it was the goddamn closet," protests an enraged voice, one I haven't heard since high school, a voice that makes me quake still.

We all freeze. We must not have heard his car pull in. Mom puts her hand on my knee. "Bill," she starts.

"Where the fuck is he," Dad growls. "Give me his fucking address." He throws open the kitchen drawer, throwing things out, looking for paper. "Bernadette, you're pressing fucking charges. Period."

Mary Catherine yanks her bathrobe belt tight and jumps up off the sofa, putting her hands to her hips.

"Now you don't worry yourself there, Grandpa," she says, shaking her derriere from side to side. "Don't you worry one bit. We women got us attorneys and shrinks out the wahzoo, and no man's gonna make us do what we no longer wanna do."

Dad stands there, his jaw on the floor. I don't know if it's Mary's attitude that's stupefied him, or if it's just the fact that she's got it back.

"Don't worry, Dad," I shrug. "I don't think I'll stay with him."

Mary swings the top half of her body around to me, keeping her hands on her hips, "You don't *think*…?"

"Okay, okay," I wave my hand. "I'm not staying with him."

"That's better, girl," she says as she bends down to hug me. But I don't feel better. In fact, I feel worse.

"Jesus, Mary, and Joseph!" Dad yells from the kitchen. We all jump, now what? But he's not yelling at me this time. It's only Mugs, so happy to "see" him that she's peeing on his shoe.

THIRTY-THREE

I am the one whom you have hidden from,
and you appear to me.
But whenever you hide yourselves,
I myself will appear.

We sleep with relative serenity that night, Mary Catherine and me in our old twin beds like we're kids again, a baby between us instead of a hamster.

Around four a.m., Kristen wakes up hungry so I reach into the crib and pull her into bed with me, holding her close to my chest. How unlike holding onto Sean, everything weighted and tight. She, on the other hand, is tiny, but so solid and strong. It doesn't follow somehow. If you're that new and that small, shouldn't you be more fragile? I'm relatively old and large, and don't feel solid at all. So why are we like that when we're babies? And where does it go?

As I hand her to Mary, something flashes through me, something like a thought, but more material. Wispy gossamer whispers around it, but suddenly it's sharp, like a searing pain running up a nerve. In milliseconds it's gone, but I can name it just the same. I served up as a wife for ten years, and I laid down as a surrogate sort of mother after that, but I never had a child. I could have and didn't. Now I watch my sister with her second baby and lie in awe at this life I've missed.

When Kristen wakes us up again, the sun lights something on the edge of our beds. I reach down and pull up new bathrobes, with the tags on even. So maybe the gods can't bear another day of Pinhead in the ancient blue rag, either.

"You take the purple one," she says, "matches your face."

I crawl out of bed, slip into a soft velour robe and then lay Mary's dark blue one over her legs. Diving back under the covers, I clumsily knock my stack of books onto the floor, a journal landing on top, open.

"Don't even think about making a comment," I snarl, leaning over to gather up the mess.

Mary shifts Kristen. "You remember writing all those diaries in high school?" she laughs. "You had about a hundred."

"Obsession belonged to me alone."

"I read them."

I flick a crumpled tissue at her. "You little bedlamite, I should have guessed."

"Well, you kept them right under the bed. Or right *on* your bed. What'd you expect?"

"It pains me to think of all that internal adolescent drama." I fall back on my pillow. "Ah, the pathetic years."

"I found one story crammed way under there after you left for college. I'll never forget it because it hit me pretty hard. But maybe my reaction was due to my prison here at home with Mom and Dad, and worse yet, Chiplerina. You abandoned me to those three!"

"Isn't that when they bought Mugs?"

"They felt sorry for me. So to replace you, they gave me a dog."

"They could have given you another hamster."

She flicks the tissue back. "I bet Mom's kept all your diaries."

"I wouldn't be surprised. She unloaded a stack of Millicent's journals a few years ago, accounts written at the beginning of the century. God, they were boring."

"Ever read Grandpa's?"

"The man wrote volumes on himself, thereby defining narcissistic personality disorder. Let's not talk about him."

"Wait, I read sad parts," she argues. "He wrote about other things besides himself, like how he loved Londa. He wrote everything they did together, how her favorite game was to be swung around by her feet."

"Well, Londa had a sister, don't forget. And look, you know he was a pervert."

"No, she would *beg* him to swing her. He conned her into thinking it was a game, and even though it killed his back, he'd swing her over and over because it got the flem or the mucous or whatever that stuff was, out of her lungs." She puts Kristen on her shoulder to burp her.

"Want to do it?" she asks.

I greedily hold out my arms, fearing the painful gossamer stab again. But as she melts into my shoulder, only the whisper happens.

"Look," Mary says, "You know he made a scrapbook of Londa's letters when she was at the hospital, taped them in chronological order, envelopes and all. But you've got to see this one letter. It wasn't glued in, so I put it in the top drawer here." She scrounges through some things in the dresser and brings out a yellowed sheet of torn looseleaf. "Read this," she says, "and tell me Grandpa was an ogre." I cradle Kristen deep into the crook of my left arm, take the letter from her hand and read it out loud:

NORTH POLE, 1941
   MY DEAR LONDA:
      MOST OF THE TIME YOU HAVE BEEN A FINE LITTLE GIRL,
      BUT YOU COULD DO BETTER KEEPING YOUR CRAYONS PUT AWAY.

I hold the letter up in the air. "See? The kid's dying and he's beating on her for not picking up the damn crayons."

"Oh chill. Keep reading."

> I HEAR YOU DO NOT ALWAYS TURN YOUR HEAD WHEN YOU COUGH. NOW THAT IS NOT SO GOOD AND I AM DEPENDING ON YOU TO NEVER DO IT AGAIN.
> YOU HAVE BEEN A FINE GIRL IN TAKING YOUR MEDICINE SO WELL. AND YOU ARE GROWING LIKE A LITTLE GIRL SHOULD.
> PRANCER AND DANCER ARE RESTLESS TO BE GOING.
> GOOD BYE LONDA UNTIL NEXT CHRISTMAS.
> S. CLAUS
> P.S. TELL YOUR DADDY I BORROWED THIS PAPER FROM HIS TABLET. I DON'T CARRY MUCH PAPER WITH ME. S.C.

I put the letter on the bed and look down at Kristen. What if she was Londa and I was her father, holding her like this, knowing full well there wouldn't be a next Christmas. Could I write that letter? Play that game? It would break me, every cell, it would break me.

"I've got an idea," Mary says, putting on her robe, ignoring the void in the room, for she knows she's made her point. "Let's go up into the attic today and begin a diary hunt. We've got nothing else to do." She grabs the letter, shoves it in the drawer and slams it shut. "C'mon, hop up, let's eat." Kristen burps in agreement.

Mom sits at the kitchen table with several shockingly uneaten pastries in front of her.

"The robes are way cool," Mary smiles, "thank you."

"Well, I wanted to save them for later," Mom says, "but I couldn't resist."

I pull out a chair and sit down to cradle Kristen in a way I can see her face and expressions. She has so many, all moving in and out like she's planned them. With this newfound picture show, food holds little value.

"Whoa," says Mary, "check out the spread. Did you do all this, Mom?"

"I couldn't sleep," she answers, pushing coffee cake towards Mary. "I'm too excited. Curtis's chance at the job up north, the court date coming soon, I just had to bake."

Mary grabs a muffin and crams it in her mouth. I don't think she has post-partem depression. "Curtis should call today to let me know how the interviews are going," she mumbles in between chews. "Got one this morning."

"Then we need to keep busy," Mom says. "Let's find a good distraction."

"Yeah," says Mary, dancing around the table. "But I ain't got no distra-action."

Mom watches her lip sync an invisible song. "We could rent a movie," she says quietly.

"Or shop at the mall," May sings.

"Let's take Kristin to the park," I interject, smoothing her soft skin. "She'd like the swings."

No one answers me. I look up. "Aren't there swings at the park?"

They just stare.

"The one on the corner by the school?"

"Dette," Mary says, "She's eleven days old."

When we return from the park, there's a message from Curtis flashing on the machine. "Hey, you guys, they've hired me. I'm catching an earlier flight back. Hang in there, girl."

Mary calls Dad at the office.

"I've already called the attorney," he says. "Forensic reports are done, I'm on my way home. Get ready to go down to Johnson's office to read 'em. Pick you up in thirty minutes."

Two hours later, Mom and I are sitting under an orange tree waiting for their return. I'm twirling purple and white pansies about two inches from Kristen's face because I read that newborns can see distinctly dark and light colors when they're right next to each other, or something like that. I don't know. Am I a mother? She seems to enjoy the game, so I keep twirling, cooing at her like an idiot.

When they pull in the driveway, I note the strain on Mary's face, but as she takes Kristen into her arms, her jaw softens and her eyes light up. Meanwhile, Dad is hyper.

"Got him by the balls," he says, clapping his hands. "You wouldn't believe it. The forensic report makes Brad and WendyJo look bad, real bad. Says WendyJo is manipulative. Manipulative! Like I couldn't have told them that six months ago. Saved everybody one hell of a lot of dough. And Mary Catherine is, how'd they put it? Something like warm and, uh, spontaneous, yeah, that's it, with Suzanna." His smile radiates accomplishment.

Mary's eyes widen and her eyebrows arch. "And the report said WendyJo was married four times, and the first time she was only fifteen."

"She has that many uncles?"

Mary stops dead in the hallway. She turns around and her face has the I-could-kill-you look. Okay, so I shouldn't have said that about the uncles. I'm sorry! I'm in a fire-ant mood because I had to give Kristen back.

Mary doesn't scold me. Instead, she hands me the child. Good, it worked. I haven't lost my old touch of tormenting her until I get what I want. "That's it," she almost yells, "I've got to get Suzanna out of there. Now." And she storms over to the phone.

"Mary, Mary, wait," Dad says nervously, "Johnson is setting up the court date, he'll call when he gets it. The report said Brad and WendyJo didn't seem abusive, remember?"

She turns her back to him, cradling the phone to her ear. "Tricky little word there, *seem*," she says.

But before she can click the on button, it rings. "Hello?" she fakes so politely. Then her eyes narrow. "No Sean, she's not here. Why would she be here?"

Dad moves towards her, but Mom grabs his arm.

"What do you mean she's missing? How can she be missing?" There's a pause. "Well you know we haven't seen her here in Texas for a couple of years. Funny, she hasn't been down for a visit since about the time she started dating *you*." She twirls her hair. "Yes, she has been very busy with her research, spends a lot of time at the library, true."

Dad's face is shifting to hotter shades of red, but Mom's standing between him and the phone.

"So say, maybe we should file a missing person's report with the police, think? But, well, having not seen her lately, I don't know if she even looks the same. Could you describe her face to the police? You saw her last, so tell me, does her face look the same?"

I panic. Mary's getting into dangerous water here, makes me want to run out back to the lake, alligators or no. I motion for her to hand me the phone.

"Are you calling me a liar, little man?" she says, turning her back to us while she vents her frustrations over court onto Sean. "I need to what? Bernadette needs to what? Do you know the definition of controlling? Of assault and battery? Are these terms in your ashram handbook? Listen up, you little white towel-headed yogi bagwan, if you so much as *speak* to my sister, much less *touch* her again, I'll plunge my fist down your throat and rip your fucking lungs out. And furthermore…"

Mom bends down near the wall and disconnects the phone. She holds the dangling cord up to me and Mary and Dad. "This is enough," she says. "For all of us, this is enough."

THIRTY-FOUR

Those who are close to me have been ignorant of me,
and those who are far away from me are the ones who have
known me.
On the day when I am close to [you],
[You] are far away [from me],
[and] on the day when I [am far away] from you,
[I am close] to you.

The lowest level of hell is not the frozen pit dominated by Lucifer. It's the Dallas airport. When normally agreeable people step through the doors of this building, they change. It's as if they suddenly develop a Tourette's of the soul, knocking you over as they sprint to catch a plane, the Armani scarf and obscenities flying. But more obscene than their mouth is their hair. Gelled and sprayed into a stylish cement, it won't move. The hair acts as a force field, a hard line of protection, common amongst women who abhor touch, but lately seen atop corporate men as their masculine borders become less defined. Get in the way of the hair and you get cut, for their mission—in this case flight service—prioritizes (*their* word) courtesy.

Worse yet are the employees with thick necks. Decked in gray uniforms edged with Stalinesque red piping, they appear out of nowhere driving tanks down the aisle, honking the horn for you to get out of the way or you'll be beaten beneath the goodyear. Sometimes they carry crippled seniors swaying in their seats, gripping their walkers, wishing they'd hobbled to the gate rather than feel their dentures shift as they ride the wild toad. But often the tanks carry no passengers and the drivers delight in blasting through the crowds solely to annoy the masses, and, of course, to vent their frustration over never being promoted to reservationist.

I don't like airports. They are the antipodes of my museful library. But standing at the baggage claim with my family, watching six foot ten Curtis lift luggage off the conveyor belt for the ravenous people below, my misanthropic nausea subsides.

I am in deep *like*. Curtis is, truly, what Mary and Mom have been lauding for a year: a basketball Buddha. Despite the shoving, he radiates equanimity not in word, but in action. He floats each bag over the heads of the crowd and places it gently down at the owner's side. Whispers grow.

"How tall do you think he is?"

"He has the strength of ten."

"Does he work here?"

I look around and note that every single person in this crowded airport has become short. Mary stands next to Curtis and although I've always considered her a tall woman, in her present position, she's a dwarf.

Driving down the highway towards home, Curtis's knees almost touch his chest even though he sits up front with the proud father-in-law. But he never complains, and he never plays the martyr by silently shifting around in frustration. Instead, he engages Dad in the latest Celtics debate and the women in back relax. This is a man who pours more in to make it half full.

We pull up to their house. Curtis unfurls himself from the car, cradles the baby in one arm and wraps the other around Mary Catherine as they walk to their door, her head leaning against his stomach. And I could swear I see those pink geraniums bowing down their blooms as they stroll by, a scene straight from the Wizard of Oz, all souls merry and content on that yellow road.

Dad puts it in reverse and we slowly roll out, Mom heaving one of her huge sighs. "It's your turn," she says, patting my knee, like the deep-end's all clear so I get to go down the slide now. "Time to find you one like that."

Mom ushers me into the trendy kitchen and slams a large and weighty machine on the counter. "I'm blending carrot juice," she says as if I'm a reluctant novice. "You remember how Jackson begged you to drink carrot juice that time you dove in the pool and scraped the whole side of your body? He pulled you out."

I narrow my eyes, tentative about the tone here, a kind of suspicious finality, like she's suddenly proactive. That never happened anyway. She's always had a penchant for rearranging the past, but now she's switching bodies and heads. I roll down my sleeve to cover the teenage scars that run up my left arm. "You drink carrots, Mom?"

Dad crouches down on all fours in the middle of the kitchen and starts rubbing noses with Mugs. "Hell, she's drinking spinach, onions, garlic, you name it. Makes me drink it, too. Pretty soon I'll be sprouting wings." He laughs and wrestles with the dog. "He sprinted out to the front yard and broke off some aloe for you, too. I'll never forget it. Damn fast runner."

Mom hauls vegetables out of the fridge like a marine on a mission. "Don't you feel healthier, Bill?"

"I have been beating those young bucks at tennis. Can't keep up with the old man," he grins as he opens the dishwasher and begins to unload cups. Are we switching heads and bodies again? Dad puts away dishes?

"What inspired you to drink fresh juice, Mom?" I ask, washing some browning stalks of celery at the sink. They appear to be organic.

"A friend at the Center cured herself of CFS this way."

"CFS?"

"Chronic Fatigue Syndrome. I've just about cured myself."

"Mom, I didn't even know you *had* a syndrome." I rinse spinach.

"Well, I don't like to talk about it." She turns on the machine and crams in an onion. "I bet this'll help your bruise, honey," she says, handing me a large glass filled to the brim with thick green muck. I sniff it politely, smiling.

"Mom, I love carrot juice, but this stuff is, uh, beyond the edge."

"If I can drink seaweed, you can," Dad chastises. "Drink it for your mother. Make her feel good."

I look at him from the corner of my eye and take a big gulp. What I wouldn't do for Sean, I will do for my mother. Dad laughs and slaps his leg. "Tastes like shit, doesn't it. Ha! But you don't eat meat, so you should like this stuff. Right?" I cannot fathom the connection, but I slug it down anyway. Maybe it really will heal something, anything.

"Okay," he says, patting his stomach as we put our empty glasses in the sink, "now you get your reward." He holds up a video and fashions a nautilus championship stance, his legs in second position, knees bent, arms flexed towards the ceiling. "*Death Inferno III*," he growls.

I feel tiny bits of onion doing cartwheels up my esophagus. "Gee, Dad, I...I -"

"Isn't it time for the news, Bill?" Mom calls out, rescuing me for the moment. "C'mere," she whispers, "back in my bedroom. I have some dresses that might fit you." We slink away as Dad settles back into the folds of the La-Z-Boy.

"Hey you girls. Get out here," he yells right as we turn on the light to Mom's closet. Our chests sink.

"Hurry, hurry!"

For the love of Job, he's only going to show us the latest Heisman Trophy winner, some guy he met on a plane somewhere. We turn off the light and skulk out to the den anyway. Somebody's got to humor him.

"Didn't you do this, Bernadette? Huh?" he asks, pointing to the TV.

I lean against the edge of the sofa and look at the screen. I see a tall, thin, heavily tanned gentleman speaking into a microphone. He looks familiar, but I can't place him.

"He's one of those egg doctors," Dad says. "Like you had."

And then it hits me. He's not one of the eggs doctors, he's THE egg doctor, the very man who loved to thrash that wand around my womb. I remember this guy all too well. Impatient, but brilliant. Maybe he's finally getting the recognition he deserves. Maybe he's cured the fertility problem after all.

"Hey, Dr. Asch," I exclaim. "Yeah, the fertility specialist at UCLA. He's the very guy who performed my surgery. Has he won the Nobel Prize?"

Dr. Asch leaves the screen and the camera focuses back on the anchorwoman. "As of yet," she says, "there is no legal precedent for fertility clinics creating embryos from unauthorized donor eggs." They break for an ad.

"What?" I ask. "Legal precedent? Did you catch any of that before we came in, Dad?"

"Well, it looks like a woman in California is charging these doctors with taking her eggs and putting them in another woman's body." He mutes the sound.

"But when you donate eggs, you *are* donating them to another woman's body. That's the point. That's why I gave mine to Madeline. It's called, rather appropriately, GIFT." I flop down on the sofa and sink into the velvet cushions. Mugs tries to scratch at my leg, a feeble plea to join me.

"This woman's saying she donated to a friend, too, but the doctors took out more eggs than he said he would, and then he gave the extras to some other woman."

I take a pillow, put it over my stomach and wrap my arms around it. "How does she know?" I hear Yeats singing in my chest. *Imagining in excited reverie / That the future years had come.*

Dad starts pacing. "Some nurses in the clinic blew the whistle. I didn't catch the whole story…but, somehow, she found out that a child was born. She discovered a two-year-old son she never knew about, living in Tucson."

I turn to Mom to check her face as I feel the color drain from my own. "You mean these guys created children without telling the egg donors, the biological mothers?" *Dancing to a frenzied drum / Out of the murderous innocence of the sea.*

He shuts his eyes and clicks off the power. "Looks that way," he mumbles. "Somebody, some physician, called it biomedical rape."

I put my hands on top of my head. Jesus Christ, what is going on here? I feel dizzy, the images of hollow needles vacuuming children, water storming from the ceiling again.

No, no, I have to think. Stay here, focus, remember.

Okay, Madeline got pregnant, but miscarried. So that was the end of it. Right? No more to the story, party over.

Wait, some eggs were frozen, I remember, I'm sure. So why now, years later, randomly hearing the six o'clock news, I find out there's more to the story? *Once more the storm is howling.*

Mom interrupts my panic. "Bernadette, honey, what does this mean?"

I look up at her without an answer. "I don't know."

"Well," she says, hesitating, "did you give all your eggs to Madeline?"

"I..., I was under anesthetic. Who knows how many eggs they took out of me, how many went into Madeline, how many were frozen." I move to the edge of the sofa and grip the frame underneath. "I could have a child. I could have, I could have, I don't know, I could have four children. Or ten. I don't know, I don't know!"

"We'll find out, honey," she says in a soft voice.

"There's no way to find out. I can't prove anything!" I slam my fist on the armrest.

"Bernadette, calm down," Dad yells. "Doctors keep records, nurses keep records. We'll just get your charts, okay—it's no problem."

"Records? I don't remember any records."

"Well, do you remember signing anything?"

"But wait," I whisper, "if I had a child then, she could be Suzanna's age by now. She wouldn't be a baby. She might be three, or four, but, then again, if they used frozen eggs, they could have waited till whenever to put them into some woman's body, and then, maybe, I've got to think this through. Maybe I'd have a child who would just be born!" But a swirl of fear, not pleasure, sweeps me over. It's like I'm standing on the white line of a road and cars are coming from each side and the force of their passing spins me round and round, I can't stop it, the whirling, I don't know how to stand still.

"What if a child of mine is hurt? Or has cruel parents? Or, god forbid, a mother like WendyJo." To be choked with hate / May well be of all evil chances chief. "And I did this to her. I wasn't thinking."

I bury my head in the corner of the couch, now angry at my irresponsibility, my carelessness. After walking out on Mikhail, my crime was absorbed by penance, but so consuming was my contrition that I created even more crime.

And the sick irony is my immersion in a religion that eschews the body, when it is my very body that has created such damage. The body does matter. For fools like me, Gnosticism is dangerous.

Mom sits beside me on the couch. "You did an act of kindness for a friend, Bernadette. Only good can come from that."

Boy, can she reinterpret.

"Mom, you don't know. I never told you how bad it was. Ending a marriage, moving to a new city, all of a sudden living alone, I embodied the traumatic. I could have signed anything without even reading it—I don't remember. And now I might have created a child who is in a harmful situation and I'm not there to do anything. I am *no*where for her. Nowhere."

"Honey, look at it this way. What wonderful children to populate the world with, children of yours. I'm sure their parents are good to them." Is this deja vu? Aren't these the exact words I used to assuage my sister? Hadn't I been lying?

We both turn when we hear Dad on the phone, talking to Mary's attorney. "Thanks Jack," he says and hangs up. Then he dials another number. "Calling Chip. He'll find some L.A. news dispatches and we can get the attorneys who are…Chip? Dad. Listen."

I straighten my back and wipe away embarrassing tears. Equanimity, I've got to practice equanimity. "This is silly," I whisper. "I'm sure I don't have kids."

"You never know, honey. It's all meant to be. But if you did know, would you want to interfere in their lives?"

I clear my throat, gather myself back. On this tangent of the plan, I was always straight. "Never," I say firmly. "Madeline and I settled that at the time. I agreed I would never interfere in any way. She wanted the child to know me as a friend, but never know my biological role." Just talking about the piece of it I prepared for, the part I once had control over, lessened the pressure.

"They were moving out of state, but I would see her, or him, whenever they visited Madeline's mother. My secret didn't matter, our fate was sealed by consideration and choice. I gave those eggs as a gift, but I knew and trusted the parents. I harbored no doubt the child would be safe and loved. Don't you see the difference?"

Mom and I turn around as Dad bangs down the phone. "Chip's checking on it. He'll call as soon as he gets something."

He opens the freezer and digs through bags of food, mumbling and cursing as he tosses things around. "We need more boxes of frozen tofu burgers, Mom. Jesus H. Christ, there's only about fifty in here. Might snow, you know. In Texas."

He slams the freezer shut and holds up a box of Dove Bars. "Hide 'em in the back."

Mom takes one bite and returns it to the wrapper. "There's got to be a better way to look at this," she muses. "I'll have to think about it. But maybe, well, maybe the universe knew you should have children and the only way to get them into this world was to trick you."

I drop my head to my resunken chest. Jesus, she just doesn't get it. If she's heard anything I've said, comprehension wasn't included.

"Finish your ice cream, Rachel," Dad mumbles, licking the stick.

The Dove Bar dangles with my head. This feels like a newly opened wound, even though there's never been a wound here before. It's old, and further back than I can remember. And it's not just because I may have children out there that could be in a rough scene. It's more than that. It's an ache that burns slowly because I cannot fully define it.

The phone rings.

"Okay," Dad says, handing me a piece of paper after he hangs up. "Here's a number for patients of this clown doctor. I don't know who will answer, though. You want me to phone or you?"

Mom hands me a paper towel to wipe off the ice cream that's run down my hand, and I feel better. *Considering that, all hatred driven hence, the soul recovers radical innocence.* "Thanks Dad. I'll call." And as I dial the number, I feel hope. This is rational, there *are* answers, I get a recording:

You have called the Task Force Repository of Files for patients of Doctors Asch and Balmaceda. The files are being stored in a secure location which is not open to the public. The purpose of this message is to provide information as to how such files may be copied by physicians so they may use them to provide medical treatment to the former patients of the above named physicians. If you are a patient of one of the above named physicians, have your current physician make arrangements with this Task Force by calling this number and leaving an appropriate message.

The government will not allow physicians or their representatives to copy such files for treatment of patients for any reason other than treatment of former patients of the previously mentioned doctors.

If you are a physician of one of the former patients of one of the above named doctors, leave your name, your phone number, your patient's name, the specific emergency medical reason, and which doctor above was the primary physician.

A Federal Agent will return your call to schedule your appointment for you or your representative to come to the Repository for the purposes of copying the file. You must bring a copier as copiers are unavailable at this time. If you need the files for an emergency, please provide the specific emergency reason the patients file must be copied immediately.

After dinner, I put on that old blue bathrobe and watch a movie with Dad. No one talks. There's no point in discussing the situation further because it's a closed case. The FBI locked my medical files and unless I bribe some physician to fictitiously say I have a specific reproductive medical emergency and then drive his eight hundred pound photocopying machine to some repository in God only knows what part of the country, I can't even look at, much less retrieve, my own fertility charts. My records do not belong to me, they belong to the government. So I will never know how many eggs they vacuumed out of my body, and I will never know into whose body they were placed. In short, I will never know if I have a child, or if I have ten children. And not one of those children will ever know about me.

I pull two sofa pillows onto my stomach. I've fallen right smack into the patriarchy-control trap. Me, the independent, the errant female. I've shifted no internal paradigms, reinvented no 'indeed.' Careless yet again, I've learned nothing.

Thank God for this video: M-16s, war paint and invasions. I can sink right down into the cushions of the Victorian sofa and feel perfectly comfortable. And as some sort of nod to my obvious failure, some sort of sympathetic panacea, Dad's even letting me hold the remote. Curled up into the armrest, I clutch it to my huddled chest like a baby.

THIRTY-FIVE

Take me [...understanding] from grief,
and take me to yourselves from places that are ugly and in ruin,
and rob from those which are good even though in ugliness.

The attorney phones the day before court. "Mary, we've got a request from the prosecution. Your ex wants the decision made only between you and him—if you don't bring Curtis into the courtroom, he won't bring WendyJo."

"It gets better," Johnson continues. "Brad's requesting a gag rule on the psych report. This means no one outside the court can read it. The psych must portray him in an unfavorable light or he wouldn't ask for it. So I'd like to make the motion to the judge that we work this out amongst ourselves, in a room off to the side of the courtroom. What do you think?"

I'm sitting at the kitchen table, watching Mary take this phone call. Her face shifts from glee to fear. "It makes me nervous," she says, turning from my scrutinizing gaze.

"Well, imagine this. Without Curtis there, Brad may be less defensive. Furthermore, he knows how the judge will rule once he reads these forensic reports. It certainly won't be in Brad's favor. Look, he's counting on you to be more lenient with him than the judge. I suggest we give it a shot."

Mom baked spinach lasagna for dinner and Dad's making faces. "No meat?"

"Quiet, Bill," she scolds, like her plan is a secret.

He gives me a look. He knows it's my fault. "Well then, where's the salt, for Christ's sake?" She hands him the salt. He pours it on.

"How 'bout cheese. Got any cheese for this?" She hands him a glass jar of fresh parmesan. He starts to shake it, but only a few pathetic chips drift onto his plate. He bangs the jar on the table and tries again. "I'm having extra mousse for dessert," he mutters, hitting the jar repeatedly, annoying us all.

"Dad, it's the Texas humidity."

"I know what the hell it is," he says, unscrewing the lid. "It's a bunch of crap." And he dumps the entire jar onto his lasagna.

Mary shifts Kristen, who's falling asleep in the baby sack she has hanging around her shoulders. "Would you like me to grind out some onion juice to help it go down, Dad?"

"Ohhh, now, Kristen, do you hear how your mother is talking to your grandpa? Eh Kristen? Kristen likes chocolate, she and Grandpa gonna have real big stockings full of it this Christmas." He takes another bite and shivers. "You damn well better appreciate this Bernadette."

I dig into the spinach and pasta with a revelry akin to as much joy as I can manage. This is my definition of celestial dining. And it's clear that Mom has done it for me, a temporary balm for the wound born of remorse.

"You know," I say, quite brightly in fact, "This will all be over in about fifteen hours. And it looks like you've won, Mary. Viva la law, let's celebrate."

"We'll go to Blockbuster and get some movies, right girls?"

No one moves.

"Uh, Dad?" Mary hesitates. "I promised Dette I'd help her find some of her old stuff in the attic tonight. Would you mind?" Kristen starts to coo, a good omen.

"Naw," he says, moving chunks of spinach to the side of his plate. "I need to haul some things out of there myself."

I move in for the save. "Hey, after the attic raid, I'll make dessert," I chirp, "those root beer floats you concocted when we were kids. How about that?" Why do I always chirp in Texas? I never chirp in my study at home. I never chirp in the stacks at the library. Did the thunder ever chirp? *I am she who chirps, yet I am the silence of the chirper.*

"Great idea! Now who'll come with me to get the root beer. We're not drinking that health food crap your mother buys."

He stands up. Mary and I look at each other in desperation. "Rachel, get in the car before I beat you like a stepchild." He slaps his leg and lets out a whoop. "With a stick. With thorns!"

I nudge Mary's foot under the table and we start to clear the dishes, keeping our eyes down until we hear the garage door close. "Is he wound up or what?" I ask. "He needs a hamster wheel."

"He's excited about court tomorrow, having all this over with," she says quietly, lifting Kristen out of her carrier.

"I don't know. Maybe Chip wasn't switched at the hospital after all."

Mary slips Kristen into her crib while I slip the dinnerware into the dishwasher. Then I get the piano stool and place it under the attic door in the ceiling, unfolding the creaky wooden stairs while Mary yanks the string for light.

"I love the smell of cedar," she says as we climb into this hot unknown, like we're pilgrims in Egypt, sisters exploring pyramids, searching together for lost gnostic writings.

"Yeah, they should keep this open, let it fill the house."

"Look," I whisper as I step into the hold, "all kinds of treasure hide up here. Millicent's trunk, what a—and my old toe shoes." I feel the ragged, dirty cloth, worn down from hours of classes after school. I twirl the long pink ribbons between my fingers and remember the sensation of feeling pretty during those rotten teenage years. The bloody toes were worth the pretension of long legs. Awkwardness vanished en pointe when the studio mirror reflected regal splendor. I stuff the toes of the shoes in my pocket and turn back to a picture of Joe Namath draped over a rusty tool box.

"Wait a minute. Who the hell would save Chip's sports collage crap?"

But Mary ignores me, rummaging further back where there's less light. I watch her. She moves easily and I think she knows this room well. She picks up a blue-flowered carton and walks back towards me.

"Here's the box, Dette. God, I remember packing up these journals when you went away to college. For*ever* ago." She's going through the box, unwrapping book after book covered in pink tissue paper. I've never wrapped anything in pink tissue paper in my life.

"Here's the story," she says. "The one I was talking about."

I'm on my knees prying open another box.

"Dette, pay attention."

"No."

She plops on the edge of a worn leather suitcase. "Now sit down, over there, on that tool box. Stop scrounging around and listen."

I continue to ignore her as she ignores me. She clears her throat.

"*I ride my bike through the orange grove to school every morning,*" she begins. "*The trees and their shadows are thick, and planted in a labyrinth I have learned well. I fly beneath the weighted branches, imagining that one more drop of mist will bring the fruit crashing down upon me. The possibility of this makes my waif-like body pedal harder. Perfectly unbrushed hair sails behind me, and my skin sings with this churning of the clandestine and the brave.*

The neighbor boy told me that if Mr. Martin caught me, I'd be shot for trespassing. Dead at seventeen. Right there on my bike. Tangled up in it. I hoped the sprinkler system would be on when they found me. I wanted to be glistening. Glistening in a grove of oranges."

She puts down the diary. "Now that's one sick teenager."

"Don't read anymore, please. Not after lasagna. Let's read Millicent's diaries instead."

"I don't remember you ever riding your bike in the orange grove. How'd you get it over the fence?"

"Oh, I made all that up."

Dad's head pops into the attic like a proud balloon. "What are you two clowns doing up here? I'm gonna get you guys. Time for floats, c'mon down!"

Mary hands me the book. "Finish it," she says.

Slumped over our floats, Mary Catherine decides to continue her dig. "Sis, is the neighbor boy in your journal our track-star Jackson?"

A lump of ice cream falls out of my mouth, back into the glass. "Yeah, I think so."

"Chip's friend," Dad interjects. "Decathelete. Damn good runner."

"But Bernadette could outrun him, dear," Mom says. "Chip couldn't."

I keep my eyes on the float. How did she know that? Had she read my diaries, too, or had she actually been paying attention all those years and the soaps were just a screen?

"Yeah, Jackson," Mary sighs. "The cute one, who always *let* you outrun him.

Remember that track picture in the school paper, titled the Oreo Team? He was standing in the middle of Jim Porter and Tim Fox, the two black running stars, and with his pale skin and blond curls, it looked like an oreo. The black guys the cookie, him the cream. And he was. Yes ma'am, he was." She twirls her hair with her spoonless hand. "And he always liked you, big seeester."

"Don't slander the Hispanic. He didn't really. He was just nice to me."

"Nice to you? How about the time he single-handedly saved your life?"

"What?" Mom asks.

"Oh nothing," Mary Catherine pshaws. "She was just mindlessly walking to class one afternoon, absorbed in her own little interior world *as usual*, when she found herself smack in the middle of a brewing race riot."

"You never told us about this," Dad says.

"It wasn't that big a deal."

"Wasn't that big a deal?" Mary exclaims. "Chip was *there*. He saw the whole thing. He said you were a dead man."

"A what?" I eyebrow up to her.

"Bernadette, you don't take care of yourself," Mom reminds me, like it's high school still, the newspaper clippings slipped beneath my morning grapefruit spoon.

"Okay, it's true. I didn't pay attention to what was going on, it's all vapid gossip anyway. So I didn't know there was this meeting of the rich snot white kids and the bussed-in black kids."

"A *meeting*? Try a gang war." Mary turns to Dad and assumes her animated actress pose, arms whipping around like she's conducting Wagner. "White kids lined up on one side of the hall, black kids lined up on the other, everybody ready to fight. Tensions been seething between the rich and the tough for months and it's come to a head at this one moment. And out of *no*where steps Bernadette. She steps right in between the line of fire, right as the kids are about to go to blows. She looks up directly into the eyes of lethal Lew Burrus with a bat in his hand. Remember him, Dad? The fullback for the football team? Charged with assault and battery after the Homecoming game?"

Dad doesn't even look up. "Black guy. I remember."

She turns to me. "God girl, you were stupid."

She turns back to Dad. "So now Dette has a *clue* she's in trouble. She freezes. Kids start yelling obscenities at her, the lines begin to close in, ready to squash her like a bug. Then out from behind steaming Lew Burrus comes this eight mile long arm, grabs her by the scruff of her blouse and hauls her over the crowd, out to the side yard and into safety." She leans back in her chair.

"Who? Who?" Dad begs.

"Jackson," she smiles, so proud, like she's proven something.

Mugs paws at the door to go out, but nobody moves.

"Well, what was Jackson doing there behind Burrus?" Dad finally asks, oblivious to Mary's coup.

"They were his buddies on the track team," she says. "He was on *their* side!"

"But how come Chip never told me about it?"

"Tell you? Are you kidding? They didn't want you guys to know they were in on a race riot."

Mom sighs. "He really was in love with you honey."

"He was my neighbor, Mom. He had to do that."

Mary slaps both her palms on the table. "Well, your brother was there and he did nothing."

"Mothers know," Dad mumbles, suddenly an expert on the Madonna archetype.

"Jackson was so respectful of you," Mom says, her eyes twinkling. "He treated you like you were, well, like you were some kind of angel."

She puts down her spoon and pushes away her half-eaten float. "He'd wait for you at the end of the driveway, just to walk you to the school bus. Then he'd ask to carry your books, but you never let him."

I widen my eyes at my float and clench my teeth. Was she like a covert Hoover? Logging my every move? Watching from behind the blinds? Mrs. Cravitz, maybe.

"You were friends with his mother, weren't you?" I ask politely. "You guys must have talked about us a lot, Mom. I remember you having coffee on the lanai, and it always got real quiet when I walked by in my bathing suit."

"That's cause you were such a shrimp," Mary says, "and you always walked like you were pinching a quarter in your ass. Who wouldn't get quiet and stare?"

"You're *supposed* to walk like that in ballet," I retort, feeling ganged upon, but certainly at home. Pinhead always made fun of my tight walk. "Swing your hips!" she'd say. "Drop the quarter or you'll never get a date." I bite my lower lip and wonder, do I walk like that now?

"Jackson's mother thought you two should marry," Mom says. "Both Catholic, both Irish."

"Two excellent reasons for marriage," Mary pipes in, rolling her eyes.

Mom leans over and whispers, "His mother said he told her you were part nun."

I freeze.

"Part nun?" Mary gasps. "Wait. Was there something I didn't know about?"

"Hold it." I defend. "There was never *any*thing between Jackson and me. Never. This conversation is getting way out of hand."

"No, no," Mom back-pedals. "She didn't mean it like that."

"Well then," Mary snorts, "which part is part nun? Which part? C'mon!"

I'm clenching my spoon and teeth. I don't want to hear this answer. But I have to, because if that guy was making up stories about me, I'm going to hunt him down and kill him.

"Which part? Which part?" Mary whines.

Mom tilts her head to one side, looks at Dad, then looks back at me and sighs. Why is she savoring this? She's sick, that's why. They're all sick.

"Your eyes," she whispers.

Silence. No one breathes. And I feel nothing but relief. That wasn't so bad. In fact, I'm sort of flattered.

Mary reaches for more rootbeer. "What a crock of shit," she says. Dad clears his throat and reaches for more ice cream.

"Do you remember that Saint Christopher medal on the silver chain? The one I gave you to wear when you flew to Aunt Grace's summer house your junior year?"

I reach down into the collar of my black blouse and pull out a necklace. "I wear him still, maw. And I ain't died in an airplane yit."

She sits up in her chair and leans toward me for a closer look. "That's the one! That was from Jackson, honey."

"It was not," I indignantly exclaim. "It was from you."

"He came to the front door when you were at ballet class. He was so sweet, so nervous, as he stood there shuffling his huge feet. He asked me to give it to you before your trip, but begged me not to tell who it was from. He said if you knew, you wouldn't wear it."

"I don't believe this," Mary smirks. "You've been walking around all these years wearing a medal from a guy you wouldn't even let carry your books? What a gas."

"Look on the back. Look for his initials."

I turn the medal over and find the small engraving—JB. "I thought it was just the manufacturer," I say, bewildered. "Damn. I never would have guessed." I feel a flush on my face and quickly put the medal back under my shirt.

"I wanted so much for you to end up with him," Mom murmurs.

I quickly regain my smartass composure. "I was seventeen for Christ's sake—a kid."

"Seventeen is a good age to be in love," she replies with a goo smile.

"And you *were* in love, Bernie girl," Pinhead smirks. "You'd just never ever admit it."

Dad stirs his ice cream and rootbeer together into one big mush. "Where'd their family move to, Rachel?"

"I don't remember, but I could find out. You could call him, Bernadette."

Is this some kind of conspiracy? To what end? To make me feel better about mindlessly creating, and subsequently losing, babies? To distract me from my violation of unborn trust, my golden rule infraction?

I push back my chair and stand up, feeling a tad warm. "Two hundred years have disappeared since then, Mom. What occurs during the darkness of high school doesn't count. Those humiliating moments of adolescence are negligible, useless, and therefore erasable." I slurp up the last of my taupe-colored foam. "And anyway, you can never go back. Thank God."

Her eyes glitter up again. "Sometimes it's better," she smiles, reaching over to pat my hand. "But we'll see. If things are meant to be, they'll happen no matter what we do."

"Uh, or *don't* do," I say, thinking while my clichés are based on fact, hers are not.

Mary licks her spoon and points it at me. "She's going to get you, girl."

"No she isn't. I'm hiding out in the attic until these ideas clear." I put my glass in the sink and melodramatically grab onto the attic steps. "You'll never find me," I gasp down at them as I march up the stairs, ascending fast into my Egyptian pyramid of grande jetes and Joe Namath babies, back into the safety of mysterious orange groves and very distant boys.

THIRTY-SIX

Out of shame, take me to yourselves shamelessly

L onda's hospital letters greet me first, spilling onto the attic floor right next to my ballet box. Don't know why I didn't notice them earlier. I was probably too taken by the pointe shoe find.

I hunch down like a woman at the Ganges and begin sifting through small weathered envelops. It's interesting that the Tucson postmark is always 1948. How irritating that my demented family pushes the Jackson scene. As if I'm going to leap out of Sean to an ancient high school flame? And then that's going to therapy me through this child crime. I can see the run-on headline of the National Enquirer: Loon Begets Rash of Children, Can't Care for Them, Has Reproductive Records Confiscated by FBI, So Finds Passionate New Romance to Forget Entire Mess.

I carefully pull brittle stationery from a yellowed envelope. In a weak and tiny scrawl she writes:

> *Dear mother and father,*
>   *Last week we saw a church-choir singing Christmas carols in the movies. And we sang with them, Miss Marlaire sad we did it good.*
>   *I am not sick.*
>   *I hope you can get mikl for the kitten.*
>   *Love,*
>   *Londa*

I open another one, all in capital letters this time, as if to emphasize her request:

DEAR DADDY
COME TO SEE ME
PRAY FOR ME
    LONDA

Then I find a Tucson postcard, unsigned.

Dear Mommy,
It is getting so very hard to breathe.
Thank you for the picture book.

I toss the note onto the floor, a well-deserved arrow of shame lancing my self-pity. Her lungs were unable to keep her in breath that I so take for granted. She couldn't breathe, but thanked her mother for a picture book.

And then it hits me: this little girl carried the gene for cystic fibrosis. This little girl is my aunt. How could I have missed the connection. How could I have repressed this critical genetic heritage?

I look around the attic, noting the stacks of souvenirs from my grandparents' antiquated lives, from my own obsolescent life, useless stacks of dust, all filled with mistakes born of carelessness and self-serving intent. There is nothing in this mishmash that helps anyone, nothing that is productive, nothing I want to see or touch or remember. Repression isn't always some necessary defense mechanism that hides painful memories so we can live a normal life. More distastefully, some repression boxes up that which doesn't suit our latest scheme, and hides its inconvenience beside an old ballet box. It isn't unconscious. We choose it. Our quest for personal redemption overrides integrity.

The ice cream turns in my stomach, backing up into my chest as I clutch my abdomen.

I hear Mom and Mary laughing down in the kitchen, putting things away. This is my secret now. I can't let on to Mom, she already feels too badly about her sister. So I sit in the attic and just stare, turning my anguish into stone, my inability to set things right into a sharp silence. It's pointless to bleed over this, there's nothing I can do but go home and work on the dissertation, turning my back on my own sweet subterfuge.

Soon Mom mounts the stairs to the attic with Mary Catherine in tow. Hearing their steps, I quickly grab an old journal and pretend to be engrossed.

They're in the attic now, walking towards me, a benignant smile upon each face. I sneeze halfway. "Nice snee," Pinhead remarks. "But only worth half a blessing. So, God *ble* you. And that diary you're pretending to read is upside-down."

I close the book, barely managing an affected smile. They make their way over to me without a word, like it's church in here. Mom sits on an old chair, putting her hand on top of mine. "Your great Aunt Grace and your grandmother Millicent made you something," she says with almost tears in her eyes. "Mary, will you get the box?"

Mary rummages through Millicent's trunk while Mom continues talking. "I see you've been going through Londa's letters."

I shoot her a desperate look. "Honey," she says, "the gene can skip generations. There's little chance you have it."

"What? You knew?"

"It was the first thing that came to me when we heard the newscast."

"And you didn't tell?"

"What would have been the point? I'm sure you don't carry the gene."

I lean over close to the side of her face so Mary won't hear. "But I *might*. Which means the babies *might*. The implications are huge." I throw my hands up, in the random way hopelessness suggests. "And there's *no* one to tell these children, or their unsuspecting parents, that this is their genetic history."

Mom squeezes my hand. "Listen, you don't know if it's true," she says loudly. I widen my eyes at her and nod my head towards Mary. "I told her about the eggs, Bernadette."

"Mom," I whisper madly. "You promised. She's got way too much going on right now—we can deal with it after—"

"Oh you idiot," Mary laughs with her large ears. "You think I'm going to go into a coma if I know?"

I just look at her and bite my tongue in earnest. Considering her recent vegetable history, that's hardly a kosher comment. "No big deal," I lie, clearing my throat to keep my voice stable. "I'm overreacting." And I'm hoping the cumulative tears will evaporate quickly if I can simply not blink. I refuse to get stupid.

"You're not overreacting," she says, holding an old hat box in front of her, walking towards me in the dim attic light, her auburn curls and long yellow chiffon dress silhouetted against the wood, cobwebs and dust rays trailing slow motion. And for just this moment, she looks like Isis—tall, regal, strikingly beautiful. And more importantly, bearing temple gifts.

I open the lid and unwrap a carefully folded quilt—similar to the one on my old twin bed—that crazed weaving of velvet and silk, each section edged with an intricate embroidery.

"When Grace died," Mom begins softly, "Millicent knew what it meant to you—how you never got to Jerusalem, how her death ended your dream. So when the hospital in Jerusalem mailed her Grace's things, she was surprised to find a partially-finished quilt with the needle still threaded in the cloth, as if Grace had been working on it right up until she died. There was a piece of paper pinned to the quilt. It said, 'For Bernadette's first child.' Your grandmother decided to finish it, as a…as a gift for you. I think you should have it now. It's sewn with both their hands."

I look down at the quilt resting in a pile on my lap, my hands beneath the folds where no one can see, clutching the velvet like if I let go, it might fly away, out the attic window, down to the orange trees in the front yard and off into the sky, back to Jerusalem.

"Here," Mom says, gently trying to take the quilt away from me. "Turn it over, honey." She pulls at the quilt again. "There's an inscription." She tugs again. "Bernadette?"

But I won't let go. I'm not letting it go. I bring it closer to my stomach and I can't look up at her. Grace knew I wasn't having children, she knew. We talked about it at length. So she stabs me with this knife? She writes to my first born child? Why? Because I didn't travel to Jerusalem, like we planned? This is it. This is why. Because I abandoned her, too. Just like her sister Millicent, I got married instead and I left her alone.

My shoulders sink with loss, like I've given birth and shadowy hands have pulled the baby away from me, the same hands that took my Grace and my innocence.

It was a dream I had once, but almost too real to be a dream. She was a slave in a dark place, on a ghostly plantation. She bore a knowledgeable beauty, not like me (immature and anorexic), she had nobility in the curve of her jaw, and she lay on the hay-swept floor of a dank and drafty barn, cradling her newly born baby in her arms, having just given birth, alone, her face joy and light as the baby slept, when all of a sudden, large dark hands, a man's rough and callused hands, appeared in the air and demanded the baby, she begged no, so much grief beginning to envelop her, but the man was wrenching the baby from her arms, and her strong face twisted in pain, not only for the loss of the baby she would never see again, but also because she loved the man, the father, the plantation owner who was now taking the baby, and this grieved her beyond understanding, that this heartless man was the one she loved, and I woke from the dream in despair because I was the woman with everything taken, and the man taking my baby away was Mikhail.

I feel an arm wrap around the back of my shoulders and my sister nestles her head near the side of my face. She says nothing, just stays there. Then, with her free hand, she turns over a corner of the quilt in my lap. "Look," she whispers, and she runs her long slender fingers over words sewn in burgundy thread. "For Bernadette," she reads, "with ageless love, Millicent and Grace. The sisters sewed this for you."

I bring a hand from beneath the folds and move my fingers over the writing. Soft satin threads, some smooth, some knotted. Their hands, those two sisters, pulled these threads through this cloth and formed my name. And now my sister and I run our own hands over the same place they wove, the four of us, holding this tapestry.

But my sister, she has not abandoned me. She is not dead, not from pills nor grief, not from drowning nor disease. With all that I have carelessly abandoned, she remains with me still.

"There's more," Mary Catherine whispers as she turns over another corner of the quilt. "Do you remember this material?" she asks, pointing to a small piece of white and red plaid flannel sewn into a corner, but noticeable because it's so unlike the dark velvets around it. My memory stirs and sifts, searching for the place I once knew this errant cloth, for it is so familiar.

"Jesus," I whisper, "those damn ugly flannel pajamas she sewed for us in Texas."

Mary giggles lightly in my ear. "Maybe Grandma had a sense of humor after all," she laughs. And then, almost like before, we all start giggling, lightly at first, but then with fullness as the release eases up our nostalgia. And I let go of the cloth, but it doesn't fly from my hands out the tower window towards my orange grove camelot. The only thing I feel taken from me is that wrenching sense of loss. It's gone, that quickly, with my sister's laugh.

THIRTY-SEVEN

I am the command of those who ask of me,
and the power of the powers in my knowledge
of the angels, who have been sent at my word,
and of spirits of every man who exists with me,
and of women who dwell within me.

It's two o'clock in the morning and I can't get back to sleep. I lie there in the glow of the moon and star nightlight and listen to Mary grind her teeth. She's been doing that since childhood. After all these years, her teeth must look like Mom's fingernails—white stubs sticking out of puffy pink flesh.

I roll over in my bed to look at Kristen. Her rosebud mouth faintly opens and her eyes dart back and forth beneath her lids. I studied R.E.M. sleep in infants in a psych course once, and I remember all the theories about whether neonates dream or not, and, if they do, what are they dreaming about? Milk? Heaven? Previous lives? Scholars studying babies always seemed somewhat oxymoronish to me. What could they possibly deduce from their notebook-tight research that even barely approaches the complexity of such sincere being?

Kristen's been up almost every hour, but it's not her fault. I know she can feel the tension in this room, in this house, as we wait, impatiently, for the final round of the legal battle over her big sister. Miniature ones feel the unseen more than us, they're closer to it. I push back the quilt and wander out into the hallway.

When I haul the leftover lasagna from the fridge, Mugs moans in his sleep, but doesn't wake up. I quietly shuffle towards the table with the cold casserole dish and a fork, but my nightgown catches on the corner of the utensil drawer, tears the pocket, and sends a loud stream of obscenities from my mouth, the Irish knee-jerk response to petty annoyance an inheritance from my father.

Unhooking myself, I eat. But on my third bite of mozzarella and spinach, it occurs to me that the level of enjoyment here is not high enough to justify the two hundred and fifty grams of fat. If you're going to enlarge your thighs, every saturated bite must be soothingly worthy. I put down the fork and stare at the wheezing dog asleep in a dark corner of the kitchen. Maybe fixing this nightgown pocket would help me. Mending could relax this anxiety and put me to sleep.

I start to rise, but then plop back down and cover my ears with my hands. These damn clocks are ticking everywhere. She hangs one in each room. Why this obsession with time? They all belonged to her father, so one would think she'd stockpile them in the garage, or throw them in a Salvation Army bin. I can't believe his damn FBI took all my fertility records. How can a supposed democracy justify such a theft? It's *my* body, they were *my* eggs, and I can only pick at *my* nails, ragged and messy, I couldn't care less. Stand up, sit back down, I hate mending, I don't mend, but she's my favorite nightgown, she must be mended, godammit, what is my problem here, rubbing my temples with the tips of my fingers.

Mom's sewing room, that's the problem. It's been forbidden by choice for years, a self-designated wasteland, only hollow women allowed. I hate it, and for good reason: it is the den of childhood neglect, a room off-limits to the young, a room where the mother sits to contrive the good-mother image because she, as saint/martyr, is sewing a pretty dress for the child, while that same child is fully alone, reprimanded to the swingset outside.

When we were kids, it seemed Mom lived in that room, if not sewing, then ironing. To this day, I don't sew. And if a clo wrinkles, it goes in the Salvation Army bag. I decided long ago that if I ever had a child, which, well, it looks like I'm not, at least not one I can hold, I decided that I'd never put her out on the swingset so I could sew her a dress, no matter how much satin and lace were on the bodice. And I'd never tell her to go play in her room while I ironed it.

If I had a child, instead of sewing or ironing, I'd gather her up in my lap and wrap big wings around her and read her politically correct fairy tales. We'd tickle each other under the kitchen table that we'd covered with sheets to make a tent. We'd play freeze tag in the middle of the white-carpeted living room and when the person who was It caught you, you'd have to freeze your body as rigid as you could until the Tagger's arms wrapped around you made you warm. And only the Tagee could decide when that thawing was complete. You'd have to hug her until she said, "Thawed!"

I jab at the pasta with my fork. Cut the crap, Bernadette. It's two thirty in the morning, you don't have any children and you're not seven. Go mend the nightgown.

I stash the lasagna in the fridge, but pull it back out for a minute to smooth the edges of the pasta, thereby omitting those ragged little lines. The cut has to look clean, like it was made with a serving knife, not a fork and my mouth.

Then it's time to tiptoe past our bedroom down the hall and quietly open the forbidden far door. God, I hate this room. Flipping the switch and expecting the harsh white light of childhood, I'm startled to see a flood of soft glow. Wait, this is no sewing room.

I step back out into the hall and rethink this dimension. Maybe too much time in the stacks, maybe too much trauma with Sean, maybe the combination of these and other discordant worlds has altered my perception. Could selective memory converge into my consciousness, too? A genetic karma for all those years of criticizing my mother's revisionist theories?

I lean in and search for some glimpse of familiarity. Still, there is none: no sewing machine, no material scraps, no fallen pins and needles, no ironing board, no iron. Instead, the walls are painted new-age lavender and the lampshades have fringe. Silk brocade cushions line the edges of a white flokati, philodendron hang from the ceiling, and white candles straight from *Kung Fu* stand among purple amethyst. Flowers and the distinct scent of sulfur hover over the room. It smells like I feel: burnt aroma therapy. One of the pastel candles mushes on touch, the wax still warm, so someone only recently blew it out. Variations on the Kuan Yin theme, one riding an intimidating dragon, another sitting on a lotus petal, rest on a shelf next to a porcelain statue of the Virgin Mary. An elaborate arrangement of yellow silk roses lay her feet and I remind myself that Mom was a Home Ec major. In accordance, only the demur goddesses of compassion reign here, no skull-waisted Kali. I push the eject button of a small stereo and pull out the cassette: *Harp and Flute for Relaxation*.

Something shifts behind me. Turning quickly, I see Mary at the doorway in her new turquoise robe, her mouth dangling. "What the hell is this?" she whispers.

"Hey, you're supposed to be asleep. Get in bed."

Ignoring me as usual, she walks into the room and sniffs the air. "Gardenias," she says.

"Close the door. Let's not wake up Kristen, too."

"Isn't this supposed to be Mom's sewing room?" she asks. "What's going on?"

"I just wanted to mend my gown, so I come in to get thread and suddenly I'm in a Sri Lankan temple. You live here. Didn't Mom ever show you this?"

"Hell no. I don't come in this room because I *refuse* to sew, don't know why, it's easy enough to do." She sits on one of the satin pillows. "I've never understood that."

"Later," I say. "We should get back to bed. I feel like we're invading a very private space."

A large and worn navy blue book resembling a Bible rests on a table. I hold it out to Mary. "Do you know what this is?"

"No. Never heard of it." She pokes at a candle. "Hey wait, this is still warm."

"We better leave and try to sleep. We'll ask her in the morning."

"Yeah, okay," she says. But we can't stop looking around, picking things up, turning them over. "I like it in here," Mary says. "Especially all the statues of Jesus' mom. She had such a nice name."

She rummages through a small gold-edged book, but I take if from her and return it to the shelf, then lock my arm through hers and lead us both towards the door. "It does feel good," I whisper, "but it isn't right. C'mon."

The next morning, fatigue burdens me to the pillow. I can't move. I turn to Mary as she puts on her robe. "Let's not say anything to Mom about that room for awhile. Not until court is over."

She doesn't answer and I sense a returning distance.

"Mary Catherine?"

She cinches the belt tight around her waist and drifts off. "Yeah sure," she says.

I quickly sit up in bed. "You need a distraction until then," I say in a panic. "Let's take Kirsten to her first mass-appeal book store. We can teach her how to make fun of all the first paragraphs of new fiction."

"I'd be afraid I'd be late," she grimaces. "I'm really scared." She pulls the belt tighter around her waist.

"How can I help, tell me."

"Um, I don't know. Nothing, really."

"A project, give me a project."

She muses absent-mindedly. "Well, want to iron my blouse?"

"Iron your blouse, are you kidding? I don't iron. Are you admitting you do?"

"No, actually, I hate ironing as much as I hate sewing. But I have to look absolutely perfect in that courtroom, Dette. You don't understand.

Every detail has to be just right. So few things can be controlled and appearance is one of them. As stupid and superficial as it seems, a starched shirt earns respect." She drifts off again. "Maybe."

"Okay, I'll iron it." She hands me the blouse. "But hey, where do you think she keeps the ironing board these days?"

Kristen gurgles to be held. "*I'm* not asking her," Mary says. "Go check behind the altar."

"Look, if one of us doesn't get some guts, you're going to court crumpled."

"All right, I'll ask. But don't look her in the eye or she'll know we've been in the shrine."

"Good morning, girls," Mom says when we slither out into the kitchen. I can't help but glance at her. She's sipping mint tea with one eyebrow up. "So tell me," she says. "What do you think of my room?"

Caught. Damn. "Uh, sorry Mom," I cringe.

"It's interesting," Mary smiles, the actress come alive. "Can we see it with you?"

I have to turn away, the cold sneer of annoyance forming in my upper lip, the involuntary twitch born of the conviction that maybe I'm the adopted one.

Mom leads us down the hall, but I hesitate in the doorway. With all the candles lit, it seems intimidating, or too private somehow. "Don't be afraid," she says, "Just come in." She pushes play on the stereo. "This is where I go to meditate."

"You meditate?" I ask, hoping my cynicism is covert.

She picks up the worn blue book I saw last night. "This makes sense," she says, looking straight at me.

Taking the book from her hands, I turn it over and look for the publisher. "I've never come across this in school. What religion is it? Looks like a bible."

"No, it's not a bible. It does bring up ideas from the Old and New Testaments, but only to show how so much has been misinterpreted."

"Sounds like just what I need for my dissertation research."

"Well, it helps me, but I don't know if it would help with your research, Bernadette, at least, not in the way you might want it to." She strikes a match and lights a pink candle. "But one idea helps me the most."

I wait for the punch line.

"Mom? And?"

"Well, we only feel two emotions. That's it. Just two. Emotions."

"Waiting?" Are they hard to pronounce? Has she forgotten them?

"Oh, right," she says. "Love and fear. Everything falls under those two categories, either love or fear."

Okay, a mere one syllable each. I lay the heavy book down next to a crystal and wonder what it says if you feel both at the same time.

"Think about it," she says. "Anger, jealousy, depression, they're all just fear. But if you feel love, no negative emotion exists."

I look over at Mary, but she purports to be uninvolved, admiring a watercolor of some blurred seraphim. There'll be no help from her. She thinks she's so tricky.

But wait, what about Rilke? Didn't he say the first face of love is terror? Fear and love woven together, yes, I can imagine that, loving someone so much you feel fear. But maybe beauty was Rilke's subject, or angels, I don't remember. I don't read poetry anymore. Sean thought poetry was too easy, like Roethke. Hence, no more Thursday night poetry readings, and our summer visit to the Hirschhorn was a disaster.

Mom clears her throat, like she's feeling fear. "I'm going to be a Reverend," she blurts out, her eyes in the headlights.

Mary interrupts the subsequent silence. "Hey, our own personal Reverend Mother. Reverend Rachel!" She bursts out laughing as she hands Kristen to me. "But why have you kept it a secret?" she asks as she analyzes a small bronze Buddha.

"I'm afraid people will laugh."

"No, Mom, no," Mary back-pedals, quickly putting down the Buddha. "I didn't mean it like that, really." She's such a liar.

I play with the fringe on a lamp. "Lon would gag on his strained carrots."

Mary shoots me a dagger look. "Oops, sorry," I whisper. Like she has tact.

"Your grandfather is past all that," Mom reminds us, her voice retaining a soft equanimity.

And harps float in the mist, played upon by winged pigs. No Mom, he's past it because he's too old to have an opinion that matters. If he disagrees, nothing changes because he no longer has power. Like a kid, he hears it, he knows it doesn't sit right, but there's nothing he can do. Does karma make that play, a collective unconscious payback for the deeds done to children? Or is it but circuitous experience, a revisitation of one's own childhood powerlessness, but with wisdom this time to see it through. There's no adulthood to look forward to, no future opportunity to set things right. The elderly can face neither their perpetrator nor themselves at a later date; they only have the hope that death means they don't have to care.

Mary pokes rude little dents in a candle. "These are intense," she says. "Do you keep them lit most of the time, like at night, when we're asleep?"

She laughs. "No, I've been in here since early this morning, working on your court appointment."

"Working on it?" Mary and I dare not look at each other. Kristen squirms.

"I pray," she says quietly.

"Prayer comes from a Latin word that means to *beg*," I snottily interject. Okay, so my cynicism is no longer concealed.

Mary assumes her best Newark voice. "So whatsa wrong with a little begging?" she brown-noses, covering her ass for her far worse slam at Mom's new airy fairyness.

"Actually, I do many things," Mom replies. "Put on music, light candles, and start relaxation exercises. Then I, well, I meditate and ask for help for whatever needs help." She giggles a little. Still sounds like begging to me.

"Uh, who do you ask for help?"

"Whoever will listen. No, wait. First you have to cover yourself with light, put a white glow all around your body so you're protected, and then…" She pauses, closes her eyes and begins ticking things off with her fingers, like it's a subtraction problem. There's a cavern forming between her eyebrows, so I suspect she's new at this. "Okay, then you ask for only *good* to listen. You request divine intervention, the highest good, and harm to none. You ask for your Higher Self, your spirit guides, your guardian angels, your ancestors of the light, Jesus, Mary and all the saints."

"Well, I'd say that about covers it. Kristen? What do you think?" I lift her up close to my face. "Aren't those the people your grandpa calls out to?"

"Your father says I'm nicer when I come out of this room. And the Virgin Marys feel like home to him, you know, his Catholic childhood. To me, she's just the feminine power in all of us, but I don't say that to him of course."

So it goes, each religion an amalgamation of others, a blend of our culture, our past, our latest perspective. Mom's new-age organization has its own tenets, but many are similar enough to Catholicism as not to threaten my father.

Even Sean doesn't see the crossover of his Catholic foundation with the American bastardization of Theravadan Buddhism. He mocks organized religion without realizing his own spiritual regime is yet another dogma. His scorn of Freudian father-in-a-faith church needs a mirror, but I'm not the one to hold it up to his face. He's strengthened my mistrust of all human structure to such a point that I've learned better than to argue anyone out of it. Dusty worn theories fascinate, but the attempted practice of such, whether it be via Sean or my mother, well, it's best to just move with it.

Mary walks towards the door to leave. "Has Chip seen this?"

"I don't think Chip would appreciate it. But I forgot to tell you, he's coming over after court. He wants us to see his new girlfriend. Apparently she's the one, and he wants to make sure you both meet her before you leave."

Mary and I look at each other and laugh. "What kind of woman would ever put up with him?"

Mom blows out the candles. "No one has so far," she says. "But things change."

THIRTY-EIGHT

Hear me in gentleness, and learn of me in roughness.
I am she who cries out,
and I am cast forth upon the face of the earth.
I appear and [...] walk in [...] seal of my [...].

After Mary and Dad leave for the courthouse, Mom slips into her lavender room. Kristen sleeps in the crib and I stretch out on my bed to hear her breathe, to be near her for only a few more hours before she leaves. I'm half happy and half sad, like Suzanna once said to me about a dead robin in the yard: half happy because the robin's in heaven, but half sad because she can't hear him sing anymore. Kristen will move to a safer place for her mother and sister, but a gap will live in my world.

I stare at the white ceiling, relaxing slowly into the scent of gardenias coming from the hall. Then I remember that diary I shoved under the bed yesterday and I reach down to fish it out. Adolescent angst would be a fitting distraction right now, solipsism fighting for my attention then as now.

I turn on my side and curl up tight, scrunching the pillow part way under my neck, scanning the pages. And there she is, *Dead at Seventeen*, the morose title scrawled at the top. I reread Mary's excerpt about wanting to be *glistening*, the words of a mere girl caught dead on her bike, *glistening in a grove of oranges.*

But the knife I used this morning at breakfast was too sharp. While I was cutting my green and brown-skin oranges for the juicer, my mother began to recite yet another rape from yet another morning newspaper clipping and the knife slipped and almost cut my hand. I must be careful with these hands, hands so critical—for my pirouettes and piano, for covering my ears and holding onto the handles of my bike. Hands not important for holding other hands. Not yet. This is all still too dangerous. Suzanne Farrell never kissed until she was 18. And now she is coveted by Balanchine. I will be Suzanne on a bike.

Soon my ride will end. I can see the edge of the grove. I can hear the cars breaking into this stillness. I brace myself for the cement and sunlight as my bike and I burst onto the sidewalk. We weave through skateboarders with backpacks and schoolbusses filled with boys. Boys who dangle their hands from the windows of condensation and whoop at me. I hate this part. The exposed part. The five hours of each weekday that I must bathe, by law, in the sweatness of peer and teacher.

I keep my eyes on the ground, where they will stay for most of this unairconditioned day, even when I am called upon to answer. But it is Friday, test-day, and I am grateful. Tests mean silence, thinking. And because I don't linger in the doorways sucking up the lungs of some desperate boy, I get a window seat. But in this Texas June, an open window means little. My bathing suit beneath my clothes is soaked. My arm sticks to my test and my bangs stick to my head while the teacher sucks loudly on ice chips from her glass. I pretend that the weight of the humidity is my cave.

Racing home, it is still sweet and dark in the grove. I cross into our backyard, throw open the lanai screen door and run to the deep end. I brace myself, smile, and dive.

The grove, the water, the solitude, these things are my heaven. These things, and the twilight visits to the lake after dinner each night. My mother doesn't know where I go. I will never tell her. I will never tell anyone. That I hide, crouched in the reeds near the far edge of the grove, pretending I'm in Egypt by the Nile, but really watching the boy who is fifth in my class fish in a solitary boat in the very middle of the lake. It is the neighbor boy again, the one who writes essays so rapturous that I sit riveted to my desk as the teacher reads them aloud to the class. This boy understands everything. That's why he's alone. That's why he's as far away from the edges as a person in a boat can get.

I hear dusk coming, and I know I must get home. There is no light on my bike. And Kung Fu *will be starting soon. I want to learn what that grasshopper learns.*

But before going to bed, I do one last thing. I sneak out and climb high into the branches of the orange tree in our front yard, and with my flashlight I read books that are too difficult: Solzhenitsyn, Joyce, Kant. I am trying to understand men. If only the Brontes had written more. They make sense.

Tonight I hear footsteps moving across my parents' lawn. I close Solzhenitsyn, turn off my flashlight and cautiously lean forward to see. It is that neighbor boy. "Hey, ready to run?" *he asks my brother at the door.* "It's just starting to cool down."

"Sure, man. But let's walk first." *The door slams.*

This neighbor boy is also the star of the track team, the one the girls at the oven drop for in the halls. I know my brother can't keep up with him and this will make my brother mad. I hold my breath as they walk beneath my tree.

"So where's your sister?" *the star asks.*

"Who knows. Forget her, will ya? Just forget her, man." *My brother is always irritated.*

I want to wipe the sweat from my forehead, but I do not dare. I move forward even more, barely steady now, to catch their words.

"She'll look at me someday. You wait." *I bite my lip and hold my breath.*

"Don't count on it, man. She's weird, an ice queen, a stone. You ever looked in her eyes, man? They're dead."

I lean. My hand slips. My flashlight falls. My hair tangles in branches, and I feel it rip from my head as curiosity tumbles my body out of the tree, landing me only two feet behind the gasps of these boys.

I am unhurt. But crumpled on the thick grass, I hear the chant of the kindergarten girl next door when her sister called her stupid: sticks and stones will break my bones, but words will break my heart. *I want to make a mad race for the grove and bury myself. I want to be shot for trespassing. I want to melt into the grass, like the wicked witch of the west.*

I hear their footsteps come close. They are surrounding me. "You okay?" they ask in unison.

I cannot answer, I cannot move. If only I can look up and gauge my position in relation to the orange grove, I can get away. I know I can outrun them. They are not so fast.

Without lifting my head, I raise my eyes and cautiously look for the silhouette of the tree line, for any path that will get me to my labyrinth of dark safety, the chant of the girl pounding break my heart, break my heart, break my heart. *But I can't see it. My vision is blocked by hands, boy's hands, open and unmoving, upturned palms before my frightened eyes. In the glow of the moon, I see that one is fair-skinned and strong, one is tanned and large. They hover here, so still, so patient. I raise my own to take them.*

I close the diary and look down at Kristen's sleeping face. Maybe by the time she's seventeen, they will have legally abolished adolescence.

Leaning closer, I note that her skin changes when she sleeps. It's translucent somehow, or softer, as if she glows. I remember that glow when those boys held their hands out to me, without saying a word, just silent, like they realized how hard it was to be that strange neighborhood girl. I lived but half a life and they knew it. Their lives were full because they weren't afraid. And how they must have pitied my penitent fear, my complete self-absorption.

Kristen's breathing rises up and down with such ease. I know from the glow of her face that she's not in this room with me. Her body sleeps, but her soul travels. The lucid skin reveals that she's flying around some alternate realm. So maybe the Gnostic idea that our body is but a shell, an outer covering for the light of Sophia, the spark of divinity held inside each one of us, maybe it isn't so wrong. Maybe Kristen is proof.

And therein lays her safety. No matter what happens to her, no matter who does or doesn't hold her, that glow stays, for the glow, not the shell, is the girl.

But the orange-grove girl in my tale of teenage torment believed she had to keep herself in trees to stay safe. She didn't know she already was. The positive and negative struggle within each of us, Psyche used to say, the old anima and animus crochet of tension. But only the negative lived in me. I allowed the negative feminine, in the guise of sacrificial duty, and the negative masculine, masquerading as self-control, inform my sun.

Meanwhile, the protective masculine ran right beside me the whole time holding out his hand. *Let me carry your books. Let me swim with you, listen to you. Let me hold you safe.*

So I was young then, and criticism solves little. Neophyte fear allows teenagers to shun help, to recede from strength, to retreat when unable to brave the promise of more. But teenagers are allowed these stupid mistakes. I toss the diary onto the floor. Adults should fucking know better.

I reach under my pillow to haul out my old blue bathrobe. Then I carefully get up off the bed, walk through the silent house and pick up the phone to dial my brother's number. I need his hand again.

"Chip, Bernadette. No, Mary's okay. She's still at the courthouse, no word. I need another favor. I'd like you to pull up whatever information you can find on these creeps Asch and Balmaceda. Anything. Newspaper articles. Personal histories. Court cases. Legal firms going after them. You name it."

I move into the kitchen, slowly slide open the utensil drawer and take out the scissors. I get down on my knees and spread the robe out in the middle of the parquet, smoothing the material until it's flat. Then I start to cut.

First I make long thick strips along the hemline. *Repository suppository. Hoover's FBI wants to confiscate my fertility records?* I start moving the scissors in zig zag jagged angles. *Then they leave me a convoluted message about how only a doctor has a right to my reproductive procedures?* I slice off random shapes and corners. *The negative masculine continues the invasion? Hoover didn't trespass the personal boundaries of wives, sisters, my grandmother, enough when he was alive so he's continuing the FBI infringement upon their descendants?* I slice off an arm. *And these doctors playing God—they can't create life, so they think they'll rob those who can?* I cut off the other arm. *I don't think so. Not this sister. I'm sewing a crazy quilt in reverse, no tears in the sink, no weights around my ankles, no pills pumped from my stomach. Because some can't create, they choose to control. But there's a place this controlling power can't go, a place we know because we create life. And it is from this place that I'll find my children.*

I put the scissors down on the floor, wrap the robe in my hands and grit my teeth. And though I'm kneeling, my back is ballet-straight as I lift it high into the air and begin to rip.

THIRTY-NINE

I am shameless; I am ashamed.

*I am the one below,
and they come up to me.
I am the judgment and the acquittal.*

Mary Catherine bursts through the door of our bedroom. "Dette, wake up. Up, up, we won!"

She runs to gather the barely squirming Kristin, her face radiant, her eyes brimming. Mom sweeps out of the shrine and wraps her wings descendent around both mother and child, while I sit up in bed, rubbing my face, comprehending little.

Mary pulls back from Mom. "Brad agreed to everything. I get Suzanna, we can move to New York, and he only wants visitation one week in the summer."

I slide off the bed and lift Kristen from Mary so they can start crying all over the place. Gardenia prayers fill the room, but I secretly think Kristen's the one who turned this around. When she's older, I'll have to remember to ask her what she did, what her connections were. She snuggles her body against my chest and reaches for the air again, her fingernails so tiny. How long, I muse, before Pinhead paints them pink.

"That damn judge didn't even look at the forensic reports," Dad yells as he paces back and forth in the hall outside our room. "All those interviews. I can't believe it. He doesn't even read a word. I'm gonna find out when he comes up for reelection, that's what I'm going to do, just find out when that asshole comes up for reelection."

"Dad, hey, it all worked out perfectly," I chirp. "What could be better?"

He stops dead in his tracks. "You're right," he mutters. A shiver courses through my spine. I love it when people tell me that, so rarely do I hear those influential words.

He starts pacing again, but now he's laughing. "You should have seen WendyJo giving Brad holy hell coming down those courthouse steps. Jesus H. Christ. He didn't say a word, just kept his eyes on the ground. But she didn't let up. Then she swings her purse around and whacks him right on the ass. Ha! Kreber walked by me, said he gave 'em six months."

"Ah poor Brad," I say quietly. "Even WendyJo thinks he's a slug."

"He said he'd bring Suzanna over in an hour, just has to get her stuff packed up."

"Then it's off to the airport," Mary cheers. "Let's run before something else happens." I hug Kristen closer to my face.

"Nothing else is going to happen," Mom says firmly. "You've been through enough, honey." She gives her another hug. "Did you call Curtis with the news?"

Dad rolls his eyes. "Pope Catholic? Called him from the car. Called Chip, too. Would have told you guys but *some*body took the phone off the hook."

The doorbell rings. "Where is everyone?" booms a male voice. It's Chip, and he's not alone. Mary and I scramble past Mom and Dad to get there first.

"Everybody, this is Beatrice," he beams. And with one look, I feel sorry for her already. But as she hovers slightly behind him during introductions and awkward banter, I feel worse. For not only is she petite, pretty and polite, she's also a student in his karate class. This means he can really abuse her, because now he's operating on the old teacher-as-God hierarchy. I hate that. She idolizes him, he gloats. I see it all the time. It bloats perennial at the university.

While Mary and Beatrice talk, Chip hands me a stack of paper. "This is everything I found online, Bernadette. But, man, I'll keep looking cause more comes up every day."

I shuffle my feet, suddenly guilty for my eyebrow-up judgmentalism about his relationship with Beatrice. "Thanks Chip," I say with extra kindness. "I'll continue the search when I return home to the library. This was really sweet of you."

I don't think I've thanked my brother for anything in my entire life. Actually, it's been decades since I even stood next to him for this long.

"Well, I looked over some of the stuff while things downloaded," he says. "One of the docs, Asch, well, it looks like he's skipped the country. He hasn't paid his attorneys and they think he's like flown the coop. And there's all kinds of people, man, who think they've got kids out there they don't know about. It's just so really weird." He shuffles his feet, too, like he doesn't know what to say next. Maybe we are related after all.

"If you're an uncle, I'll be the first to let you know," I smile.

"Uh, I don't want to say rough stuff, Bernadette, but one article said that those doctors might have not even *kept* any records about whose eggs went to who, how many they took out…or, like, they might have written down what they *wanted* to write down, you know, like not what really happened."

"Like you mean they lied, right?"

"Uh, yeah man. But how can you prove it, you know?"

Now he's making me mad. "I intend to find out."

"Well, one article said that doctor would write on the files if a woman was, uh, you know, in her twenties and pretty. And he'd take more of her eggs, for like, older women. And you were in your twenties, and you, well," he hesitates and sort of chuckles, "you know you're really pretty."

I stand there and just look at him, incredulity brimming at the edge of shock. So he's come a long way from telling Jackson my eyes are dead. There's a step. But admitting it in front of me is quite the leap.

"I never saw commentary to that effect written on any of my charts," I contradict.

He puts his hands in his jean front pockets and looks at the silk rug. "Mom, uh, told me you never checked out any of your charts, or your records, or anything." And then he blushes, knowing full well he's turning me in again.

My mouth opens to answer, but no sound emanates as I become the queen of shame. I feel my body furl with her constricting crown. Her grip tightens the skin on my face, hardens the line of my lips and locks my knees. It's like I've been hit in the face again, but I don't fight back because I know I had it coming. Surely I deserve this.

"Chip," Dad interrupts. "Help your sister with her bags."

We quickly turn away from each other and help Mary put the last few pieces of luggage next to the garage door. Together, still silent, we join Mom and Beatrice on the sofa. My embarrassment subsides now as Beatrice, so unaware, warms to the innocuous conversation. She even slaps Chip's leg when he tells a joke.

"Hey, Dette," he says, playfully smacking Beatrice's leg in return. "How much were you paid for donating your eggs?"

All eyes proceed to me. Mom's mouth drops open. "Paid?" I ask, sitting up straighter, wondering how his sadist little self could return so soon. He never *did* know when to drop the knife.

"I couldn't get paid. It's against the law to get paid for donating eggs."

"Well, who told you that?" he asks.

"Madeline, the friend I donated to."

Beatrice flicks his arm and gives him some kind of look. I glance at Mary. "She flicked him. Did you see that?" This small movement is our private testimonial to Beatrice's worthiness as sister-in-law. But Chip seems uncomfortable, and not from the flick.

"Oh, just wondered," he says nervously.

Mary, however, is not going to let this one pass. "Why are you asking her about getting paid?" she demands. "Where did you get that idea? What aren't you telling her? Don't even think about holding out on us."

Chip looks at Beatrice. "We read that donors got thousands of dollars for donating their eggs," he says. "And it's perfectly legal. Your friend was, well, misinformed, I guess. She should have paid you."

"Thousands?" Mary shouts. "Boy were you dumb, Dette."

Beatrice moves away from Chip and leans towards me. "But you must have received something. Surely you didn't go into this kind of experimental fertility treatment and subsequent surgery for free, did you?"

Subsequent? Did she use the word subsequent? I've misread her. Maybe she dyes her hair blonde.

"No," I stutter, remembering the card from Madeline last Christmas, the photo of her two adopted girls, sisters in handmade red velvet dresses. "I didn't give them for free."

"Well then, what did they pay you?" Mary digs. She can never let anything rest, not even my unexpiated guilt. She should be an attorney.

"I, uh…"

Beatrice bounces on the sofa. "Altruism!" she chimes. "You were just being nice. You got nothing back." She continues to bounce her derriere up and down, ponytail bobbing. This chick is *on* something. "That is so, so noble."

"It wasn't altruism," I mumble. "There's no such thing. I had other reasons. Proof being that I damn sure would have taken the money had my friend offered. I could have used it for tuition."

"But, but, what about…"

"Beatrice, we have to leave," Chip interrupts.

Mom stands up and Mary follows suit, like no one wants to have *this* conversation. "Beatrice, you have so much energy," Mary says with a demure smile. "You must really enjoy karate." But I know my sister's not interested in martial arts. The three-syllable adjectives caught her attention, too. Like me, she's looking for dark roots.

Chip beams. "She's, like, the best in the class."

Beatrice stands up and chirps, "I can reach his face. Watch!" She does a roundhouse kick over his head. My hopes begin to rise, but he was sitting down when she did it. Still, I like her more and more. And it doesn't slip by me that in front of my family, she too may have a tendency to chirp.

"We have to go now, Beatrice, or we'll be late for class," Chip says, standing up a full foot taller than the blonde ponytail atop her head.

"But I thought we were going to see your niece, Suzanna?" she pouts. He leads her towards the front door and we all follow for one last A-frame hug.

"Wait!" Beatrice chirps again as she pulls away from his directive arm. Then she manages another roundhouse karate kick right at his face, missing his nose by about an inch. None of us say a word.

"Beatrice, stop man!" he cries out, groping for the door handle, trying to pull her out. But she jumps away and kicks at his face again. He trips outside while she follows one roundhouse kick after another, calling out "eeeeee-AH," or some such guttural sound with every jump. He runs to the car, alternately yelling, "Hey stop! Okay man!"

Dad closes the door. "Jesus," he says, shaking his head.

Mary and I look at each other with pride. "Payback," she pronounces. "And it's about time. He's finally met his match."

"It all comes around, doesn't it?" I murmur. "But I sort of wish I would have had the guts to do that to him when we were in high school." But then I hesitate. "Oh, I don't know. Maybe not."

Mary Catherine puts one hand on her hip and points at me. "Bullshit," she says, "You should have had the guts to do that about two weeks ago."

FORTY

... the judge and partiality exist in you.

For what is inside of you is what is outside of you,
and the one who fashions you on the outside
is the one who shaped the inside of you.
And what you see outside of you,
you see inside of you;
it is visible and it is your garment

"**M**om, one of my nails broke packing up the crib. Do you have that kit?"

We sit at the kitchen table while Dad trances out on a tennis match. I file away at the broken edge. "Miss my sister," I mumble. "Miss her already." I feel about three, but without any innocence anymore. Like I feel the lines around my eyes even though I can't see them.

"I know, honey," Mom answers, rubbing lotion into her hands. "Sisters missing sisters."

My shoulders drop and hunch. "God, I'm sorry. How rude of me."

She laughs with a lightness I love to hear, "Bernadette, that was almost fifty years ago."

"So, well..." I hesitate, "don't you miss her still?"

She squirts a glob of lotion onto her hands and holds them out to me. I put down the file and give her my own, my palms together in a tired prayer. Wait, how did I know to do that?

She starts rubbing her extra lotion into my skin, stroking my weary knuckles until the slow drip of memory seeps back into the hardened dirt of my brain. I remember this! In Texas, after she washed the dishes, her skin dried to an alligator texture, she'd call to me. *Bernadette! I have too much lotion!* And I came running to give her my hands.

I loved it. I lived for it. This child's massage seemed to forgive the trespasses of the day, soothing my guilt like the Act of Contrition: *Oh my God, I am heartily sorry for having offended thee...*

Saying that prayer in bed every night, my hands and feet pressed together so no energy might escape, always allowed for easy sleep. Lifting those words off my huddled chest proffered such relief, like a Catholic caress, expiation soothing the muscles of my embattled little seven-year-old heart.

With this childhood memory, the dark confessional of a church suddenly lures me. I need penance. *Forgive me father, for I have sinned.*

Mom takes away her hands. No! More, more. I need kneading. Don't ever stop.

"I've spent most of my life trying *not* to miss Londa," she says, putting the lid back on the lotion. I stare at the tube with a contumacious longing. She doesn't notice, but that's probably a good thing. "I've spent years trying not to think of her," she continues. "When I started going to the Center, it all just came out. A half-century's worth of crying." She folds her hands together and leans on her elbows.

"Can you tell me about her?" I ask gingerly, looking away from the tube, hoping the old mom doesn't resurface and go to the sink to run the hot water, hosing down the kitchen parquet with the nozzle.

She stays seated and smiles at me instead. "It's okay, honey. Don't be nervous. I can talk about her now." She looks over to Londa's photo framed on the wall by the phone. She never did give me that picture.

"My sister meant everything to me," she says. "Her breathing, the way she smelled, her long dark hair. She was such a fragile spirit. When I was little and she started one of her coughing spasms, I became so frightened. I'd sneak out of my bed and climb under her covers and put my arms around her, trying to hold onto her so tight that I would make the coughing stop. I'd close my eyes hard and grit my teeth, and imagine her as a tiny angel shivering inside a rain drop. And all I needed to do was crawl inside the rain drop and keep her warm."

Now I know why she would let me stay up late to watch the movie <u>Jane Eyre</u>, even on a school night, the scene where young Jane climbs into Helen's dying bed and they fall asleep together. I stare at Londa's airbrushed photograph. She even looks like Elizabeth Taylor, the dark hair and eyes, that mesmerizing smile, like she understands more than a child should.

"Eventually Londa would stop coughing and fall asleep in my arms. But I knew that if Mom or Dad found me in her bed, which they did a few times, they'd scold me good. They'd say I was too close, breathing on her, giving her germs. So when her body became still, I'd carefully crawl back to my own bed and lie there on my side, trying to keep my eyes on her, trying so hard not to fall asleep, in case she woke up again and needed me. When they couldn't keep her at home anymore, and she had to go live alone in Tucson, I thought I'd failed."

"Oh Mom," I can barely say, reaching out to touch her arm, "you never told us. I'm so *sorry*."

"But in the end, even the Tucson doctors knew she should be near her family when she died. So they sent her back, straight from the airport to the hospital. And my Dad would ask her what she wanted most, some little treat he could bring, something that might make her feel better. And she always answered, '*My sister.*'

"But I wouldn't go. She lived in an oxygen tent by then. I'd overhear Mom and Dad talking late at night after they'd get home from the hospital, how wet everything in her room was, the walls, the chairs, the ceiling dripping water, and how it smelled, and how awful she looked.

You know," she glances up at me and smiles. "Hoover almost fired your grandfather for all the time he spent at that hospital, reading to Londa, coloring with her. He refused to go to the office those last few weeks. Can you imagine Lon coloring?"

I try to giggle. I can't.

"Anyway," she continues, "I just couldn't make myself go. I didn't want to see her that way. And I knew I'd want to crawl in the oxygen tent with her, and I knew they wouldn't let me. So I kept waiting for her to come home, so I could hug her again, but do a better job this time and make her really well. But she died in that oxygen tent and they said she died still asking for me."

I think I see Mom's lower lip quiver, but it's slight, and only for a second. I search her face for more clues as to how this lies with her now, but it is only a path to avoid the tightening in my own throat. I can hardly find my voice. "Mom," I manage to whisper, "you were just a little girl."

"Yes, I was," she says with clarity. "And I should have done a heck of a lot of crying then. But I never did." She smiles at me. It's easy to see she's has resolved it. No unfinished business remains. She's worked through it somehow and found her reconciliation. I want to learn how.

"You said the Center helped you. When did you start going there?"

"About the time I couldn't take it anymore with Brad and WendyJo. I had to take drastic measures. It was change, or go swimming again."

I about choke on that comment, but she chuckles and flips over the lotion tube. "Funny how those two and all their crazy antics brought me to a place where I began to learn all kinds of things. My dad, my sister, so much to work through. I came to see everything as an opportunity to learn a lesson."

"The death of a child? What lesson did losing Londa teach you?"

"Forgiveness. I came here to master it in many forms."

"I know them well."

Mom starts to talk, but then closes her mouth, shakes her head like she's changed her mind. "What?" I ask.

"Well, I was just going to say that maybe Brad and WendyJo were a God-send. They created a lot of change in our lives, change for the good." One of her eyebrows goes up. "Maybe we should bless them."

"Let's not get carried away, Mom. Should Suzanna bless them? What change for the good did they do her?"

"Okay," she says, "see it how you will. Say they're *tools*. Does that help? You know, we can't know why anything happens to any of us. It's all of a purpose."

"Sounds like the Bible," I snap, pushing my shoulders back. "Can't know the will of God, can't change it. Well, I plan on changing a few things, like finding my records regardless of what the FBI or the will of God intends."

"Then that *is* the will of God," she says. "And anyway, you don't know that maybe the FBI is doing this to *protect* you and your records."

"Jesus, Mom!"

"Okay, okay, honey," she whispers. But I hope I haven't hurt her feelings. I've never known death at such a young age, someone she loved so much.

"Mom, I'd like to go there…to the Center I mean, if I could. Their ideas might give me some insight into my research."

She looks up, surprised. "We could go tomorrow," she says, too merrily.

Her enthusiasm heralds a retreat. "Yeah, but it's really time to head back, face the music so to speak." I suddenly feel down again, like the leftover stone-ground-wheat bread pudding in the fridge. The drama right here trumps the drama I'll return to.

There's a deafening silence. Finally Mom talks. "What will you do, honey? Will you go back to him?" I don't answer. "I apologize for asking this," she says. "I know it's none of my business, but uh…" She starts squirming, so I prepare myself for the worst. "Why have you stayed?"

Good, an easy seminar question. I answered it awhile ago, about the time he shoved me across the foyer. My reply is ready to wear. "I have a debt, Mom."

"A debt?" she asks. "To him?"

"To God. Or the universe. Or whatever you call it. I broke a vow and walked out on a man who was never unkind to me. That must be worked off. I have to earn the forgiveness."

"Oh my...well, um, I don't know," she stutters. "I believe that everything is only how you perceive it."

"No, Mom. In some cases, everything is just how it *is*. As another fine example, let's take irresponsibly creating children who may have cys..." I catch myself. "Who may have sisters they don't know, who may be completely lost in the world." I'm sinking fast, falling deeper and deeper into the pit of dejection and heaped-up laundry. Two major crimes have been committed and just when the penance for at least one of them appears, my own mother tells me I'm wrong.

"Your perception is a choice you make," she continues, ignoring my rebuttal. "But be careful because in this choice the purpose of the world you see is chosen, and will be justified."

"That sounds a *tad* scary."

She laughs, full of herself now, like she's on a roll. "Only if you perceive it as scary," she grins.

What *are* they teaching her down at that Center? She opens the lotion lid and my pulse quickens. But then she tightens it back up again. "So, tell me," she asks, loosening the lid, tightening it, teasing me without mercy, "how does being with Sean earn this forgiveness you're convinced you need?"

Kneading my own hands in my lap, I try to organize the theory so she'll understand. "Remaining committed this time, offering compassion, working hard, maybe this will atone for leaving before. Well, that was the plan."

I close my eyes and rub my temples. "God, I was such a spoiled girl in my marriage. I had such a rich world. I thought everything had to ring some ethereal version of perfect or…or else. But perfection already lived strong with us. How many women know a faithful, gentle husband, a beautiful home, a full life—and never even work at it, ever. Our friendship came naturally, with no effort. So I walked. How completely inexplicable."

Mom doesn't say anything. She stands up, opens the fridge and brings back two beers. Slams them on the table. My mother? "You never had to *work* at it?" she asks with exasperation. "What do you mean? You worked two jobs—demeaning, minimum-wage jobs far beneath your capabilities. And you did it all to put *him* through school. And buy *his* books, floor to ceiling bookcases on every wall and always filled. It pained your father so much to see you slave away, day after day, even on weekends, year after year."

I guessed Dad was a little apprehensive about me supporting Mikhail's dreams, but I thought it was just because he was majoring in English, or because Dad's ancient generation wanted the wife at home scrubbing.

"But he brought me wine before dinner," I say sheepishly.

"And who cooked that dinner?" Mom drills.

I have no answer, my illusions are slanting.

"Maybe that was a way to control?" I suggest. "There's your foundation. If I do everything, then I'm the one in charge. Right?"

"Bernadette, it's not for me to say," she continues, her face softer now, "but you idolized him."

"Well?" I answer. Big surprise. He was perfect, a man with a perfect mind. I thought everyone idolized him. Everyone but Pinhead.

"You put him on a pedestal."

Okay, now I'm getting mad.

"But isn't that exactly how it should be, Mom? Aren't you *supposed* to think well of your spouse. Isn't that what love is?" I gulp down about half my beer. "This fits your perception theory—perceive him as perfect and then he is? Isn't that why you wanted me with Jackson? Because he put *me* up there?" I'd figured it out. I love closure. The eldest is always the most brilliant.

"You're right, that is how love should be. And so, for a brief second, you thought that maybe you should love yourself enough to put yourself up on that pedestal, too. And in order to do it, you had to leave. And you did." She takes a swig. "But then you forgot, Bernadette, then you forgot."

I drop my head down onto my arms on the table. "I want to hold Kristen."

She reaches over and slowly smoothes my wayward hair. "When did I lose my wild first-born daughter?" she asks. "That long-legged girl who swung so high in her swing I thought the whole set would topple over? I remember watching you from the window, praying you would slow down, only to have my heart stop beating as you pumped that swing as high as you could, then opened your eyes wide, let go and sailed off, your body flying through the air, your arms stretched out wide, your head thrown back, screaming with delight. You'd land on the ground in a heap. I couldn't look."

"I was probably aiming for the dog," I mumble into my arm.

She doesn't hear me. She just keeps right on remembering. And the whispery edge to her voice tells me she's almost all the way back thirty years ago, looking out the window to that dead dry dirt of a backyard.

"I was so afraid you'd die. Like Londa, I'd lose you, too. I would tear away from the window and force myself to iron and iron and iron, never allowing my eyes off the TV screen because when it happened, when you broke every bone in your body, I didn't want to be there to witness it."

I lift my head two inches from the table and look at her. But she is not looking at me. She's staring at Londa's picture.

"But your screams," she went on, "you screamed so loud, all three of you kids. I could never tell the difference between laughing and crying screams. I mean, I knew in my mind they were teasing playful shrieks, children's fun, but the constant fear that one of them, just one was all it took, would be a cry for help. And with your father out of town so much, only me there to save you, if I could. And what if I couldn't? What if I ran outside too late? So I'd turn the TV volume up higher and higher, trying to drown out your voices. Sometimes I grew so scared, it was close to unbearable."

I slowly rise up on my elbows. "And that's when you'd come out and hose us down," I whisper. "God, I get it now, why you had to do that. I get it."

She turns away from Londa. "What?" she says, with the certainty of being back in the present. "Hose you down? What are you talking about?"

"Remember? You'd get so frustrated with our yelling, you'd slam the screen door and blast us with the hose."

"I never did such a thing," she gasps. "Are you kidding? Now and then, you'd call to me through the window and beg me to squirt you with the hose because you were burning up out there. This is Texas! And I'd do it, but never ever as a punishment. You begged me. You loved it."

I am stunned, speechless. I'd held this crime against my mother for decades only to find I'd imagined it? "But wait, Mom, I know Pinhead never got wet. I specifically remember you turning off the hose, going inside, and the kid standing there stone dry. Don't tell me you squirted her, too, please don't."

"Of course I didn't get her wet—she had on all those damn dresses. I wasn't going to wash and iron twelve outfits! I told her repeatedly that if she wanted to play in the water, she'd have to wear only one clo, like you and Chip." She throws back her head and laughs, then picks up her beer and toasts the air. "See, we perceive how we wish, eh?"

I drop my head back down to the table. This uninteresting game is boring me too much to elevate me from my mental sitting position. My mother is winning and I'm sinking. I can't even trust my memory anymore. She's glass half-emptying me. She's taking the mournful cello

Budokan version of *Tangled Up in Blue* and adding castanets. Even Dylan knew that everything's just how you play it.

"Look honey," she says softly, "that girl flying off the swing is still you. I see her in your eyes when you laugh with Mary Catherine. I see her in your face when you get angry with the doctors who stole your eggs. I see her in your whole body when you hold Kristen. It's time to move away from the guilt you feel. I really believe that's what's holding you back."

I say nothing. I can hear her drinking.

"About a year into your marriage, you wrote me a letter, most of it filled with *his* accomplishments. At the end of the letter, you said he was your very breath. Your very breath! I knew then that you'd have to leave him one day. That you stayed for years amazes me."

I raise my head and look into her eyes. I feel overwhelmed and shaky. "So you think I was wrong to be that way? That I was naive and foolish and young? Was I not more pure then? Was I not holier than I have become, than I am now?"

"Bernadette, you told me once that if he died, you were joining a convent."

"I still *do* think about joining a convent."

"You are just as holy now as you ever were. You don't have to work your skin to the bone to be holy; you don't have to serve and serve and serve in order to get love." She coughs. "And you spend too much time in the library."

The library? What the hell has the library got to do with it?

"And now this punishment you've given to yourself, living with an abusive man, like that solves anything! To tell the truth, you're still a slave, but in a different form. Mikhail never hit you, but you were injured just the same."

"Mikhail was a good man. Period."

"He was. I imagine he still is. I meant that you were the one who injured you."

We stare at each other, locked in our knowledge that even though she's right, I can't take it all in. It is too much for one woman, too much to be sorted, analyzed, fixed, healed. Just like the Thunder—all paradox and confusion and meaning that is simply out of my reach. *I don't understand.*

Anger, jealousy, betrayal, they're nothing compared to not knowing. Who can blame Eve? She had a tree that contained knowledge and she leapt for it, tried to taste it. Eve didn't do anything wrong, she just wanted to understand, and for this she was punished. For this, we are. What kind of religion goes there? What kind of God?

Mom breaks our stare with a smile and leans over towards my face in earnest. "Bernadette, you talk about forgiveness when you don't even know—"

I pull my now rigid body away from her. "Yeah, yeah, yeah. I *do* know. You're supposed to forgive your*self*. Well Mom, that's a clichéd crock. It may work for most people, but no matter how much I read and work and study, I knelt in a Catholic church my entire childhood and adolescence, six o'clock in the morning six days a week. Guilt can't help but win."

She crumples up her empty beer can and her voice takes on a firm tone. Her smile is gone. "That's not what I'm saying, not even close. Study, you say? Study? What has your studying got to do with it? And this forgive-yourself business? You talk about forgiveness and you don't even know there's nothing *to* forgive. Ever. There should be no guilt. No guilt! And why? Because nothing real can be threatened. And nothing unreal exists."

I just stare at her. She's drunk. One beer and she's under the table, raving like Rochester's wife in the attic, talking nonsense and believing every word of it.

"Mom, what religion is this?" I quasi-snarl back, feeling a little sarcastic and sloshed myself. I've never argued like this with my mother before, but we're on a roll. "What in the hell have you been reading? Sounds like Heidegger to me. He's so boy. I just skim him."

She slaps her hand on the table. "Stop it. Just stop it! You've got to learn, Bernadette. You've go to learn that you haven't done anything wrong, and in turn you'll learn that *none* of us have. There's purpose everywhere, in everything, even if we can't see it. There's just *movement*, that's all, there's just—"

"To the steakhouse!" Dad cries out, leaping from his La-Z-boy chair and clicking off the news. Mom and I both jump in our seats and turn to him, our jaws caught open. We're both shocked at our arguing and both shocked at how far we've gone into another space from here.

But Dad's oblivious. Or not so oblivious. Either way, whether he's conscious of what he's doing or not, he's bringing the silliness of it all back into the room. He's taking our convoluted notions of the logical and the true and singing out to us that we're both way over our heads.

He stops at the table. "Hey, what's this?" he says. "Your mother's drinking a beer? Jesus, Mary and Joseph!" He holds up the crimped beer can. "Non-alcoholic? Near-beer? Who bought this stuff? Whoa, you better get in there and light some candles, Rachel Jane. And start praying. I'm calling the Center, calling the Center!"

He slaps the beer can down on the table and puts both his hands up in the air above his head, palms forward. His face is flushed and beaming with laughter, and he's got a grin from big ear to big ear that only an Irishman can muster. "I am the Walk of the Life. The Walk of the Life!" he calls out to the ceiling. "Hallelujah!"

Well, that about sums it up. Jesus as hamster. Mom and I look at each other and bust out laughing. This family, who invented it? I go to get my sandals.

FORTY-ONE

Hear me, you hearers,
I am the hearing that is attainable to everything;
I am the speech that cannot be grasped.
d.I am the name of the sound

I am the sign of the letter
And I [...].
[...] light [...].
[...] to the one who created me.
And I will speak his name

"So where do you two drunks want to eat?" Dad asks as we get into the Lexus. "Drunk on near-beer. Ha!" He slams the steering wheel.

"Take Bernadette to a place with vegetarian food." My mother says, such an angel.

"Jesus," he moans. "Seaweed burgers. Okay, but we'll stop in the nursing home first."

"Wait!" I say, opening my door as he starts to back out of the garage. "In that case, I forgot something." And I run into the house to grab the crazy quilt Grace gave me. If we're sitting in the home of the living dead playing dead ourselves, I want something to do.

"Why in the hell do you want to bring that for?" Dad asks as he puts it in reverse.

"Well, certain features confuse me—like why some sections sort of crunch? To look at it closely, I'd say it seems to be the parts Grace sewed."

"Crunchy?" Dad asks. "What'd you mean crunchy?"

Mom turns around and looks at me in the back seat. "Oh, I know, honey," she smiles. "Grace probably didn't have much money. She believed in spending it all on travel, or she spent it on the children at the hospital. It was common to stuff a quilt with old paper. Sort of like recycling. I meant to say that when I gave it to you. It's not crunchy on the sections Millicent sewed because she probably stuffed it with material scraps." She leans over the seat. "Can I see it for a minute?"

I pass the small quilt and she moves her hands over the embroidery on the crackly side. "You're right. These sections look a little more wild. It's definitely Grace's sewing."

"Well, do you think I could take out the paper?" I ask gingerly, not wanting to sound like a snob. "I mean, not because it would be softer then, but because the crunch could be old newspapers from Jerusalem or Egypt, something Grace read."

"Sure," Mom answers, handing the quilt back over the edge of the seat. "In fact," she continues, "I store a sewing kit right in here." She opens the glove compartment.

"You keep a sewing kit in the car?"

"Mother of God," Dad cries out, slapping his thigh. "She's got the whole house in there. What'd ya need? A sandwich? Shoe polish?"

"Uh, just a scissors, Dad."

He pulls into the nursing home and Mom hands me a pair as we get out of the car. "You can do it carefully while we talk to Dad," she says. I smile to myself, my plan exactly. Hey, she called him Dad. Never heard that before.

I chuckle. "You guys want me keeping real busy, don't you. You're still afraid I'll ask him about Hoover?"

"Naw, fire away." Dad says, opening the large entrance door and nodding to the receptionist. "He won't even know who we are."

When I first see Grandpa in his room, I'm sort of shocked. He's still strapped in his wheelchair and the news blares on the TV, just like the other times I've visited, but he looks so much worse. The leather belt wrapped across his chest and around the back of the metal chair seems to be digging into his skin. He leans on the strap, his shoulders weighted forward and his head hanging down, drool dripping onto his legs, the folds of loose clothing masking the withered legs, the loss of a lap. Kissing him on the forehead, I say my name and could swear he smiles, but then again, maybe it's a grimace. I step back and stare at him. Gray skin masks a face devoid of passion. His eyes are without intention and his wrinkles are more like grooves. He must be near death, I think, his body losing life, sinking further and further into the final dejection that there's absolutely nothing he can do to salvage the mess he's made.

I sit in the corner chair and look for a good place to open the quilt, while Mom and Dad sit on the edge of the bed and yell meaningless conversation which he doesn't hear or doesn't care about because he's mumbling totally random and demented responses. But they keep right on talking to him as if he's taking in every word.

I find a space where Grace sewed simple straight stitches, easy ones I can sew back up once the job is done, and I start to cut these lines, gently pulling out the threads one by one. I open the quilt a few inches and peer inside. Actually, the stuffing looks fairly flat. Two fingers barely fit through my opening, just enough to pull it out, but nothing moves. I pull again. It's stuck. Lifting the quilt to my face and looking inside, I see the filling isn't bits of newsprint in pieces. Instead, there appear to be several sheets of eight by eleven paper, some layered, some folded in half, thereby giving the slightly padded and crinkled effect. So I cut more thread and make a larger opening. Meanwhile, the conversation from *Alice in Wonderland* continues on the other side of the room.

"What'd you eat for breakfast today, Lon?" Dad yells.

"Took an oath. The letter," he answers, still drooling onto his would-be lap.

"Looks like they put a new bulletin board up in the hall," Dad yells.

"The organization. Didn't see the satchel. I took an oath."

"Dad."

"Eat your banana, Lon. Good for your eyes."

"Dad."

"Bernadette?" Mom says. "Honey? What's wrong? Are you okay? Bill, quick, pull up a chair for her."

I'm standing in front of him now, shaky and scared, holding out the crinkled sheets from Grace's quilt. "These aren't Jerusalem newspapers," I say quietly. "I don't know what they are, but they look official."

Dad makes a face. "The stuffing from that blanket?"

"Grandpa's name is all over them. And the title—he's said this to me before. Repeatedly."

Mom points to the headline. "Polar Expedition."

"I always thought he was babbling."

"These are securities," Dad whispers.

"Securities? What are securities?"

"Jesus H. Christ," Dad continues. "Do you know what these are worth? Holy Mother of God."

Mom holds my wrist out to Lon. "Dad," she says without yelling, "Do you know what these are?"

Grandpa takes the papers from my hand and looks at Mom. His face lights up like Kristen's. Then his whole body starts shaking, and his mouth contorts, as if he's trying to say something, but can't get it out. The drool doubles, sliding down his chin and neck, while his spotted ashen hands are trying to bang the sides of the wheelchair. I think he's having a stroke or a seizure, but his face seems brilliant almost; he may even be smiling. His eyes have become missives and he keeps looking at Mom, his lips moving, desperately trying to talk or to scream or to die.

"Call the nurse," Dad yells. "Rachel, get the nurse!"

Mom jumps up to run for the door while Dad tries to hold Lon's shoulders, keeping them from shaking, then he grabs Lon's hands to keep them from banging the sides of the wheelchair. Grandpa lets out a shriek, a deafening cry of exasperation because his tiny skeleton just can't articulate his need.

Dad steps back in shock, but grandpa's cry wasn't frightening, it was more like the howl of a wolf who's finally seen an eclipsed moon. And I'm thinking he's recognized these papers.

Mom, her hands on the doorframe, turns back to the room.

"Rachel!" Dad yells. "What the hell?"

"No," Mom says, now kneeling beside her father's wheelchair. "Look at him. He's trying to laugh. He doesn't need a nurse, he's happy."

And she's right. Lon's face is aglow and his gray grooves have softened and he's not having a stroke, he's laughing—laughing without a sound, just like my sister does.

"You found them," he says with amazingly articulate speech.

"Lon. Lon," Dad bends down and yells in his ear. "What are they?"

"You found them."

"Lon?"

Grandpa stops laughing. He clears his throat. He looks up at Mom and gazes at her as if he's seeing a Gauguin for the first time. He smiles, only slightly, and tears start to run down his wrinkled face.

"Rachel Jane," he says, in a cogent and lucid voice, "I am sorry, so very very sorry." And his head drops back down to his chest, as if the sincerity of the thought took all his strength. We cannot answer, for how does one respond to an apology half a century late? *It's okay? Everything worked out fine? I forgave you long ago?*

Dad steps up to the wheelchair to wipe the drool off grandpa's chin when all of a sudden he raises his head to Mom again. He swallows slowly, pausing to form the right ideas in his debilitated brain. His mouth moves but nothing comes out as he strains to construct the words. We wait.

"Thank you for coming to visit me," he slowly says, the pain from unused muscles, the ache of overwhelming gratitude, intent inside his voice. Then his eyes close, from exhaustion, from recompense, from closure, while the tears drip onto his lap. His head falls to his chest and the papers slide out of his hands and drift slowly down to the carpet.

The Thunder
1990 A.D.

FORTY-TWO

I am the one whose image is great in Egypt
and the one who has no image among the barbarians.
I am the silence that is incomprehensible
and the word whose appearance is multiple.
I am the utterance of my name.

Lon died a few days later. He refused to eat, turning down the ice cream even. Of course I went in to see him, trying to get him to talk, but he'd never answer a single question. No seemingly random phrases, either. He'd just lie in his bed all day and stare at that picture of himself in the red sweater, careless drool flowing from his elfish grin.

I took the cell phone into the branches of the orange tree, called Mary Catherine. "It's over," I said. "He starved himself to death." But Mom was under the canopy, don't know how, a bucket of mulch in one hand and pruning scissors in the other.

"No," she said sort of softly, squinting up into the tree. "Dad died from serenity. He finally lost his fear."

No one ever did find out how Lon acquired those securities or how they came to Grace in Jerusalem. When they did make their way into her hands, however, she knew they needed to be hidden for a long time. No safety deposit box was safe, not from the FBI nor the brother-in-law she knew too well. She stashed them in a place no man like Lon would ever suspect, sewed them into a quilt no one would ever own. She intentionally labeled it 'To Bernadette's first child,' fully aware I wasn't having children. Chances of Lon's money being found within such a gift were slim. The discovery wouldn't come for decades, if at all, but surely not until well after Millicent and Lon were dead.

What Grace couldn't have anticipated was Gamete Intrafallopian Transfer. Who would have believed that I might conceive, instead of zero children, maybe ten or more; not to mention the sweet little fact that they could all be the same age, slip from different wombs, and carry the genes of different fathers.

Or maybe Grace did know. Maybe she divined I'd bear that first child one way or another, not only physically, but emotionally. Sequestered in a land of holy feminine wisdom, with caves full of secrets, maybe she understood more than I did then, more than she allowed herself to say.

The lost and buried papers were surely what haunted Lon all these years, his paranoia reducing him to banana storage. And of course we all felt foolish that we considered his ambiguous prattle to be just that, when it was, in fact, full of meaning. If only I had listened more closely, or written some of it down, we might have a clue what happened.

Dad tried to date the securities. He thought they originated shortly after Londa died. And Mom suspected that all the gossip about Lon getting fired had more to do with some scandal involving this money than it did with him hanging out in the hospital, coloring.

He probably stole the money out of desperation to send Londa to Arizona. But the money came only weeks too late and was therefore no use to him. So he hid it, and grew his bitterness into the ideal Hoover investigator, barbaric and merciless.

But what gangster did he steal it from? What satchel did he find? Could he have blackmailed Hoover? He was certainly close enough to the neo-Napolean, and he despised him with the force necessary to pull it off. When the government named the FBI building in DC after Hoover, Lon was beside himself. He raged through the house, destroying more lamps and books. Then he loaded up his guns and left. Millicent didn't hear from him for days, and when he finally returned, he never spoke of the J. Edgar Hoover FBI building on Pennsylvania Avenue again.

And finally, what was the Polar Expedition? If anyone knows, and we've checked, they're not telling. Maybe some things are better left unspoken. Regardless, all those years of fear ended the moment he saw the papers. It showed on his face and in his apology to Rachel Jane.

My mother gave me the money from the securities. She said Grace chose the benefactor and the issue was closed, no questions asked.

And she added that it wouldn't surprise her a bit to find out that Millicent was in on it all along, that maybe she'd accidentally discovered the papers in the attic, or wherever Lon had hidden them, and she guessed their value and secretly mailed them to her sister so far away he'd never recover them. And she remained silent. Lon had taught his wife well how to keep her mouth shut.

"Payback," Pinhead smirked. "Grandma wasn't smart for nothing. She never got mad because she got even. All those years she put up with him because she had his secret and his money and she could just revel in watching him squirm. Swearing and scratching around up there in the attic over her head while she sat grinning in the living room, quietly crocheting for the Church Bazaar. And we felt sorry for her, what a crock. Grandma was no fool. She took care of him good." We doubled over, laughing at the irony.

But I stopped laughing when Mom told me what I should do with the money. "Use it to find your children," she said. "And don't stop until you've found each and every one. Any money left over can go for their education, or for whatever they need. This is forgiveness money."

I went back home and told Sean I perceived him as needing to be alone and if he contacted me in any form, I would perceive myself down to the county magistrate's office to file assault and battery charges. I haven't heard from him since, how nice to have a closed door. I'm not angry, but I'm clear—in some situations, there is no ambiguity. Sean taught me when to walk away. With Mikhail, the door never fit snug in its jamb and still has a tendency to swing: I had to leave, I didn't have to leave. I may never know where it stops. I'm learning to live with that.

I found Jackson. It took awhile because this was all on my own, with neither advice nor commentary. Eventually, however, I did reveal my findings to Mary Catherine.

"Okay listen, Bernadette. You've already had the proverbial transition relationship. It took years to get around to it, and you chose a violent Buddhist for the task, but now you're clear. You can proceed with confidence. And remember, he's never seen you in a ballet leotard, so there's a chance he'll like you for your soul. Unsound as it is."

"He saw me in a two-piece at the lake almost every day."

"We were in high school for Christ's sake. You look a little better now."

Jackson works for the Department of Justice, how ironic. And convenient. After months of lengthy, and fearful, phone conversations, I decided to acquiesce to the inevitable: we must meet.

To retain independence, it had to be on my terms, in my car. I drove to DC, ostensibly to do research at the Library of Congress, but really with the intent of straightening out my karma.

I pulled up to his townhouse and he was sitting on the stoop. Waiting. Oh God oh God. I slowly tripped out of the car, he stood up, and at first glance, it all flooded back.

"Bernadette," he waved, running down the steps. I couldn't breathe. Here, in person, much more than his voice pulled at me. His very presence drew me, just as it did in the orange grove decades ago.

"It's so nice to see you again, Jackson."

And without a trace of *my* adolescent awkwardness, he maturely held out his hand to me. No hug attempt, ever chivalrous, still knowing who I am. Then he nodded to the medal around my neck.

"Nice," he smiled. Athletes are so damn confident.

"I can't believe you wouldn't let me carry your ton of books, skinny as you were," he said.

"Well, I'm not skinny now," I said, admiring his smile from behind my RayBans, scanning his tall and lanky body, his dark blond hair now cut close to his face.

He raised an eyebrow and gave me the once over, still smiling. "No, you're not skinny now." Then he whistled some Disney theme song, something about dreams coming true, just to make me laugh as he lifted my books from the trunk. "But you can take off those sunglasses Bernadette, because I can tell you're looking at me. And I knew you would someday. I just didn't think I'd have to wait twenty years."

I looked at you all the time, from high in the trees, a view more FBI covert than these sunglasses. You just don't remember.

I whipped them off my face, but I kept my eyes on the ground, a slight fear they might still be dead. "Well," I said, "you'll be carrying *these* books to make up for lost time." And I just stood there, my hands on my hips, smirking nervously as he loaded up his arms and trudged up the steps of his brownstone, feigning a ball and chain around his ankle. Paradox is such a fine thing.

But I couldn't resist. Memories of the years I watched him pass me by propelled me into action and I ran to help. But as I tried to take some of the weight from him, our arms became entangled and he let go of the books, sending them sprawling across the small stoop. Then he scooped me up in his arms, just like on the cover of one of Edna's bodice buster romance novels and we kissed like we should have kissed back in that orange grove years ago. And it felt like heaven to me, felt like my mother, felt like God—safe and kind and strong, like I'd fallen in the snow and sound arms had scooped me up and laid me before a fire—large hands now gently untying the wool scarf that had been choking me for so long. I was half-unconscious, a concussion from years before lingering still, and I was finally being kissed slowly awake. I leaned deep into his warm body, my chosen place of rest ever since.

And now, curled up together on his velour sofa, weekend after weekend, trading our decades of catch-up stories, we even talk of having children, an idea that finally doesn't frighten me.

I hired a legal firm in Los Angeles to investigate my situation with the fertility clinic, but so far the FBI has sealed all evidence. Doctors Asch and Balmaceda will be put on trial and the grand jury subpoenaed all records and no one can see them except the judge and a jury of my peers. Not even FBI agents. Nothing is available to me, to my attorney, or to the public until Asch and Balmaceda are found innocent or guilty, and sentenced. That's when my records will be released. And I won't be able to miss it because their sentencing will be headline news across the country.

However, minor detail, before the feds were able to arrest them, Asch and Balmaceda sold their Rolls and racehorses and fled the country, their millions from playing God sewn into their tridents. Their extradition depends on the treaty laws with the specific country, Asch fleeing to Mexico and Balmeceda possibly to Argentina.

But what country has laws on human egg-stealing in a treaty with the U.S.? It's unheard of. So there will be little to no basis for their extradition, and there can be no criminal trial in this country without the defendants. So in a worst case scenario, Asch and Balmaceda won't be extraditable, there won't be a criminal trial, and my records will remain in some vault in a cave in the Wyoming desert forever.

Now that she's in law school, Mary Catherine keeps watch. She found out one of the chief law suits, of the seventy that have been filed to date against the clinic, comes from a woman who has proof her eggs were stolen—a woman who watches "her" twins, born from her stolen eggs, walk past her house to school every day.

"Those children look just like her," Mary Catherine tells me. "And she can't say a word to them until this is settled."

"But she sees them nonetheless," I argue.

"Who cares? Aren't they her children? And she can do nothing?"

"She can do nothing? Are you aware of the real definition of nothing? She knows who their parents are, she knows if they are smiling or crying while they walk, she knows if one has a scraped knee, or if one finds a monarch butterfly lying on the edge of the sidewalk. She knows if they are safe, Mary. She has at least *some*thing."

But then she stung me with the worst, the sword to my side, but surely a source of all Mary's anger and motivation to find my children. "Dette," she told me, hesitation in her voice, like she knew how this would set me back, "I didn't want to tell you this, but her eggs were taken from her body and implanted into that other woman the exact same month you stayed at the clinic. She's listed in the same fertility series as you and Madeline. Do you know what that means?"

I know what that means. I know exactly what that means.

So Mary's obsessed, involving all her law professors even. Actually, I think the entire law school is following the scandal as it unfolds, the way she talks. There's no legal precedent for egg or embryo-stealing, the only regs on the books being for *farm* animals, so, jokes aside, it's a new and fascinating case for her crowd. They can't wait to see how the feds are going to get Asch and Balmaceda back into the country to stand trial. And then she says they want the criminal case to end, for then, just like with O.J., the civil case begins and they'll dive in head first and break new ground. Mary says they're going at it with all guns loaded. My sister, someday she'll drop those murderous metaphors.

Mom asked me for help in choosing a topic for her final paper for Reverendhood. Of course I suggested Gnosticism, but she rejected that one, saying it sounded "too Christian." Too Christian? What a far cry from the accusations of heresy the Church Fathers made two thousand years ago. Mom wanted to research something as far away from Catholicism as one could get, so we bantered various religions back and forth and finally chose Taoism. By the end of her research, she concluded that Taoism and Catholicism had, at their core, much in common, the same conclusion I'd made by the end of grad school: that is, that most religions tell the same story—just love one another. But I'm still not real sure about *some* people.

So Mom and I continue our ongoing debate about the concept of forgiveness. I still say you can't forgive people like Hoover or the fertility doctors, she says not only can you, but you don't even need to and who do I think I am anyway? She says that when I get clear about my children, I'll feel differently about everything. She thinks that when my own guilt ends, I'll be able to ease up on everyone else's.

And I know she's right. Most days, I can look in the antique vanity mirror and say it's all okay, even if I never find them. Because ultimately, on this level, records or no records, I can't ever really know. Like with Mikhail, ambiguity and inconclusiveness are friends The Thunder has taught me to accept.

Now Reverend Rachel helps a friend lead healing workshops. They teach relaxation techniques, mindfulness meditation, and ways to find the positive masculine and feminine. Dad attended a few of her workshops and became jealous that young men, after the sessions were over, thanked Mom with a hug. Dad wanted her to quit the workshops, but she held firm, said he was starting to sound like Lon. So he refused to go with her anymore. "I'm sixty-seven!" she'd say. But I guess to him, she was still twenty-one.

Brad is on probation for some petty criminal activity, probably loitering or sloth, and is not allowed to leave the state of Florida, so Mary doesn't worry about that one-week visitation. But he does phone Suzanna every Sunday, asking her about school, about boys, about TV shows.

"But Aunt Bernadette, I'm not sure if I *like* him or not."

"Well, does Brad say things that upset you?" I ask when we talk on the phone.

"No, he always says nice things," she tells me. "But I feel sorry for him."

"Why?"

"Aunt Bernadette," she sighs, "he always asks me the same question every single time he calls. He keeps asking me if I can for*give* him."

"And what do you say, honey?" I murmur, turning away from the phone, wondering if my children, when we find them, will be telling this same story about me, fear and love weaving together as I wonder if they will view me as careless with their lives. Wondering, years from now, if I will.

"I say the same thing every time he asks," Suzanna says. "I just tell him I'm *thinking* about it. But, but..." She hesitates. I hear her grinding her teeth, just like her mother. "But I don't know how long I can go on saying that. He wants an answer!"

I pull the magenta thread through the lime-green bead on her latest poodle skirt and I burst out laughing, for there is only one answer to the ever-perplexing forgiveness question. "Oh Suzanna," I sigh, "you tell that man that a sister can think about it for as long as she likes." And I tie a knot, remove the needle, and tuck the embroidery threads beneath the velvet, smiling at the way we all end up with this same hand, wondering where our boundaries are. My sister grabs the phone.

"Are you making her another clo?" she barks. "Enough already with the fruffy tulle and boas."

She's such a whiner. When I visit my nieces in upstate New York, I load myself down with toys and books and flouncy dresses upon which I've sewn fluorescent beads and feathers. It drives Mary Catherine crazy. She wants them dressed only in solids from L.L. Bean. My sister, still the fashion plate.

"They like frivolous," I argue. "Let them revel in it. If you make it taboo now, you're going to pay later."

"They look like Barbie and Midge." She muffles the phone and yells at Suzanna to turn down the TV.

"They look silly and happy," I say, "how kids are *supposed* to look."

"You, the feminist. What a crock."

"Strong women can wear anything, even pale pink," I say coolly. "I read somewhere that Isis had all her robes died in beet juice. That makes Isis pretty pink."

"They grew beets in Egypt? *Beets?*"

"Beets."

"You just send me a beet when you get there, you hear me? I want a beet from Egypt."

"Listen, I shouldn't go. I know I shouldn't go."

"Because you'll miss Jackson so much, aren't you finally sweet. I always knew you could change."

"I should stay here because I should find those children."

"Stay here? Are you kidding? Go. Go to Cairo. Ride the sphinx. Climb a pyramid."

God, this girl. "I'm not going there to climb pyramids, Pinhead."

"I know, I know. You're going to study the chopticks language."

"Coptic. It's *Cop*tic." She never gets me.

"Coptic, schmoptic, no one cares."

I cringe, knowing she's right.

"Even if you did turn down that job in Texas," she continues, "you're an academic and that makes you *use*less. All you can do is theorize. And since you can do that anywhere, get on the damn plane. Go to Cairo. *I said turn down that TV!* Attorneys do the real work in the world. We're the ones with the power. I'm going to find your kids, got it? You just go think. Go talk to the thunder, or whomever."

I slide open my desk drawer and take out my plane ticket for Cairo. Not all the money's going to the lawyers, Grace. Some of it's going to Egypt. Here I will visit the original Coptic manuscript of *The Thunder* held in the Coptic Museum. And not only for reasons of scholarship; I want to see for myself alone what the Thunder said. And, maybe more importantly, I want to see, with my own eyes, the places where the ellipses are, the places where we *don't* know what she said, the places where we're supposed to guess, or imagine, or wish. Because that's what I do so much of the time anyway.

But *The Thunder: Perfect Mind* was not originally written in Coptic. It was written in Greek. Unfortunately, there are no extant copies. When I lie in my disheveled bed at night, listening to the Virginia mountain rain, my Jerusalem artifacts on my nightstand, I think of Grace and I know the Greek original is out there somewhere, as yet undiscovered. And I think I just might be the very person, or the very idiot, to search for it. I know finding it will fill in some of the gaps, will tell us what The Thunder meant in all those places where we can't make out what she wanted to say. But I also know the original will have gaps of its own, new spaces we can't account for, difficult phrases to translate, cryptic passages we can't understand.

If only I could walk the stone steps of a temple in Alexandria, the city where I believe *The Thunder* was composed, and ask for help. But ancient Alexandria is under the sea, temples and libraries lost hundreds of years ago. Excavations continue to uncover new findings and I hope to be standing on a dock watching when the next statue of Isis is raised from the water. Or the next Gnostic scroll, perfectly preserved.

In the richest part of me, though, I know I've already found The Thunder, in all her paradox and enigmatic wisdom. She's been here all the time, quietly waiting, like she waited under the sand for two thousand years. She's not why I'm going to Egypt.

I'm going to Egypt for you, Grace, a pilgrimage of sorts, closure on an old dream I could never forget. How long it did take me to get here, how curved and afraid the path has been. I imagine the photograph I'll send back to Suzanna and Kristen, me on a camel, pyramid in the background, thin wisps of my graying hair hanging about my face, shaded eyes searching for the thunder.

My sister is there, her snarling self capably taking the pictures. My medal glints the sun back to her, swinging about my neck as I sway, trying to keep my balance. And we're laughing so hard at my clumsy fumbling on the camel that I start to slip. She's yelling that I'm still a nerd, all those years of ballet lessons for naught, and I'm grabbing at the blankets and camel hair, yelling back that she should try sitting still on this angel and then make fun of me, when oh my God, there I go. All the way down, it feels like ten stories my slow motion fall to the ground. I hear her running through the sand, calling my name, *are you okay? Are you okay?*

I land on my hands and knees and it's so hot to touch, it's burning my skin, but I refuse to stand up. She's kneeling before me now, holding out her arm, but I don't take it. I'm staring at my own hands, spread out and pressed into the stinging sand, making an indentation, forcing the grains to push up between my fingers. I feel like crying, but I'm too happy. "Look," I smile. "Look at the sand."

She bends down close to me, our foreheads almost touching. Then she presses her hands into the sand, too, lining up our fingertips end to end, the sand overflowing our outstretched fingers. Our palms and kneecaps are on fire, but we stay anyway, hand to hand, staring down together. "You've done it, Bernadette," she whispers.

"We've done it, Mary Catherine." I whisper back. "We've filled the gaps."

Look then
at all the writings which have been completed
Give heed then, you hearers
and you also, the angels and those who have been sent,
and you spirits who have arisen from the dead.
For I am the one who alone exists,
and I have no one who will judge me.

For many are the pleasant forms which exist in
numerous sins,
and incontinencies,
and disgraceful passions,
and fleeting pleasures,
which (men) embrace until they become sober
and go up to their resting-place.
And they will find me there,
and they will live,
and they will not die again.

The Thunder: Perfect Mind,
The Nag Hammadi Library

Made in the USA
Charleston, SC
16 September 2015